SHOW **...** TV®

Special Books by Special Writers
The Book:

My Fair Gentleman

A contemporary, provocative and just plain funny story about changing *your* life—and *other people's*. This is a book to be read and *reread*. A book to cherish.

The Characters:
Catherine Eliza Hamilton. A lady (actually, an *engaged* lady). A dedicated psychologist who's in danger of being turned into "the perfect hostess." Faultlessly polite, compulsively neat, she's also (of all things) a pool hustler. And a woman who takes risks....

Joe Tucker. An ex-baseball player who's looking for a new job—one that doesn't entail modeling underwear. A single father who's never quite picked up the knack of parenting. A man's man—a woman's sex object. And definitely not housebroken.

The Author:
Jan Freed first burst onto the Superromance scene in May 1995, and readers can't stop talking about her! Her first novel—*Too Many Bosses*—is nominated for three *Romantic Times* awards, and she's still getting fan letters about her second, *The Texas Way.*

"Jan Freed...has a truly gifted light touch with characters who still manage to tug at the reader's heart."
                                                                        —Alexandra Thorn

ABOUT THE AUTHOR

Jan Freed is proud to write in a genre that "presents a hopeful view of life without diminishing its hardships." A huge fan of musical theater, Jan enjoyed creating her own Americanized and modernized version of *My Fair Lady* with the roles reversed. "In writing Catherine and Joe's story, I realized that the strongest romantic partnerships are forged by a willingness to learn from each other. In other words, mutual respect."

Jan lives in Texas with her husband and two children. She loves to hear from readers and invites you to write her at: P.O. Box 5009-572, Sugar Land, Texas, 77487.

Jan Freed

MY FAIR GENTLEMAN

Harlequin Books

TORONTO • NEW YORK • LONDON
AMSTERDAM • PARIS • SYDNEY • HAMBURG
STOCKHOLM • ATHENS • TOKYO • MILAN
MADRID • WARSAW • BUDAPEST • AUCKLAND

With love and thanks to my parents,
Alta and Vilbry White
For giving me the confidence to try,
a belief in "happily ever after"
and a normal name

ISBN 0-373-70713-4

MY FAIR GENTLEMAN

Copyright © 1996 by Jan Freed.

Printed in U.S.A.

MY FAIR
GENTLEMAN

CHAPTER ONE

CATHERINE ELIZA HAMILTON swallowed hard as the duck à l'orange sitting in her stomach threatened to take wing up her throat. If anyone had told her two hours ago she'd wind up in a dive like The Pig's Gut, she would have choked on her cognac.

Glancing toward the adjacent bar stool, she noted her fiancé's expression and mentally cringed. Carl was feeling particularly smug tonight. And why not? Driving from the posh Houston restaurant to this small industrial town had been a brilliant tactical move.

She should have set recruiting rules of course. Or at least tried to slant the odds in her favor. Instead, she'd let anger overcome a mind trained in the science of emotional processes. Some psychologist she was. No wonder Carl had seemed amused at dinner by the idea of her establishing a private counseling practice. She'd "counseled" herself into a situation Freud would have sold his id to analyze. Catherine sniffed in self-disgust.

Flat beer, acrid smoke and the smell of male bodies straight from a shift at the oil refinery made her wrinkle her nose. The noise was almost as bad. A country-and-western tune hissed and crackled from an ancient jukebox. Billiard balls clacked. Gruff voices cursed or whooped according to the shot.

Who would have thought Carl Wilson, heir to one of the oldest fortunes in Houston, would have known this hole-in-the-wall existed? Then again, who would have predicted he'd ask her out at all, much less propose marriage after only three months of dating? No one but his parents, that was for sure.

Carl had been disarmingly candid from the beginning. After two failed marriages with beautiful bimbos, he had to choose a "suitable" wife and provide grandchildren soon, or be cut from his parents' financial cord once and for all. So this time he'd looked deeper than superficial beauty. This time he'd bypassed lovelier candidates and chosen Catherine for what was in her heart.

Her blue blood.

A fair exchange, all things considered. She was thirty-two years old and both plainer and smarter than most men liked. She'd always longed to have children, and now she had a shot at starting both a family and a new career.

Impatience set her fingertips drumming on the bar. She wished Carl would hurry up and select a guinea pig. One beer-swilling, belly-scratching Cro-Magnon would do as well as another.

"Why not just take the shirt off my back!"

Catherine swiveled her bar stool toward the bellowing voice.

A dark-haired giant of a man whacked down his cue stick, grabbed the hem of his baseball jersey and jerked it over his head. Muscles rippled and stretched. A garish tattoo flashed on one arm.

"How 'bout my pants, too? They should be worth a few bucks." He reached for his belt and fumbled with the buckle.

Uh-oh. Catherine squeezed her eyes shut. Maybe Carl wasn't watching the spectacle. Maybe he'd spotted himself in the mirror behind the bar.

"I've decided," Carl said in her ear, excitement lending a shrill edge to his voice.

She pressed her eyelids tighter. "Which one?"

Guffaws and whistles broke out in the room. Carl chortled in triumph. "The one mooning his opponent at the second table!"

Wincing, Catherine cracked open one lid and stared through a carcinogenic haze. Bare buttocks glowed red beneath a neon Budweiser sign.

She closed her eye and thought rapidly. No good to panic. On the civilization scale, the man was an amoeba. But the stakes were too high for her to back down now.

Resting his chin on her shoulder from behind, Carl slipped both arms around her midriff and rubbed his dark blond hair against her cheek. "You know, darling, you can still call off this whole thing. Dr. Hamilton would definitely not approve, and he trusted me to take care of you this summer."

The pleasant tingle his uncharacteristic caress evoked vanished. "Dr. Hamil—*Father* won't ever have to know about our little wager, unless you tell him." Catherine pried away Carl's forearms and swiveled to face her handsome fiancé. "Are you afraid I'll win?"

His condescending smile reflected forty years of too much money and too little challenge. "You constantly amaze me, Catherine. By all means, if you insist on conducting this experiment, go ahead." He waved his hand airily and propped an elbow on the bar. "I can't wait to watch you try and convince your subject to cooperate."

You and me, both. Catherine slipped off the stool and nervously smoothed her black linen sheath. How did one sway a man who looked as if "fee, fie, fo, fum" were the extent of his vocabulary?

Carl reached out suddenly and caught her hand, his expression earnest. "If he gives you any trouble, darling, I'll be here."

Although fit and trim, her fiancé only stood nose to nose with her own five feet nine inches. She squeezed his fingers with a rush of affection.

"Thanks, Carl. That's nice to know." Turning, she faced at least a dozen death-row-inmate stares.

Her chin came up. Her aristocratic mask came down. Fixing her gaze above billed caps and cowboy hats, she located her quarry. He'd managed to pull up his jeans, thank heavens.

The man stood bare-chested, his arms crossed and boots planted wide. Thick black eyebrows pulled together to form a V. A square dark-shadowed jaw angled aggressively. His bold nose appeared to have been broken at some point in his questionable past.

He needed a haircut, a shave and a strong cup of coffee, from the looks of his bleary expression and swaying stance.

His opponent, a scrawny grizzle-haired man clutching a baseball jersey, shook the fisted material high. "Dammit, Joe! I'm the best man with a cue this town ever seen, and you know it. You had no call to make me play, 'specially with you bettin' money you don't have. Now go on home and sleep it off."

"Joe" was muscular without being muscle-bound and at least six foot four. Maybe taller.

As Catherine drew nearer, she began to feel almost petite. It was a new unsettling experience.

"Don' wan' your charity." Joe scowled fiercely. "I can take you, Earl—double or nothin'."

"You got a dry well for brains, son? I said go home." Earl flung the jersey on the table. "I ain't gonna play you."

Joe's biceps bulged, his forearms corded, his long fingers curled into fists. He clenched his jaw and shifted slightly. The garish tattoo on one arm sharpened into red-and-blue dancing teddy bears.

Staring, Catherine walked smack into a billiard table and had to brace her palms on the felt top to catch her balance. Catcalls and whistles rang in her ears.

"Another one bites the dust, Joe."

"This one fell harder'n most."

"Think what she'd do for an autograph, lover boy."

Her cheeks burned. Then a hard arm was draping her shoulder, steadying her. She tilted her head back and stared into deep brown eyes warm with concern—and so bloodshot they were painful to view.

"You okay, miss?"

He smelled like a brewery. "I—I'm fine, thank you." She lifted the oak log of his arm from her shoulders and stepped back. Several voices urged Joe to follow.

His expression darkened. He swept a meaningful look full circle, waited for the clack of ivory and rumble of conversation to resume, then looked back at her.

"I'm not usually so clumsy," she admitted. "But then, it's not every day I see a tattoo like yours."

He glanced down at his arm as if startled. A dull flush stained his neck. "It's, um, practice," he mumbled. "My, um, daughter. You know...for a carnival?"

She blinked.

"You know...face-painting booth? To raise money for her softball team."

Catherine didn't know. A fund-raising carnival—or any kind of carnival, for that matter—was beyond her sheltered experience.

His flush deepened. He looked somewhere over her shoulder and shrugged. "Didn't expect to shuck my shirt."

Recalling his naked bottom, she felt her lips twitch. "Those bears wouldn't have been safe *anywhere,* tonight."

His dark gaze snapped to hers and lit with devilment. One corner of his mouth lifted in a rakish grin. He was as swarthy as a pirate and certainly as cocky. And suddenly she wished Carl had picked anyone in the bar but this man.

"I'm Catherine Hamilton," she said, extending her hand.

He reached out simultaneously, his hair-dusted chest filling her vision. "Joe Tucker."

Her hand disappeared, swallowed to the wrist by his grasp. Against his bronzed skin her forearm looked pale and fragile. Flustered, she withdrew her fingers. No wedding ring on his left hand, though he'd mentioned a daughter. No telltale tan line, either. Divorced? She hoped so. A wife would complicate things.

Cloth whizzed past her face. Joe snatched the bundle from midair with lightning reflexes.

"Mind your manners and put your shirt on, fool," Earl commanded. "Can't you see she's a lady?"

The words had a startling effect. All traces of affability fled as Joe pulled the wrinkled Astros jersey over his head. Propping his knuckles on his hips, he cocked his head. "What're you doing here, Catherine Hamilton? Looking for excitement on the wrong side of the tracks?"

Yes. But not the way he meant. She drew a calming breath. "I'd like to talk with you in private."

His lids drooped. He gave her a leisurely head-to-toe inspection. "Sorry, doll. You're not my type."

So what else is new? "Ditto, beefcake. Now, can we talk—or not?"

"Not." He turned to the billiard table and began plunking balls into a triangular rack. "So what d'ya say, Earl? Double or nothin'?"

The infernal man was going to ruin everything for her!

"I done said I won't play you, Joe, so quit askin'."

"How about me?" Catherine blurted.

Both men's heads whipped around.

She held Earl's incredulous gaze. "Eight ball, regulation rules. If I win, Joe's debts are wiped clean. If I lose, I'll pay you double his current losses, whatever they are, and leave you both in peace—"

"Wait the hell one minute," Joe interrupted, his eyes narrowed. "What do *you* get outta this, lady?"

A long story. Too long to explain now. "Your charming undivided attention for fifteen minutes." She arched a brow and looked from one man to the other. "Well, boys, what d'ya say? Double or nothing?"

JOE LEANED against the paneled wall and chugged from a long-neck beer. Not that it helped any. His pleasant buzz was history, thanks to a stranger meddling in his business.

He'd driven to The Pig's Gut knowing the regulars would lynch any sports reporter daring to shove a microphone up his nose. After all, he was a local legend, the first major-league baseball player Littleton had ever produced. If their boy Tucker wanted to get wasted in private, they'd see to it he could.

It was his own fault they'd let Catherine Hamilton get near him. He'd never met a woman he didn't like. They'd heard him say so over and over, and it was true, except for a certain type of bored socialite—the "ladies" who pursued him behind their husbands' backs in private, but looked right through him in public.

During eight seasons with the Houston Astros, he'd learned to keep his nose—and other important appendages—out of tight spots that could spell trouble. In the end he'd still screwed up.

His celebrity status had fallen a bit once news was out that his contract hadn't been renewed. But not as much as he'd deserved. Grimacing, Joe plunked his empty Lone Star bottle on the concrete floor.

He was thirty-four and his career was over, destroyed along with the cartilage of his left knee on a ski slope this past winter. Tomorrow he would assume full responsibility of his daughter for the first time in twelve years. And he was dead broke. A man couldn't sink much lower.

Don't look now, Tucker, but you're letting a woman try to clear your debt.

Resettling against the wall, he glared at Earl. The inveterate pool hustler had won the break and was positioning the cue ball. Catherine stood to one side, her expression disinterested as Earl bridged his cue stick and took aim. The shattering crack of the opening break didn't even make her blink.

Something wasn't right. There'd been no sultry glances Joe's way. No accidental touches. No hair tossed coyly out of her face. He focused on details that had escaped him before.

A tall thin body in a shapeless black dress. Discreet gold jewelry. Straight black hair swept back from her face with a tortoiseshell headband. A longish nose, hollow cheeks and extremely pale skin. Definitely not a beauty. And yet...

She looked up and met his gaze. Challenge, determination and keen intelligence blazed from her light green eyes with laser-beam impact.

"Get out your wallet, miss," Earl said, cackling. "You're gonna need it soon."

She turned again to the table, and Joe released his breath.

"Excuse me if I don't rush," she said dryly.

"Suit yourself." Earl drew back his cue stick and let fly. A solid orange ball dropped into the side pocket. Moving farther down the rail, he lined up a second shot. "Two in the corner," he called, sending the solid blue ball rocketing home.

Catherine watched poker-faced while Earl shuffled here and hunched there over his cue, slamming or finessing balls into pockets at will. One by one, players from nearby tables abandoned their own game to watch the master at work. Within minutes, only the eight ball and a solid red ball stood between

Earl and more money than he made in a month at the refinery.

Scanning Catherine's seven striped balls, Joe accepted the inevitable with a twinge of disappointment. He'd been curious as to what she wanted to talk about. Now he would always wonder.

Propping his cue stick against the rail, Earl made a show of chalking the tip. "Sorry t'hafta do this, Miss Hamilton, but you can't say you wasn't warned."

Catherine moved into the light from a bare bulb hanging over the table. "Don't apologize, Earl." Her eyes flashed with catlike luminosity. "You're going to miss the next shot."

Billy Tremont raised the bill of his Texaco cap and grinned. "Hooee, listen to her, would ya?"

Skeeter Johnson snickered around a wad of chewing tobacco. "He's shakin' in his boots, ain't ya, Earl?"

Joe pushed off the wall and shouldered his way through the crowding circle of men.

"You're very good, Earl," Catherine admitted. "But putting left English on the ball requires a steady touch. Now that I look closely, you seem a little shaky to me." Her glittering green eyes locked with the old man's baby blues for a long moment.

Skeeter moved forward and jabbed the undisputed Pig's Gut pool champ between his narrow shoulder blades. "C'mon, Earl, get this over with. I've got a run goin' at table five."

Frowning, Earl slid grimy-nailed fingers up and down his standing cue stick before hoisting it up into shooting position. Was it Joe's imagination, or did the old buzzard take longer than usual lining up the shot?

"Three in the side," Earl finally announced, drawing back his elbow.

Ivory clacked.

Patsy Cline crooned.

"You miscued," Billy said on a groan, sending his idol a stunned look. "You *never* miscue."

Curses and disbelieving grumbles broke out. Earl stared at the undisturbed red ball as if it had just sprouted horns. Lifting a trembling hand, he rubbed the back of his neck.

Joe moved close and spoke low in his friend's ear. "Don't worry, buddy. She'll screw up her first shot, and then you can finish her off."

Earl glanced up with a shaken expression. "I think she's a damn witch. Did you see them eyes?"

Joe'd seen them. "She psyched you out, all right. But remember, we've got the home-stadium advantage."

He searched the room and found Catherine removing several cue sticks from the back-wall storage rack. After rolling each one on a nearby table, she settled on the twenty-one-ounce cue with an Astros sticker on the handle. Coincidence, or had she picked his cue on purpose? It was much too long for her, but comparatively new and unwarped.

Ignoring the suggestions for what to do with a "man-size shaft," she headed for the table, balancing the cue on one shoulder with all the nonchalance of Huck Finn carrying a cane pole.

The lady had guts, Joe admitted. He almost hated to see her razzed by the guys. But she'd invaded their turf, not vice versa, which made her fair game.

She laid her cue on the table rail and studied the scattered balls intently. A red-haired man Joe didn't recognize thrust a blue chalk cube under her nose.

"Here you go, babe," the stranger said, checking to make sure he had his audience's full attention. "Rub the tip real good now. You look like you could use some friction."

Ribald laughter erupted all around. Pinkening cheeks were the only sign that Catherine heard. She took the cube and calmly rotated the end of her cue stick in the chalk.

"Ooh, that's it, babe, don't stop," the man continued, urged on by hoots and whistles. "With hands like that, who cares if you ain't much to look at?"

The laughter trailed off nervously.

Joe saw the flash of hurt in her clear green eyes. Anger and shame clenched his fists. He headed around the table, aiming to plug the jackass's mouth with his knuckles.

Catherine set the chalk cube on the rail. Turning to the leering redhead, she pressed the tip of her cue on his crotch seam and met his astonished eyes. "What's your name?"

His Adam's apple bobbed. "G-Gary."

"Well, Gary. I can explode a rack of billiard balls into all four rails with a single stroke. What do you think I could do to these itty bitty things?" she asked, her voice coldly speculating. Sweeping the circle of men with a contemptuous look, she lifted her chin. "One more word out of *any* of you, and I just might have to satisfy my curiosity. Do we understand each other?"

Heads nodded, none more vigorously than Gary's.

She smiled and lifted her cue stick from chalk-marked denim. "Excellent. Now, everyone please step back three paces from the table so I can breathe."

Joe obeyed along with the rest, intrigued by a woman who could be Olive Oyl one instant and Pop-eye the next. He suddenly found himself rooting for *her,* the money be damned.

For the second time that night, she examined the table end to end. When she finally moved into action, Joe had the feeling every shot had been planned.

She was an ace pool player of course. Sometime during the past half hour he'd decided she would be. Her strokes were strong, her aim damn near scary, her movements graceful and efficient. When she stretched over the table for a double-bank shot, her dress tightened and his eyebrows rose. She might be thin, but she sure as hell wasn't shapeless.

As striped balls spun, whammed or lipped over into pockets, he started to believe she would run the table.

Earl did, too, from the grim look on his leathery face. The reigning champion turned slightly green watching her last ball ricochet toward a side pocket. It hit hard, almost jawed out, then dropped out of sight.

Once she nailed the eight ball, history would be made at The Pig's Gut. Earl studied the table... and slowly grinned. Murmurs broke out in the crowd. Joe followed their gazes and silently groaned.

The eight ball guarded a corner pocket. Blocking it from a clean shot sat doom—the solid red ball that had defeated Earl. There was no way around it, un-less...

He watched Catherine assess the situation from several angles and knew the exact moment she made her decision. When she stepped up to the table and positioned her cue, his muscles tensed in empathy. Bottom of the ninth, two outs, winning run on third. Been there, done that.

She struck the cue ball hard, low and at precisely the right angle to lift it up and over the red ball. It landed with a thud and nicked black ivory, sending the eight ball rolling with agonizing slowness toward the pocket. Was it enough? Would it fall?

Yess!

Joe's whoop rang out in the stunned silence. Catherine straightened and sent him a grateful smile, her flush of triumph giving him a glimpse of the woman she might be, given a little happiness or makeup.

She looked toward the bar as if seeking someone's congratulations. Her smile dimmed.

Joe's head snapped around.

A man watched her from a bar stool. Blond hair, medium build, disapproving expression. Obviously her companion for the evening. Joe didn't like him.

The man's gaze moved to him, and Joe stiffened. Pretty Boy's appraisal was cold, amused and very thorough. Joe's dislike verged on something stronger.

"I've been hustled," Earl protested, breaking the hostile moment.

Joe turned and grinned at the old man's sour expression. "No, you were beat fair and square. My debt's canceled and you owe the lady a handshake."

Earl glanced at Catherine with grudging respect. "Maybe she could show me how she did that jump shot. I never been able to do it worth a damn." He shuffled over to the table, where Catherine stood racking balls with awkward jerky movements.

Where had her gracefulness gone? Joe eyed the blond-haired man at the bar thoughtfully, then looked back at the disgruntled customers returning to their own interrupted games. Manhood had suffered a blow tonight. They were not happy campers. An irresistible idea hit him.

He went with the moment and cupped his hand to his mouth. "Listen up, guys. There's a free beer for anyone who's interested."

Heads turned and faces lit. Skeeter took three steps forward then stopped, his expression suspicious. "Hey, you couldn't even pay off Earl. How're you gonna buy us all a beer?"

Joe couldn't contain his slow grin. "I'm not buyin'." His thumb jerked toward Pretty Boy at the bar. "*He* is."

CATHERINE GLARED across the small round table at Joe's casual sprawl and straightened her spine. He'd insisted on waiting for their beers to arrive before listening to her proposal. The delay gave her too much time to think. Too much time to analyze.

She, Catherine Eliza Hamilton, who could trace her paternal ancestry back to English royalty, had threatened a man's family jewels with her cue stick. She'd used her Ph.D. in psychology to rattle Earl's composure and win a game of billiards. And as if that wasn't enough, she'd enjoyed herself tremendously during both activities.

Thank heavens her father was away, lecturing at Oxford University. She wouldn't have to hear him rant about her appalling lack of decorum—the product of her mother's working-class genes of course. He'd blamed Mary Lou Hamilton for his daughter's every fall from grace since Catherine was three years old.

Mary Lou had been a waitress before marrying Lawrence Hamilton, of the impoverished but socially prominent Connecticut Hamiltons. He'd divulged that tidbit the year Catherine had turned sixteen and begged to work at a movie theater with her friends. Instead of serving popcorn, she'd spent the summer serving up research for his latest *Psychology Journal* article.

Although she now cowrote those articles, her father had never gotten around to adding her name to the byline.

Sighing, she watched a miniskirted blonde approach their table carrying a tray. Joe's teeth flashed white against his dark stubble as he drew in his long legs. The woman's faux-leather hips swayed harder. Her breasts jiggled in the aftershock. Disgusting. Why, she looked old enough to be his... older sister. And that smile was positively incestuous.

Bending low, the buxom waitress set two frosty bottles on the turquoise Formica. "Here they are, Joe, nice'n cold."

He wiggled his brows at the plump cleavage six inches from his nose. "Want me to warm 'em up for ya, Tammy?"

She bopped him on the head with her plastic tray, ignoring his indignant yelp. "Behave yourself, Joe Tucker, or I'll tell Allie you dropped your pants for the whole bar." Splaying hot-pink fingernails on one hip, she turned toward Catherine. "You watch yourself, hon. Allie's the only one who can control her dad. Always clownin' around, he is. Either that, or breakin' hearts. He's a real smooth talker.''

An unintelligible grunt sounded from behind her back.

"See what I mean?" Tammy's blue eyes twinkled as she turned. "That'll be three bucks for your beer, Joe." She winked to take the sting out of her demand.

Frowning, he fumbled in his back pocket. "What about the lady?"

"Are you kiddin'? Any woman who can shut Gary up and kick Earl's butt in the same night deserves a reward. Her beer's on me."

Meeting Tammy's admiring gaze, Catherine took back her snide thought about silicone implants.

Joe flipped open his worn wallet and extracted a five-dollar bill. Catherine couldn't help seeing it was the last of his cash. She glanced toward the bar where Carl sat brooding over his American Express receipt. Before tonight, she'd never seen her fiancé forced to do *anything* he hadn't planned.

"Wait," she said, halting Tammy's outstretched hand. "Put them both on Mr. Wilson's tab, please. And be sure to give yourself a big tip."

Tammy glanced over her shoulder at Carl and looked back grinning. "Anything you say, hon. The customer's always right." Tucking the tray under her arm, she swished off toward the bar.

Joe twisted the cap off one beer, wiped the glass lip with his sleeve and offered it to Catherine. No quaint mug in sight. Repressing a shudder, she accepted the bottle and told herself his jersey was cleaner than it looked.

He opened the second bottle for himself and cocked his head. "Okay, Catherine, I'm all ears. What's so all-fired important you wanted to talk to me about?"

At last. "My future counseling practice."

"Your future... Are you a shrink?" He spat the word out as if it were castor oil.

"I'm a psychologist," she corrected. "Up until now I've acted as research assistant to my father. I'm sure you've seen him interviewed on TV—Dr. Lawrence Hamilton? He heads up the Department of Counseling and Educational Psychology at Richmond College?"

Joe looked remarkably unimpressed.

"He wrote *The Five-Minute Intelligence Test*. All the major talk shows booked him as a guest," she added helpfully.

Shrugging, Joe spread his hands. "Sorry. Never heard of him."

Catherine felt a shocking surge of satisfaction. "Where have you *been* the past year?"

Eyeing her closely through slitted lids, he tilted his head back and took a deep swallow of beer. When he rested the bottle on his muscular thigh, over a third of its contents had vanished. "You really don't know who I am, do you?"

She drew her brows together. "Should I?"

He chuckled ruefully. "Guess not. On paper I played for the Astros, but my knees were on ice half the time."

"You're a hockey player?" This was terrible.

"I said Astros, not Aeros. As in the baseball team," he explained, his male disgust palpable.

Baseball, hockey—they both meant road trips, lots of publicity... "Wait a minute. Did you say *played?*"

"Yeah." His bleak tone matched his eyes. "Right now I'm kinda at loose ends."

She broke into a joyful smile, then smothered it at his startled look. "I'm changing jobs, too. That is, I'd like to establish my own family counseling practice. But my fiancé—the man buying the drinks tonight— wants a more ... traditional relationship."

Joe knuckled his eye sockets, blew out a breath and held her gaze. "Catherine...work with me here. What the hell do I have to do with any of this?"

Oh, God. She took a tiny sip of beer and grimaced. What she wouldn't give right now for a snifter of Remy Martin to bolster her courage. "I need you to win a bet I made with Carl."

"A bet."

"That's right. Over dinner, we were discussing Father's theory that intelligent sophisticates are born, not made. Carl agrees with the theory. I don't." She cleared her throat. "I'm afraid I became a tad... vehement."

Her fiancé had stepped into her father's shoes for the summer and triggered years of suppressed rebellion. She'd actually raised her voice in a chic restaurant defending environmental versus genetic influence on behavior. Every paternal slur regarding her own "tainted" gene pool had fueled her heated challenge.

"You might wanna speed things up, doll. This place closes soon." Joe's dark eyes gleamed with amusement.

She rubbed damp palms down her dress, then folded them on the table. "I wagered I could tutor anyone of Carl's choosing and pass that person off as a member of high society to the world's biggest snob."

He cocked a brow.

"My father," she said.

"I see." His rapidly cooling stare sent a shiver down her spine. "So your boyfriend went slumming for a lowlife sure to flunk and picked me?"

It sounded awful put that way. She peeled at the sodden label on her beer bottle. "Please don't be offended. Carl is very competitive. He hates to lose. And let's face it, you *were* mooning the ceiling when he picked you."

Joe's hooded gaze never wavered. "Just out of curiosity, what do you get for winning?"

"If I win, Carl has agreed to finance my private practice until I develop a clientele." She read his unspoken question and shrugged. "The Hamiltons may have impeccable breeding and a history of academic brilliance—but they have no head for managing money."

Glancing toward the bar, Joe twisted his mouth. "I take it Pretty Boy doesn't think you can turn a sandlot player into a major-league all-star. What does he get for winning?"

"Stop calling him that."

"Pretty? Or Boy?"

He wanted sarcasm? Fine. "*Carl* gets a pedigreed hostess for his parties. Someone who'll dote on him and his children, instead of her career."

"You mean he'll get a slave, while you give up your dream."

"No, he'll get a *wife*, whether I establish a practice or become a stay-at-home mom. When it comes to family, Carl and I have the same dream, the same values. Once I win, he'll see that my personal obligations won't suffer for my career.''

Joe snorted and shook his head.

"Are you married?" she asked bluntly.

"No." His expression grew shuttered.

"Sounds like you don't think too highly of the institution."

"Since my wife died, I don't think about it at *all* if I can help it. Can we get back to the point, here?"

Embarrassment held her mute. He obviously still grieved for his wife, and she'd intruded on his privacy.

"Earth to Catherine," he drawled as if addressing an airhead.

Her sympathy vanished. "The point is, I need your help, and you admitted you're at loose ends right now. So will you do it?"

He looked off into space for so long she thought he wasn't going to answer.

"And just what do I get for helping you win your bet?" he asked, his keen gaze sliding back to hers.

Her mind went blank. "Well, let's see..." She hadn't prepared beyond his acceptance. "What do you want?"

Joe drained his bottle of beer in two gulps, wiped his mouth with the back of one hand and delivered a volcanic burp.

"I thought you'd never ask."

CHAPTER TWO

THE BURP WAS a nice touch, Joe thought, watching Catherine's opinion of him dip lower than a sinker ball. The disgusted fascination on her face might've been funny—if it wasn't so damned insulting.

That was how shrinks were of course. Arrogant sons of bitches, playing God with people's lives. He'd wised up to their crap long ago and sworn to handle problems *his* way. Not that he'd done such a hot job.

Catherine drummed her short nails on the table. "Well? What do you want?"

He narrowed his eyes, his guilt converting into a more tolerable emotion. "I'm thinking."

Wouldn't he just love telling her exactly where to put her high-and-mighty bet? Except that her proposition might be the break he needed. His chance to secure Allie's future. To make amends. He'd be a fool not to explore his options.

But he could sure as hell make the woman squirm first.

"Before we take this any farther, doll, I need you to fill in some gaps for me." Noting her flinch at the word "doll," he slouched back and scratched his belly for good measure.

She watched his fingers with a distracted frown. "Gaps?"

"Yeah. Like what you mean by 'tutoring.' And what the terms are for winning or losing this bet. Minor stuff like that." He crossed his arms with a deliberate flex of muscles.

"Oh. Well..." Her gaze lit briefly on his biceps and fluttered away. Then drifted back.

His slouch slowly straightened.

"First I would evaluate your social skills to see which ones need polishing..." Her stare grew languid, sliding as softly as a chamois cloth over his throat. His chest. His abdomen.

Lord have mercy.

"Second I would schedule lessons in those areas where you seem to be lacking—" her gaze moved lower, stopped, and rose swiftly to focus somewhere over his shoulder "—n-not that you *are* lacking. Anywhere. Th-that is, I'll have to look harder—I m-mean longer..." A mottled flush crept up her neck. "What I *mean* is, I'll have to analyze you further before developing a specific tutorial plan," she finished primly.

Joe managed a stunned grunt. Vowing to use his little black book soon, he willed the blood back into his brain. "So how long will all this tutoring take?"

Relief flooded her face. "Carl's parents are hosting an engagement party at the end of June. My father is flying in from London to attend. That gives us a little over four weeks to get you ready."

"For what?"

"For the party. That's where Father will meet you."

"What about your mother?"

Some indefinable emotion flickered in her eyes. "Mother...died when I was very young." She leaned forward, her manner brisk and professional once more. "You'll be introduced as a fictional member of a prominent East Coast family. If neither my father nor any of the guests discover your deception by midnight, Carl will concede victory to us."

Too weird. "How many drinks did you two have before cooking up this bet?"

"One glass of brandy," she said, taking him literally. "But I assure you we're both very sober."

No kidding. They'd turned a lovers' spat into cold contract negotiations for spouse job descriptions. And maybe that was smart. He sure as hell knew impulse marriages were dumb.

Joe lifted his size-twelve sneaker and pointed the toe this way and that. "Midnight, huh? Think a glass slipper'll fit?"

Her straight dark brows drew together.

Lowering his foot to the floor, he sighed. "Never mind. If someone finds me out, won't you and Carl be embarrassed? Won't your parents be—"

"Cinderella! I get it." A delighted smile softened and lit her face.

He smothered a wave of uneasiness. *She's a shrink,* he reminded himself. *She'll probably never crack another smile the whole four weeks.*

Reaching for his beer, Joe realized it was empty and recrossed his arms. "As I was saying, what happens if I'm recognized at this party? Granted, I spent a lot of time in the dugout, but it's possible a real sports fan would remember me."

"If you were a polo player maybe. Or even a tennis pro. But this crowd will be too highbrow to follow a sport like baseball."

He made himself count to five before answering. "Yeah, those Columbia Star Suites in the Astrodome draw a pretty raunchy crowd. CEOs of major corporations, senators, *polo players* . . ." Noting her startled expression, he snorted. "We're not talking mud wrestling, here, Catherine. Baseball is a sport for *all* fans. Young and old, rich and poor—snobs and just plain folk. Lord have mercy if that ever changes."

She'd grown paler as he'd talked. "You're absolutely right. I sounded just like Father. Please accept my apology."

Joe nodded uncomfortably. He hadn't meant to get on his soapbox. But she'd insulted baseball, dammit.

"Of course it's possible someone could recognize you at the party," she admitted. "Or that you could—that I won't have done my job properly . . . Well, you know."

"I'll keep my pants on, if that's what you mean," he said dryly.

"I don't anticipate a problem, but if you're discovered, Carl and I will explain everything to the guests. You won't be held responsible."

"How comforting." Unfolding his arms, Joe examined the fading callus on his glove hand. "Okay, Catherine, I think I have the general picture now. And I figure a month of my time to help you win this bet should be worth . . . oh, at least five grand." He looked up. "Not including expenses."

Her nostrils flared. "*Five grand?* You must be joking!"

"'Fraid not, doll."

He thought of the rent due next week, Allie's softball camp fees, the humiliating thong-bikini-endorsement contract waiting to be signed. His agent had mailed out a slew of his sports-broadcasting demo tapes with no response. Yet a woman reporter in Chicago had salvaged his tape from the reject pile and forwarded it to a swimsuit manufacturer with immediate results.

Catherine twisted toward the bar. Joe followed her gaze, his hackles rising at the sight of Pretty Boy's smug little smirk. When she turned back around, he steeled himself to hang tough.

"Let's negotiate," she said, her features taut.

Billiard balls clacked. A throaty love ballad wound down; a lively two-step started up. Yet Catherine's gaze never wavered.

Joe was the first to look away. He glared at her nearly full beer, glad he hadn't paid for it. "I have obligations. You have money. What's the problem?"

"I told you, I *don't* have money. If I did, I would have started my own practice years ago, instead of struggling to pay off student loans. Do you have any idea what research assistants earn?"

He glanced up, moved in spite of himself by the hint of desperation in her eyes. She was either a damn good actress, or honestly couldn't afford his price.

"If you can't offer money, Catherine, just how in hell *did* you expect to sucker someone into going along with your crazy scheme?"

Her gaze faltered, dropping to her tightly clasped hands. "To be honest, I hadn't thought that far ahead. This whole thing sort of snowballed out of control." She peeked up through surprisingly long lashes. "I know it's hard to believe, but I'm usually very disciplined, very careful to consider all the facts before making a decision."

"Oh, I believe you."

Her lashes swept up, exposing her shy pleasure. "You do?"

She'd taken it as a compliment, and suddenly he was glad. All the fun had gone out of playing a goon.

"Sure I do. Everybody breaks loose and acts crazy sometimes. Guess this was your night." He scooted back his chair and stood. "Now if you're ready, we'll chalk this up to a full moon and go about our separate—"

"Wait! We haven't finished negotiating."

There was that hint of desperation again. He frowned at her upturned face. "Let it go, Catherine. It's just a stupid bet."

"It's *not* a stupid bet. Well, it is, but the principle it represents isn't. Oh, I can't *think* with you looming over me like that. Sit down. Please."

He sat, cursing himself for a fool.

"Look, what you said earlier about Carl coming here specifically to find someone who would 'flunk' the bet...well, you were right. He simply can't imagine anyone without a background and family tree similar to his being able to move comfortably among elite society." Her expression gentled. "Frankly, Joe, right now you couldn't."

He grabbed the neck of her beer bottle, draining half the contents and suppressing his rising belch. "Frankly, my dear, I don't give a damn."

She choked on a laugh. "I don't blame you. Elite society is filled with boring people. But there's no doubt in my mind that with four weeks of tutoring, you can be just as boring."

"You mean just as good, don't you?"

The teasing glint in her eyes faded. "No, I don't. You would simply be proving a point. And you might find that having a little savoir faire—learning a bit about the arts and sophisticated pursuits—will open doors that would otherwise be closed. That could be of real benefit to someone in the job market."

"I'd benefit from some *money,* dammit." Spending four weeks just to get hoity-toity was nuts. It was time to cut his losses and go home. "I sure as hell don't need savoir faire to work for the refinery."

"You're going to work for the refinery?"

"I've got a standing job offer." He'd wear a thong bikini before accepting any position not related to sports, but Catherine didn't have to know that.

She studied him shrewdly. "I can see that you'd hate working there, but at the same time you're skeptical about the return on a four-week investment in my plan."

A chill prickled his arms. Earl was right. She was a damn witch.

"I promise after we win the bet you'll have employers standing in line to make you an offer—in the field of your choice."

A damn *good* witch, Joe amended.

"Did you know that savoir faire means literally 'to know how'? As Father says—" her expression turned snooty "—it separates those who *are* cosmopolitan from those who read *Cosmopolitan.*"

Her father sounded like a prick. "What do *you* say, Catherine?"

"Me?" She looked startled, as if no one asked her opinion much. "I believe we all have the power to change the circumstances of our birth, to become whatever we choose. Winning this bet will show Father and Carl I'm right."

Something about her intensity made him think there was more to it than that.

"And it will help you land that job you're after," she continued. "Coaching, perhaps? Sports broadcasting?" Her brow arched knowingly. "Ah, sports broadcasting."

He hastily closed his mouth.

"I was running out of guesses," she admitted with a chuckle. "Just think. Two candidates. Each knowledgeable about sports. One articulate, polished and experienced on camera. One articulate, polished and an ex-major-league player. Which candidate do you think the station manager knows will attract more viewers?"

She'd made one helluva case, he had to give her that.

A close-the-sale gleam entered her eyes. "I'd say that's a pretty fair return on four weeks of your time, wouldn't you?"

Still, a man had to be practical. "It won't pay my rent next week."

With a strangled sound of frustration, she yanked the beer bottle from his hand, tipped it to her mouth and threw back her head. Glossy hair slipped away, revealing an arched white throat. Sensual. Feminine. Totally uninhibited.

Joe stared at each rippling gulp and felt his blood head south again. A neck like that rated special attention. Starting at the delicate hollow where her pulse beat, then nibbling up to her smooth jawline—

She clunked the bottle down, snapping Joe out of his fantasy. He scrubbed his face in his palms.

"Did I mention the vacant apartment that comes with my offer?"

His head came up. "It must've slipped your mind."

"It's a darling little place."

"I'm all ears." Hell, he was Dumbo.

"Very cozy. Completely furnished. And it's free."

He could fly! "Where's it located?"

"On the outskirts of Richmond College. Right behind our house, so you could walk up for lessons—"

"*Our* house?" Everything in him bristled.

"Actually it's my father's house, although I don't see what difference..." She let the sentence trail off and followed the direction of his gaze. "Good heavens, no! I mean, Carl and I don't... That is, I live with Father. It's convenient for me to conduct my research where he keeps his private notes." Her tone could've corroded batteries.

What was the story with these three?

She brightened. "He'll lease the apartment to a student in the fall, but right now it's just collecting dust."

His thoughts were already rounding third base. His agent needed a place to park and think for a while. If he sublet his apartment to him for a month, he could tear up that thong-bikini-endorsement contract. And a little polish was exactly what several sports directors had said he lacked.

"What about expenses?"

"I'll take care of lesson-related costs—tickets, gasoline, rentals and the like—but meals are your responsibility."

He didn't have a clue what she was talking about, but meals he could handle. Allie was a whiz at stretching hamburger... Oh, God, Allie. Lately she'd been so moody he didn't know what to expect from his little pal anymore.

"How many bedrooms did you say this apartment has?"

A wary glint entered Catherine's eyes. "One. But it's very large."

"Is there a sofa bed by any chance?" He'd slept on worse, and it was only for a month.

"As a matter of fact, yes."

"Is there a pool?" Allie loved to swim.

"There's a lap pool nearby. . . for adults only." He could see her busy little mind working. "But the tennis courts are open to anyone," she added hopefully.

Allie loved all sports. She'd be a natural at tennis. "If I did this, my daughter, Allie, would be living with me."

"How old is she?"

He didn't like the way she was biting her lip. "Twelve. Is that a problem? I mean, are there restrictions against children at this place?"

"No."

"You don't sound too sure of that."

"No," she said more forcefully. "In fact, the management loves children."

He searched her face, reassured by the honest conviction he saw there. "I must be crazy," he muttered to himself.

"You mean you'll do it?"

"I have to tie up some loose ends in the next couple of days, and I can't commit before then, but if everything falls into place—"

The impact of her lithe body hitting his chest whooshed the air from his lungs. Slim arms circled his neck and squeezed. He registered soft skin, silky hair, a flowery scent—and then Catherine drew back.

"Thank you, Joe! I promise you won't regret your decision."

Watching her smile light up the dingy pool hall, Joe had a sick feeling he already did.

"I WON'T GO!" Allie slammed the door hard enough to rattle her row of softball trophies.

Stalking to her dresser, she moved the tallest trophy a fraction to the left and rubbed the brass-plate inscription: Allison Tucker, Most Valuable Player. Instead of feeling her usual burst of pride, she blinked back the horrible sting of tears.

The doorknob rattled. "C'mon Allie, it's only for a month. It'll be fun."

Fun. Joe's solution to everything from her earliest memory, from the time she'd actually believed in magic. She glared at the door. "You go on, then. I'll stay here with Norman."

"You can't, honey. Norman needs time alone since Doris kicked him out. Besides, I'd miss you too much. You're my best pal, remember?" His deep voice was sentimental, wheedling.

She closed her eyes against the images crowding her mind. Making ice-cream sundaes for dinner on Gram's bingo night, playing hooky from school to share popcorn at a movie—saving a place at her team awards banquet for a father who never showed up.

"Allie, please open the door."

The ache in her chest moved higher, swelling her throat. Her stomach churned worse than before a big game. She wanted to fling the door open and throw herself into Joe's strong arms. She wanted to fling the door open and scream the bitter words clogging her windpipe.

"Allie?"

She wanted to be a little kid again, too dumb to know anything about anything.

The silence stretched. Joe sighed, then walked away.

Released, Allie dove for the top of her bed and buried her face in a pillow. The tears she'd been holding back burst free. Why had Gram married that snowbird and moved to Minnesota? Didn't she know her granddaughter needed her? Depended on her, if not for love and approval, at least for adult common sense?

Now Joe wanted to pack up and move to some place Allie'd never heard of, away from her friends, away from Tommy Burton in apartment 34C. And for what? Some stupid plan some stupid lady'd made that might help Joe get some stupid job. He wasn't a Houston Astros player anymore, he'd told her, and she would bet her MVP trophy Gram didn't know. If she did, she never would've left two days ago. Allie clenched her soaked pillowcase and gave in to a fresh surge of tears. Why couldn't things stay the same?

Stretching out her arm, she groped blindly, connected with a soft shape and dragged it close. The stuffed monkey was the closest she'd come to having a pet. Joe had won it for her last year at her softball team's annual carnival.

Yesterday, when she'd practiced face painting on his arm, he'd promised to win her another animal at this year's fund-raiser. It was one promise she believed. After all, hadn't he wiped out the tower of bottles on his first throw last year? Her friends had said later what a cool father he was. And they were half-right. He was strong and cute and a super athlete and way cool about blowing off rules and making people laugh.

But he was no father. At least, not like her friends had.

Flipping onto her back, Allie sniffed hard and gritted her teeth. She *hated* crying. Only wusses cried. But lately she was out of control. A real loser.

Like when Tommy'd smiled at her by the pool twenty-six hours and forty minutes ago, and she'd giggled like a demented hyena. If he hadn't already thought she wasn't worth his super-fine smile, he sure did now. Sarah Sokol had whispered something to him behind her hand, and they'd both laughed. Allie wanted to die just thinking about it.

Lifting the hem of her T-shirt, she scrubbed her face and frowned at the Boyz II Men poster on her wall. Joe'd said his teacher lady friend was real classy. That she'd show him how to act like he'd grown up in a mansion, instead of a run-down shack behind Big Joe's filling station. Anyone who could teach a guy all that fancy stuff probably knew a lot about girl stuff, too.

Allie lay quietly, feeling more like herself by the minute. She would quit being a baby and face facts. Joe was Joe. She was old enough to take care of herself—and him, too. He needed her.

Swinging her legs to the stained beige carpet, she walked to the door and stood finger-combing her snarled hair, instead of brushing it. Gram would've thrown a hissy fit, but Joe wouldn't notice. Pulling her door open, she moved down the hall and stopped short of the den entrance.

Just like every morning, Joe sat reading the sports page in his old recliner, his bare feet sticking out well past the footrest. He'd dragged his favorite cutoffs and tank top out of the dirty clothes hamper. Again. She'd have to sneak them into the wash before the neighbors complained.

From the looks of the teddy bears on his arm, he hadn't showered after getting home last night. A bowl of soggy cereal sat on one chair arm. The other supported his tightly clutched beer. He looked scruffy, tired and . . . sad.

She'd hurt him, Allie realized with a start. *Both* of him. The playmate she adored and the man who'd disappointed her so many times over the years. Her wonderful impossible dad.

He glanced up and noticed her in the doorway. "Hi there."

"Hi."

"Feeling a little better?"

She nodded, hating this awkward politeness.

"Good." His gaze sharpened. "Then who was named most valuable player for the 1974 World Series? There's a hamburger in it for the winner."

It was a game they'd played for years, familiar and safe. She crossed her arms and waited for him to up the ante.

He sighed. "Okay, *with* fries."

"Finley with the Oakland A's. Piece'a cake."

"I'll get you one of these days," he promised, ruining the threat by grinning proudly.

"In your dreams. Can I have a milk shake, too?"

"Not for that no-brainer. Now go do something with that rat's nest on your head while I get my shoes." He pushed down on the footrest and sat straight.

Allie slowly touched her head. He'd noticed her hair? "Joe?"

He finished a huge yawn and rolled his shoulders. "Hmm?"

"I'm sorry I slammed the door in your face."

His eyes met hers, all trace of grogginess gone. "That's okay. I know you miss Gram, and you're kind of scared about the two of us getting along without her. I know I haven't always been there for you. But now I won't be on the road half the year. Things'll be different."

He'd known how she felt? Staring into his anxious eyes, she couldn't breathe for the love filling her heart.

"We can do this, pal," he said with forced heartiness. "Together."

This time Allie didn't hesitate. Running forward, she threw herself into Joe's strong arms and held on tight. After a long moment she lifted her head and smiled.

"Course we can, Joe. It'll be fun."

CATHERINE STOOD behind father and daughter while they studied the "apartment" she'd promised Joe three nights ago. Heat radiated up from the driveway in brutal waves. How could they look so fresh in this Amazonian hell?

Allie's cap of short dark hair reached just above Joe's elbow. Wearing shorts and a ribbed knit shirt, she revealed the compact body of a young gymnast. Yet her budding curves promised future havoc for adolescent male hormones—and Joe's peace of mind.

When had Joe's wife died? Catherine wondered briefly. She knew only too well how rough the next few years could be for the girl without a mother's guidance. Ignoring the odd catch in her heart, she focused on Joe.

He'd shaved recently, a definite improvement over the last time she'd seen him. His khaki slacks and hunter green shirt flattered his broad shoulders and lean hips. Or maybe it was the other way around. She had a feeling he'd look good wearing anything. Especially his bare skin. She glanced away. Then looked slowly back.

Something about his quietness made her nervous. Possibly the fists hanging by his sides like small hams.

"This is it?" Allie finally asked her father, her up-tilted face a delicate version of his—yet not like his at all. "This is what we'll be living in for a month? It's a *garage* apartment, Joe."

"I can see that." His tone matched his fists.

Okay, Catherine admitted silently, maybe she'd been a wee bit hasty describing it as she had.

"This sucks big-time," Allie said, grabbing Joe's arm. "Let's go call Norman and tell him he can't lease our apartment."

"Too late, pal. He's halfway here from Dallas by now."

They turned to Catherine in unison, their identical brown glares prodding her guilty conscience. Her sweeten-the-pot offer didn't seem nearly as brilliant today as it had in The Pig's Gut.

"Where is my fully furnished apartment with a very large bedroom?" Joe asked carefully.

She looked up and squinted at the redbrick structure shimmering over the garage. "Technically speaking, it's right in front of you. Just because the one bedroom happens to be the living and dining room, too, doesn't mean it's not large." If her peripheral vision could be trusted, Joe wasn't amused. "Now calm down. Once you see the inside, you'll feel much—"

"You lied to me," he interrupted.

She met his gaze at that. "I never lie."

"Oh, excuse me. You messed with my head. Psychotherapy, I believe you couch doctors call it."

This man was no amoeba. "Actually we prefer to think of it as creative ego management." Her feeble smile died in the face of his deepening scowl. "That was a joke."

A bad joke, but then, she doubted David Letterman could've cracked Joe's contempt. Someone in his past had really done her profession a disservice.

He lowered his brows. "Where are the tennis courts you promised?"

Relieved, she turned and pointed toward the east. "See those big trees? The courts are right behind them. An indoor lap pool, also. The neighbors love pairing up for a tennis match, if you're interested. We're very friendly around here." Didn't she always wave at the sweating fools when she walked by on her way to swim laps in cool indoor comfort?

"And I suppose you'll tell me the management that 'loves children' isn't a lie, either."

At last, firm ground. "I love children," she stated unequivocally, frowning when he continued to look skeptical. "You certainly are being unreasonable for someone who's expecting a Norman from Dallas any minute."

"Gimme a break, doll. Am I supposed to be happy I gave up my big apartment for a doghouse in your backyard?"

She narrowed her eyes.

The makeup she'd carefully applied after his unexpected phone call was no doubt melting with her sweat. The wraparound denim skirt she'd anxiously selected clung, hot and itchy, to her hose. She'd worked every spare minute for the last month on the haven he'd just called a doghouse, hoping to use it as her summer office. Enough was enough.

"You called *me,* remember? You were the one who made plans to move into an apartment without seeing it first. I've been standing out here without the benefit of air-conditioning for fifteen minutes—ten minutes past my previous record—and I have nothing to show for it but sunburn and your verbal abuse." She lifted her stinging nose high enough to do her Hamilton ancestors proud. "Considering you have the manners of a mongrel, a doghouse is exactly what you deserve. However, I'm offering you a charming efficiency apartment any number of people would be thrilled to lease. I decorated it myself. Now, do you want it or not?"

Joe looked as if he were choking on his answer.

"No?" Catherine inclined her head regally. "Well, then, perhaps I'll call *Norman* when he arrives and see if he's interested. Can you give me the telephone number, Allie?"

The wide-eyed girl nodded.

"Leave my daughter out of this," Joe practically snarled. "Show me the damn apartment." Spinning around, he glared ahead.

Catherine almost felt sorry for him. Almost.

"How can I refuse such a gracious request?" Pulling the keys from her skirt pocket, she brushed by Joe and mouthed "ego management" to his daughter in passing. After a startled second, Allie's brown eyes sparked with feminine comprehension and amusement.

A warm glow spread through Catherine as she headed for the stairs leading up to the efficiency. Hearing footsteps behind her, she grinned in triumph.

"What are you smiling at?" Joe snapped.

Catherine started to turn.

"Would you chill?" Allie said to her dad, sounding thoroughly exasperated. "First you want me to be happy about moving. Now you don't want me to smile. Make up your mind."

His grumbled "Sorry" restored Catherine's grin. She'd felt an instant rapport with Allie and looked forward to gaining the girl's friendship.

Reaching the unshaded staircase, Catherine began climbing the steps, the biting smell of hot cedar reminding her not to touch the railing. At the small landing she stopped and inserted her key into the cherry red door.

"Well, here we are," she stated the obvious, turning the knob and pushing forward with a sudden feeling of doom.

Maybe she'd been a wee bit hasty not telling Joe about his roommates.

CHAPTER THREE

HALFWAY UP THE STEPS Joe paused to rest. He'd come a long way since his surgery two months ago, but climbing reminded him why his contract hadn't been renewed. Rubbing his left knee, he watched Allie tentatively follow their new landlord into the apartment. He should take his daughter's advice and "chill." But it was damn hard to do with Catherine's little speech ringing in his ears.

The nerve of her, implying he'd been gullible, or worse—foolish—to act decisively and quickly. How many opportunities, how many good times would've passed him by in the past year alone if he'd waited to plan every detail in advance? More than she'd experienced in her entire uptight life, he'd be willing to bet.

His mosquito of a conscience buzzed out of nowhere and bit deep.

If he'd planned the off-season vacation his daughter'd begged him for, instead of flying off to Vail on impulse, maybe he'd still be on the Astros roster. Maybe Allie wouldn't have cried her heart out when his mother left. Maybe—

"C'mon, poky," Allie called down from the doorway.

Joe straightened and blinked. She had the filled-to-bursting look of someone hiding a good secret. Thank

God. The apartment must meet with her approval. He waved and she ducked back inside.

Climbing the remaining steps without much enthusiasm, he reached the landing. The place would be sophisticated of course. And probably as sterile as the woman who'd decorated it. He hoped like hell the carpet wasn't white. Assuming a carefully bland expression, he drew in a breath and crossed the threshold.

A riot of colors assaulted him.

Green. Purple. Red. Orange. Some others he'd seen on paint chips that never got taken home. Closing his eyes, he gave his pupils a minute to adjust from sunlight to lamplight, then risked another peek. He hadn't hallucinated.

Lord have mercy, he'd just committed to living in a crayon box for a month.

"So what d'ya think?" His daughter's eyes, soothing pools of familiar brown, had never seemed more beautiful. She gestured widely and grinned. "Does this place rule or what?"

Rule? It conquered. Overwhelmed.

"Catherine did everything herself. The kitchen curtains. The wallpaper. Even that painting over the sofa. Can you believe it?"

He turned and studied the rectangular canvas of purple and orange flowers, saved from dime-a-dozen blandness by rich texture and disturbing boldness. His mind stumbled. The artist of this painting was no uptight sterile woman. Even his untrained eye detected passion in the vibrant brush strokes.

Catherine laughed uneasily from somewhere behind him. "I'm sure your father's more interested in the practical features of the apartment. For example, the sofa folds out to a bed."

He heard the swish of her long denim skirt. Felt the fabric brush the back of his slacks. Inhaled the scent of lush summer blooms and heated female skin. *She smells like the painting looks,* he thought, spinning around to confront this unforeseen threat to his plans.

She took half a step back. "It's…it's a brand-new mattress. Top of the line."

Noting Allie had wandered to the kitchen, he gave Catherine a thorough inspection. Mascara smudged her left eyelid. Her nose glowed with sunburn. A tight low ponytail did nothing to flatter her narrow face. Hardly a femme fatale. Hardly a threat.

Relaxing, he slid one hand into his pocket. "Where's Allie going to sleep?"

"There's a roll-away bed in the closet. I'm told it's fairly comfortable."

"What about this thing?" He measured the sofa with a doubtful eye. "I'm not exactly petite."

"Oh, that mattress is big enough for two and quite comfortable—" She broke off with a frown and glanced away.

Oh-ho! So that's how it is! He jiggled his pocket change irritably. "Big enough for two, is it?" he said for her ears alone.

Her cheeks pinkened to match her lifting nose. "Three, if everyone cooperates." She held his gaze long enough for him to feel like a fool, then walked toward the kitchen. "There's a trick to unfolding the roll-away bed, Allie. And the pilot light sometimes goes out on the stove. How about taking the ten-cent guided tour?"

Allie's enthusiastic nod made Joe stare. Whatever happened to "This sucks big-time"?

Ignoring him completely, Catherine glided around the apartment touching features with the grace of Vanna White turning letters of the alphabet. He'd never seen a woman move like that. So erect, yet so fluid a book on her head wouldn't have wobbled.

They spent a long time in the walk-in closet talking about bed latches, linens and storage space. The bathroom tour drew Allie's appreciative, "Cool." After that Joe quit paying attention and sat on the sofa with a sigh.

For a man who supposedly understood women, he couldn't seem to get a handle on Catherine. Take this apartment, for instance.

In his living-room experience acceptable colors ranged from beige to dark brown. Fabrics matched. Walls were covered with family photographs or framed prints. The only purple in sight was grape-juice stains on the carpet. But *this*...

He stretched out his legs and gazed around. This place was as foreign to him as a subtitled movie.

Now that the shock had worn off, he could tell there was a weird sort of order to everything. Somehow the green-checked sofa blended with the floral-patterned armchair. The glossy green patio table and chairs looked good against the purple back wall. Even the Mardi Gras masks hanging like pictures didn't spook him the way they had at first. The black iron doorstop, though, would definitely have to go.

Joe examined the thing with a shudder. He *hated* cats. All cats. Even fake ones. He leaned forward and squinted. Stood up and moved closer. Bent down and reached out.

The doorstop opened slitted green eyes and hissed. Something gray streaked up close and bit Joe's outstretched hand.

"Son of a *bitch!*"

"Romeo!" Catherine rushed forward and scooped the gray cat from the floor.

Clutching his injured hand, Joe glared at the scruffiest, ugliest, meanest-looking excuse for a famous lover he'd ever seen. Satanic yellow eyes glared back from the cradle of Catherine's arms. At her feet, the black doorstop yowled plaintively.

She looked down, her expression softening. "It's okay, Juliet, he's not hurt. See?" Catherine lowered the huge gray tomcat to the floor, where he began grooming himself as if soiled irreparably by the incident.

Joe pointed a wounded finger. "*He's* not hurt? I need a rabies shot, for cryin' out loud."

Frowning, she reached for Joe's hand, examined his punctured skin with a small sound of dismay, then twisted toward Allie. "Honey, would you get antiseptic and bandages from the medicine cabinet please?

Crouched on the floor stroking the black cat, Allie looked up and met Joe's stare. *Traitor,* he accused silently.

Her golden skin flushed. "Sure thing," she mumbled, loping off to the bathroom.

"Romeo's had all his vaccinations. You won't need a rabies shot," Catherine assured him.

"Where the hell was he hiding all that time?"

"Under the couch. He probably thought you were going to hurt Juliet. He doesn't like men."

"No kidding," Joe muttered.

Bending her head, Catherine probed his wound. "Does it hurt much?"

Like he'd been stabbed with hot pokers. "Nah."

"Such a manly man," she said, amusement lacing her voice. "Is this my cue to swoon?"

"You wouldn't be the first one, doll."

Her green gaze lifted. The air hummed between them. Her shift in mood from skeptical to speculative didn't surprise him. His fierce desire to satisfy her curiosity did.

Allie ran up, breaking their locked gazes. "Here's the stuff you wanted," she said breathlessly.

Catherine released his hand and reached for the supplies.

"Does it hurt real bad, Joe?" Allie's expression offered an apology for not asking him earlier.

"Nah." He grinned and deepened his voice. "I'm a manly ma— *Ow-w-w!*"

"It's only a little iodine," Catherine said sternly, dabbing his fingers with the stinging liquid. "Quit fussing. Manly men don't whine."

He dropped his chin to his chest and thrust out his lower lip in an exaggerated pout. Allie giggled. Catherine glanced up and snorted. Reclaiming his hand with a shake of her head, she set to work.

Absurdly pleased, he nodded toward the two cats now vying for Allie's attention. "What the hell are they doing here?"

She froze, then continued bandaging his fingers. "They live here."

His good humor fled. "Excuse me?"

"They live here," she said louder, as if the problem were his hearing, not the cats.

"Don't you mean they *lived* here?"

"No." She finished wrapping his last puncture wound and offered a bright smile. "There you are. Good as new."

He caught her wrist as she stepped back. "Cats weren't part of our deal."

"Didn't I mention them?" She shrugged elegantly. "Oh, well, they're so little trouble it must have slipped my mind."

"Catherine..." he warned.

Her expression sobered, all flippancy gone. "I can't keep them at the house, Joe. My father is allergic to cats."

"So have the house cleaned before he comes back from England."

"I tried that after his book tour. It nearly put him in the hospital. He's *severely* allergic."

"So keep 'em outside. This neighborhood is a friggin' cat paradise. All those trees to climb, birds to chase—"

"Dogs to chase them," Catherine finished, her tone grim. "Juliet's declawed. She couldn't defend herself or even climb a tree for safety. I have to keep her inside. And Romeo is devoted to her. He'd die if I separated them."

Joe made a sound of disgust and released her wrist. "Gimme a break. They're just *cats,* for God's sake."

Some emotion veiled her face, a vulnerability that said the animals were much more than casual pets, much more than he could comprehend. The next instant her eyes narrowed, so like the doorstop's it was eerie.

"The students who rent this apartment come and go, but Romeo and Juliet stay. This is their home. If you can't share it with them, I'm afraid our deal is off."

Allie moved up and tugged on Joe's arm. "They won't be any trouble. I'll take care of them myself. You won't have to do a thing. Please, Joe, can we stay?"

He looked into doe brown eyes and remembered a little girl of six pleading for a kitten, a little girl of eight pleading for a puppy.

"You said yourself it was only for a month," she persisted, turning his own words against him.

He'd vetoed the kitten and puppy. The subsequent rabbit and bird, too. His mother wouldn't tolerate an animal in the house, and, as she'd told him, *he* wouldn't be there to help care for them.

Before Allie's imploring eyes grew disillusioned, before his gut could churn with guilt, he cupped her head and rumpled her silky hair. "Okay, pal, tomorrow we'll bring a load of stuff over and get settled in. But when it comes to those two monsters, forget what I said about us sticking together. You're on your own."

Whether his sudden difficulty in breathing came from Allie's crushing bear hug or the quiet thanks in Catherine's eyes, he couldn't have said.

FIFTY MILES AWAY, Mary Lou Denton eased behind the counter of Columbus Truck Stop's diner and tied an apron over her slim black skirt. The luncheon special—chicken-fried steak as big as a hubcap— would keep things hopping for hours yet. She might run the place now, but she couldn't sit on her duff in the manager's office while the waitresses up front ran

themselves ragged. She'd walked too many years in
their shoes.

Grabbing an order pad and pencil, she slipped into
the stream of action without a ripple. Dishes clat-
tered. Voices rumbled. Steam clouded or curled,
spreading the smells of grease, coffee and fresh-baked
bread. A waitress's telltale perfume. She'd have to
wash and rinse her hair twice tonight, but the thought
didn't annoy her as it used to. She pushed back a
surge of uneasiness.

If there was an extra spring in her step, it wasn't
because today was Wednesday. She hadn't worn her
hair up in a French twist for any particular reason.
Her heart didn't leap each time the door jangled
open. No, not hers. That would mean she cared who
came in. And she was way too smart for that.

Irene whizzed past balancing loaded plates on both
arms. The harried waitress's well-timed mumble
found its mark and Mary Lou scanned the eating
customers. Ah. So Grace had discovered the new
driver for Valley Produce, had she?

When the pretty young woman tossed him a parting smile and headed toward the kitchen, Mary Lou
stepped into her path. "The family in booth three
finished five minutes ago."

Grace blushed, knowing she'd been caught flirting. "Yes, ma'am."

Mary Lou nodded and moved out of the way. *Yes,
ma'am, old lady, ma'am.* As if she'd never experienced the thrill of a man's appreciative gaze. As if she
never would.

Without vanity, she knew her thick dark hair had
very little gray, her skin few wrinkles, her body little
excess flesh for a woman of fifty-two years. Men still

cast her second glances. She stared at the front door, realized what she was doing and turned back to the counter wearing a blush of her own.

Drivers sat hunched over their plates in a long row. Cattle at the trough, she'd called them once upon a time, when her dreams were big and her patience shrank in proportion to her swelling feet. She'd been so disdainful then. So... naive. Funny how tragedy changed a person's outlook. She'd returned from the East a whole lot sadder but wiser.

These men had names. Families. Troubles and triumphs. Her feet swelled worse than ever, but thank God her head didn't.

"Hey, beautiful, c'mere a minute," a familiar voice boomed.

Irene, Grace and Mary Lou swiveled their heads at the same time. Nate Dawson grinned at all three but crooked his finger at Mary Lou. The younger women rolled their eyes fondly and returned to their duties.

Smiling, Mary Lou walked to the barrel-shaped trucker who'd become a true friend over the years. The birth of his two daughters, his problems with various employers, the glorious day he'd bought his own rig—she'd shared them all with Nate. Just as he'd cheered her promotion to manager two years ago. She suspected he'd put the original bug in the new owner's ear that led to a serious interview.

She stopped in front of Nate and patted his arm. "How's it going, stranger? You haven't stopped by my office in ages."

"Been workin' against the clock the last coupla months. Only stopped today 'cause I was runnin' on fumes. By the way, pump 9 is knockin' real bad."

"I know. It's on my list." Along with a hundred other details to take care of. She tapped Nate's polished plate and chuckled. "Sorry you didn't like the special."

"I couldn't hurt Danny's feelings now, could I? In fact, maybe I'd better have some of his peach cobbler."

"Mmm. Aren't you forgetting those size-forty pants you were going to fit into for Cindy's wedding?" His daughter was getting married in three weeks. Short of liposuction, Nate was out of time.

His hopeful expression fell. "I stuck to my diet all morning. Didn't stop for a doughnut or nothin', you can ask Frank. He's been tailin' my mud flaps since San Antonio. Tell her I didn't stop, will ya, Frank?" Nate elbowed the driver on his right, nearly knocking the smaller man off his stool.

Frank resettled his skinny rump and slanted his colleague a lethal glance. "Touch me again and Cindy'll be wearing black to her wedding."

"Ooh. Big talk from such a little man."

"It ain't the size of the dog that counts, buddy. It's the fight *in* the dog—"

"Guys," Mary Lou interrupted before the reference to size could turn sexual. And it would, as surely as men would be boys. "I'll get you the cobbler, Nate, if you'll promise to reserve a larger tux for the wedding while there's still time. They may have to ship one in from another store location."

Nate threw up his hands. "Forget the damn cobbler! Jeez, you're worse than Barb. It's not like I haven't tried to lose weight. I have. It's just that I've got this...condition."

Mary Lou stared. Nate *never* lost his temper. "What do you mean, condition?"

Looking as if he wished he'd kept his mouth shut, Nate glanced from side to side, then leaned forward. Alarm shot through her.

"I saw a doctor in Dallas," he confessed grimly. "There's a problem with my stomach, Mary Lou."

"Oh, Nate, no."

"'Fraid so. Something called dunlop disease."

"Dunlop disease?" She reached for his beefy forearm and squeezed. "It's going to be okay, Nate. You'll do what the doctor says and everything will be fine."

Eyes cast down, he shook his head, his jowls swaying. "Ain't nothin' anyone can do. My belly done lopped over my belt, and that's all there is to it."

He raised mischievous hazel eyes an instant before he sputtered into laughter. Frank joined in.

Releasing Nate's arm with a shove, Mary Lou felt her face heat. Gullible to the end, that's what she was.

Still hooting, Nate pointed a stubby finger. "Got you good that time, honey, didn't I, Frank?"

Frank met her narrowed gaze and wisely kept quiet.

Stabbing her pencil into her coiled hair, she stacked the men's empty dishes with clattering force.

Nate sobered. "Aw hell, Mary Lou, I'm sorry for pulling your leg like that. This damn wedding is making me real mean. It's all Barb nags me about day and night." He rubbed at a water ring on the counter. "She expects me to be happy, ya know? But the truth is, I'll miss Cindy somethin' terrible."

Mary Lou scooped up the pile of dishes. "Would you like that cobbler now?"

"Guess I'd better not." He studied her closely and sighed. "Those cat eyes of yours are still hissing mad. I don't blame you. I can't expect you to understand what losing a daughter feels like."

Her fingers slackened. Crockery hit the floor and shattered. Cursing, she lowered her knees to the black and white tiles and stared at the mess. She hadn't dropped a dish in at least fifteen years.

"You okay?" Nate's concerned voice drifted over her head.

"I'm fine," she managed to croak.

"For a minute there, you turned white as a sheet. You see a ghost or somethin'?"

Did a memory qualify? "No. I'm fine," she repeated, as much for herself as for him.

Grace rushed up, sympathy in her cluck and glee in her eyes. "Would you like me to clean that up, Ms. Denton?"

Mary Lou sent her a wry look. "No, just give Nate and Frank their checks, please."

"Yes, ma'am."

Feeling as fractured as the smashed earthenware on the floor, Mary Lou struggled for composure. She'd thought her past safely buried. Yet one innocent comment had unearthed her clawing guilt.

Is she married? Is she a mother? Is she happy?

Not knowing sliced her heart. She bled as much now as thirty, twenty, ten years ago. Time had only changed the questions.

"Here you go, Ms. Denton."

Blinking, she smoothed back her hair with trembling fingers. Irene had placed a whisk, dustpan and paper bag within reach. Mary Lou slowly began gathering broken shards. Movement flowed unchecked around her—a stream purling around the rock suddenly dropped in its midst. At some point Nate apologized again and left. Grace announced she was going on break.

Mary Lou's awareness returned by degrees. She dumped the last dish fragments into the paper bag and sank back on her heels. For the tenth time in as many minutes the front door jangled open.

It was him.

She didn't question how she knew, she just did. And that scared the hell out of her. Despite her earlier thoughts to the contrary, she'd let herself care too much about someone in her life. If she needed a reminder of the consequences, the past few agonizing minutes provided ample proof.

Very quietly she eased backward until her fanny hit storage drawers. From the other side of the counter, she would be invisible.

Bustling toward the kitchen, Irene paused in midstride, her startled gaze flicking from Mary Lou to someone at the counter. Someone tall. "H-hi there, Mr. Chandler. What can I get you?"

"A Diet Coke please. No, better make that two. I'll take one to Ms. Denton in her office." The deep cultured voice soaked through the surrounding Texas twangs like wine through beer nuts.

Mary Lou's pulse accelerated. The moment for revealing herself came and went.

Irene, bless her heart, never faltered. "Just let me turn this order in and I'll get your drinks right away."

"Take your time. I'm not going anywhere."

Swell. Mary Lou swallowed hard and forced herself to think. Once John headed for her office with the drinks, she'd slip out the front door and think up an excuse later. She was simply too shaken—too vulnerable—to face her monthly meeting with the owner of Columbus Truck Stop today.

Thank God the lunch crowd had thinned. Thank God for Irene's quick wit. Thank God Grace was lingering outside with the new driver for Valley Produce.

"Not that I'm complaining," John said conversationally. "But worshiping at my feet might be more effective without a counter between us."

She stopped breathing.

"The game's up, Ms. Denton."

Thanks a lot, God.

There was no hope for dignity. Nothing left to do. She rose slowly, her popping joints a crowning addition to her complete and utter mortification.

"How'd you know I was there?" she asked miserably, unable to meet his eyes.

A beat of silence. "I just knew."

Her gaze snapped up. She caught her breath and stared.

John Chandler's eyes were the color of fresh-ground coffee, his hair a distinguished salt-and-pepper gray. His European-cut suit complemented his lean body and outdoorsman's tan. Recently divorced and spectacularly rich, he was a debutante's dream, a society matron's fantasy—a truck-stop manager's delusion. A delusion five years her junior.

His attention shifted to Irene, who hurried forward carrying two fizzing Cokes.

"Ah, thank you, Irene." His charming smile disappeared the instant he turned back to Mary Lou.

"Shall we go to your office now, Ms. Denton?"

She noted the interested stares of nearby truckers and silently groaned. This had to be a nightmare. "Yes, of course."

Untying her apron, she tossed it into a hamper and slipped around the counter. She sensed his intense gaze while he followed her through the diner, the adjacent minimart, the unmarked door next to the beer cooler, the short hallway sprouting several rooms on each side. By the time she reached her small office she was ready to scream from the tension.

John entered behind her and all the oxygen left her lungs. As discreetly as possible, she placed her desk between them and settled in her high-back chair.

His eyes flashed. "Feel safer now?"

"I don't know what you're talking about," she bluffed, forced to dilute her advantage by craning her neck. "Please, have a seat."

He placed the drinks on her desk, sat in the guest chair and crossed his leg with an elegance that should've looked sissy, but made her feel fluttery inside.

"Come on now, don't play dumb. We both know you're anything but. My portfolio manager says I should clone you to shore up my other weak investments."

The compliment surprised and warmed her. She'd worked very hard to turn around a failing business and warrant this man's faith in her.

"Why are you hiding behind four feet of wood? What's wrong, Mary Lou?"

She wanted more than his faith, that's what was wrong. "I think we should stick to surnames, don't you?"

His surprisingly dark eyebrows lifted and fell. "Funny. Last month you called me John in this very office. If you insist on formality in front of the staff that's one thing, but after two years of working together—"

"We don't work *together*. I work for you. No, that's not right, either. I work for your portfolio. I'm a weak investment, remember?"

His mouth quirked. "I'd hardly call you weak. You're one of the strongest people I've ever met. Quite unusual for a beautiful woman, in my experience."

Hot pleasure spilled through her veins. It was the first time he'd stepped from a traditional employer's role, other than to brag about his college-age daughter. She reminded herself sternly he was out of her league.

"Do you take such a personal interest in all of your investments, Mr. Chandler?"

"It depends on the potential for return, Ms. Denton."

She licked suddenly dry lips. "And what kind of return do you expect from me?"

"I *expect* nothing. I speculate that patience with you would be well rewarded in the long run."

Oh, God. "What if you're overestimating my abilities?"

"I don't believe I am. I've given it a lot of thought."

Her heart was thumping like diesel-pump 9. "You have?"

For an instant his eyes blazed. "Oh, yes, I have." He lowered his lashes and tweaked the crease in his pants. "Perhaps we should discuss this more fully over dinner tonight."

She wanted to say yes more than anything she'd wanted in a very long time. "I don't think that's a good idea."

"You've got to eat, don't you? When was the last time you had dinner in a nice restaurant?"

She smiled briefly. "I think I'm insulted."

"Don't be. I know how hard you work, that's all I meant."

What else did he know about her? "Mr. Chandler...John," she conceded, amazed at the fierce triumph that crossed his face. "Thank you for the invitation, but I really don't believe in mixing business and pleasure."

His eyes widened innocently. "Did you think we would have fun? That this would be a date?" He wagged his head and hand. "I'm sorry to disappoint you, but I'd like to discuss the quarterly profit-and-loss report if you don't mind. And there's an interesting treatise about the effect of religious cults on the price of oil and gas I'd like you to look at. You can take a peek over dessert if you're a fast reader."

By this time she was chuckling. He made her fears seem ridiculous. Still...

"You can pick the spot. What do you feel like eating? Chinese? Italian? You name it, you've got it."

His boyish eagerness was irresistible. With a rush of defiance, she caved in. "Any place is fine with me—as long as it doesn't smell like grease!"

CHAPTER FOUR

CATHERINE MEASURED coffee, poured water and started the automatic brewer in her father's spotless white kitchen. Her new tenants had moved into the garage apartment the day before. Joe was due at nine o'clock for his "orientation" session. She'd no sooner returned from her morning swim about eight than she'd heard his Bronco back out of the driveway. Round trip, the drive to Allie's softball camp at the Y shouldn't take more than forty-five minutes.

Father and daughter were very close from what Catherine had observed. Still, something about their relationship had nagged at her in the hours after she'd shown them the apartment. It wasn't just that Allie called her father by his first name, although that indicated a disturbing equality between the two. No, there'd been something else. An interaction she'd recognized and responded to on a deeply personal level.

Then last night an image had crystallized in Catherine's mind: Allie's face, pleading with Joe to stay for the month.

The girl's expression had been resigned, as if she'd experienced disappointment many times in her young life. She'd obviously expected her father to say no and reverse the plans they'd discussed. Yet she hadn't been able to mask her trace of hopefulness.

Catherine paused now in the act of sponging stray coffee grounds from the counter. How well she understood the adoration, the sick disappointment, the renewed hope. In her case, she'd never been able to meet her father's expectations. The adoration/disappointment cycle had continued until hope had finally died. The same would happen to Allie unless Joe's pattern of behavior changed.

Glancing over her shoulder at the wall clock, Catherine winced and massaged her tender neck muscles. Curiosity didn't always kill the cat. Sometimes it just injured.

Her tenants' many trips up and down the apartment stairs yesterday had been clearly visible from her office window—if she twisted her head just so. When Joe had spun around unexpectedly and headed for her back kitchen door, she'd nearly sprained her ankle scrambling away from the closed miniblinds.

Foolish, really. He couldn't possibly have seen her, despite the knowing glance he'd directed at her window.

She'd taken her sweet time answering his knock. Then wished she could slam the door on his cocky smirk. Instead, she'd invited him inside to wait while she retrieved the apartment keys he requested from her office.

Inhaling deeply, Catherine closed her eyes at the heavenly aroma of baking cinnamon rolls. The man couldn't say her kitchen smelled like a hospital today. When Joe arrived for his lesson, every salivary gland in his mouth would activate. Just the ticket for establishing a cooperative mood. She hoped.

Humming under her breath, she set the smoked-glass breakfast table and centered an arrangement of her father's look-but-don't-touch hybrid tea roses. The ones Carl had scolded her for picking just last night. A shrill buzz startled the frown from her face. The cinnamon rolls!

Five minutes later she fanned all twelve on a china serving platter and drizzled them with icing. Another glance at the clock sent her rushing to the refrigerator for a glass pitcher of orange juice. Setting it on the table, she stepped back and cocked her head. There. The stage was set. Where was the leading man?

Casting a hopeful look out the window above the sink, she sighed. No Bronco in sight. Perhaps he'd stopped for gas or a newspaper.

She refolded the linen napkins and angled them this way and that. Pulled an only marginally perfect rose from the vase and tossed it in the trash. Dashed into the bathroom and freshened her lipstick.

Time passed. Wandering to her office, she opened the miniblinds and settled behind her mahogany desk where she had an unobstructed view of the driveway. What could be keeping him? She forced herself to relax and decided to pay bills. When the last envelope was sealed, she sprang up and returned to the kitchen.

Could he have been in an accident? Surely he would've called her by now if he could, knowing she'd expected him an hour and a half ago.

At the sound of a vehicle pulling into the driveway, she stopped pacing and ran to the window. A blue Bronco, thank God. Smoothing her black tunic T-shirt over matching leggings, she took a deep breath and reminded herself she was a professional, trained to listen before jumping to conclusions.

A large shadow blocked the kitchen door's frosted window. Three loud knocks rattled the frame. Flinging the door open, she noted the conspicuous absence of blood, bruises or bandages.

"You're late," she said, unable to keep the hard edge from her tone.

Joe looked startled, then wary. Flipping off his Astros cap, he shoved back his shaggy dark hair, resettled his cap and tugged down the bill. "Good morning to you, too."

"Morning? Morning was one and a half hours ago, the time we agreed to start your session." She eyed his disreputable army green tank top and gym shorts, the bits of damp grass clinging to his calves and sneakers. "Obviously something more important came up."

Following her gaze downward, he toed off his shoes and stamped large, startlingly white bare feet. "Allie's coach asked me to give a few pointers to the kids. Guess I lost track of time."

His boyish shrug and crooked smile were undeniably appealing—and far too practiced to her discerning eye. Catherine had no doubt they'd served him well over the years.

"Are those cinnamon rolls I smell?" He sniffed the air and peered over her shoulder. The grin he flashed this time reflected genuine delight. "Hey, would you look at that table! This is great. I didn't eat breakfast before I left." Starting forward, he pulled up short when she moved to block the doorway.

"I don't recall inviting you in."

"Oh, yeah." He ducked his head endearingly. "Sorry."

Somehow she managed to hold both her ground and his expectant dark gaze without wavering.

"May I come in?" he asked finally, his voice a bit strained.

"No."

His eyes rounded. "No?"

"No."

He thrust out his unshaven jaw and straightened to his full height. She wondered if he always fell back on intimidation when his attempts to charm failed.

"We had an appointment," he reminded her grimly.

"That's right, we did. You missed it. Maybe I could've rearranged my schedule if you'd called about your delay. But as it is, I've got other things to do now."

He braced a palm high on the door frame, his biceps swelling. "I didn't *miss* the appointment. I was late. What's the big deal?"

His body curved loverlike above her—powerful, dominating, smelling of new-mown grass and musky male. Her skin prickled. Only years of self-discipline enabled her to focus on his question.

"Being late shows you're not committed to winning the bet, and that affects three lives. Mine, yours—and Allie's. She's a very big deal, in my opinion."

He stepped back suddenly and turned around, staring toward the rosebushes lining the cedar fence. A mockingbird's full-throated song rose and fell.

"I already apologized," he muttered. "What the hell more do you want?"

She released her pent-up breath. If it had been just her future at stake she might've eased up. But memory of Allie's pleading face drove Catherine on. "Turn around, Joe."

He grew very still.

"Please."

Shaking his head, he turned, a sorely tried man humoring the little woman.

"You didn't lose track of time, Joe. For some reason, you wanted to be late." The emotion in his eyes flickered so fast she almost missed it. "You were afraid," she stated with a flash of insight.

He paled beneath his tan. "That's crazy."

"No. It's a rational, valid feeling."

"I'm not—I wasn't afraid. That doesn't make any sense."

"Why not?"

He propped his knuckles on lean hips and snorted, as if to say, *Look at me.*

She did. He stood with the easy masculine arrogance of a superb athlete, his size and physical strength undeniably impressive.

"So what are you saying?" she challenged. "That a big strong guy like you can't be afraid? Or at least, that you shouldn't be?" From his expression, that was exactly what he thought. She huffed softly. "Give yourself a break, macho man. Experiencing a *feeling* of weakness doesn't make you weak. People are afraid all the time. It's how we humans *react* to fear that makes us strong or weak."

A light glimmered and faded in his eyes, returning as a cynical gleam. He executed a mocking bow. "Thank you, Dr. Hamilton, for clearing that up for me. I feel so much more in touch now with my feminine self. Or is it my inner child breaking free?"

"My money's on the brat," she said wryly. "And I'm not a practicing counselor. Yet."

He bowed again, this time with grudging respect, and studied her a long moment. "You're really not going to start my lessons today, are you?"

She already had, but fortunately he was oblivious. "I told you, I have other things to do. Life doesn't revolve around your whims or convenience, no matter how much you'd like to think so."

Supremely indifferent, he squinted up at the sun. "Beautiful day." He slanted her a casual look. "Think I'll drive to Galveston and check out the beach action. I can work on my tan and still make it back to the Y before softball camp is over."

She shrugged. "Maybe. If you don't lose track of time, that is." Bending over, she plucked his sneakers from the flagstone patio and dangled them out from two fingertips. "The sand gets pretty hot. Wouldn't want you to burn your feet."

He stepped forward and snatched the shoes from her hand, his glittering stare promising retribution. She waited until he'd turned and was halfway across the patio before calling, "Oh, Joe?"

He stopped, his back muscles bunched with tension.

"We start tomorrow at nine o'clock sharp. No shoes, no proper shirt—no service. A shower wouldn't hurt, either."

His free hand clenched and unclenched once. Without acknowledging her in any other way, he continued on toward the apartment stairs.

Catherine closed the kitchen door and slowly walked to the table. Lifting the pitcher of orange juice from a puddle of condensation, she poured herself a glass, pinched off a piece of brittle white icing from a cinnamon roll and popped it into her mouth. The sugary confection melted on contact.

She'd more than likely just robbed herself of a private counseling practice, Catherine realized, staring into a whorl of rose petals. Yet concern for Allie had left her no choice. Her goading remarks had been catalysts for change, necessary risks. Well, most of them, anyway. She probably should've resisted that last dig about the shower.

If Joe accepted the concept that his "self" and his feelings were two separate entities—and Catherine thought she'd seen a breakthrough—they could move on to exploring deeper issues. Like what motivated his fear. And why his daughter expected him to disappoint her. And of course, how a blue-collar jock could transform into a member of the beau monde in twenty-eight days.

She had no idea if Joe would even show up tomorrow after the tough stand she'd taken. Everything hinged on whether or not the seed she'd planted today would germinate. Or whether he was rooted too deep in never-never land to ever grow up.

JOE COMBED BACK his wet hair, turned away from the mirror and spread his arms wide. "So what d'ya think? Will she let me in the door this morning?"

Juliet blinked once from her perch on the toilet tank and let out an approving meow.

"She speaks." Grinning, Joe sank to one knee and clasped a hand over his heart. "'O, speak again, bright angel! for thou art as glorious to this night, being o'er my head, as is a wingèd messenger of heaven unto the white-upturnèd wond'ring eyes of mortals…that fell—that *fall* back to…to…' et cetera, et cetera.''

He rose, sucked in a breath and hitched up his jeans. ''Yep. Playing Romeo got me more dates in high school than playing ball. Betcha didn't know I was so talented.''

Juliet stretched her elegant black paws and yawned, her tongue pink and curled.

''Everyone's a critic,'' Joe mumbled, turning back to the mirror. He rubbed a speck of dried shaving cream from his chin, smoothed his cowlick, met his own anxious eyes—and snorted.

Unbelievable. That self-righteous stick of a woman had him worried about passing muster. Him. A guy who hadn't been rejected since Lindy McGehee decked him for looking up her dress while she skipped rope.

Shoving his blue cambric shirttail into his jeans, he stalked into the kitchen and jerked open the refrigerator door. Juliet streaked up and wove a sensual figure eight through his legs.

''The doctor could take a lesson from you,'' Joe said, knowing it was a lie.

He'd admired Catherine's graceful way of moving from the first. In all honesty, he didn't think she looked like a stick, either. Her tall slim body had intriguing hints of softness. And there was the rub, or rather, lack of it. Because while he'd been fighting a surprising urge to make her purr, she'd been finding him offensive.

Her crack about his taking a shower still stung.

Juliet meowed impatiently.

''All right, all right. Don't get snippy. There's something in here with your name on it.'' He wouldn't even have to sneak it behind Allie's back, since he'd already driven her to the Y.

Pulling a plastic container from the refrigerator, he popped open the lid. Juliet instantly collapsed on his cowboy boots. He looked down into rapt green eyes.

"Does Romeo know you're this easy?"

She rolled to her back in a decadent sprawl.

Munching on a cold fish stick, Joe almost felt sorry for the big tomcat he'd let outside earlier. He dropped a second stick into Juliet's bowl and watched the cat spring up, all trace of sultriness gone now that she'd gotten what she wanted.

"Women," he muttered, closing the refrigerator door and washing his hands.

He glanced at his watch. Five minutes to nine. His stomach lurched. This was worse than confronting his dad after a three-error Little League game. At least Big Joe's reaction had been predictable. Joe would gladly trade hours of practice without supper for whatever awaited him this morning. Everyone knew facing unpleasantness wasn't his style. Yet no one had *ever* accused him of being afraid.

Until Catherine.

Her penetrating gaze had seen through both his smile and his bluster right to the core of his fear. Somehow the fact that she recognized him for a coward had calmed the panic he couldn't explain, the instinct to flee that usually followed. And damned if she hadn't cinched his cooperation by bringing Allie into the picture.

Unlatching the front door, he paused at an ungodly eruption of sound from the other side—a cross between grinding gears and a colicky infant. Forewarned, he cautiously opened the door.

Romeo catapulted past his knees, slowed to an arrogant walk and rounded the corner into the kitchen. Joe could hear Juliet's purr from where he stood. What the hell did she see in that guy?

Closing the door, he clomped down the stairs and eyed the two-story plantation-style home Catherine shared with her father. Huge pecan trees shaded much of the backyard except for a rose bed along one fence line. A wrought-iron umbrella table and matching chairs filled a corner of the flagstone patio. The Hamiltons might not have the kind of money they wanted, but they *had* it. More than he'd ever saved, anyway.

Ignoring a pang of guilt, he crossed the patio, knocked firmly on the kitchen door and prepared himself for his tutor's smugness. The door opened immediately. Catherine moved into a filtered sunbeam.

That had to be why her eyes lit up as if in pleasure.

"Good morning, Joe, I'm so glad you came!" She studied him from head to toe and met his gaze again, her smile warm with approval. "How nice you look today. Come in, please." Stepping aside, she opened the door wider.

And his heart expanded in his chest.

He crossed the threshold with a bounce in his step and glanced hopefully toward the breakfast table. Clean as a pinch hitter's uniform. In fact, the whole kitchen smelled like disinfectant again.

"Have you eaten anything this morning?" she asked.

He shrugged a shoulder and tried to look gaunt. "A fish stick. Cold. Kinda greasy." *Cinnamon rolls, come to Papa!*

"Good. Then you'll have a clean palate. Follow me." She smiled and walked to an open doorway on the right, her loose white knit dress cupping and releasing her bottom in a rhythm he found mesmerizing. Turning, she caught him staring and blushed, the color intensifying the green of her eyes.

Careful, Tucker. She's on Pretty Boy's menu, not yours.

Recovering her poise, she arched a brow. "Well?"

"I'm right behind you," he said, his long stride making up ground fast. He followed her through the door and pulled up short. "What the . . . ?"

The room's large oval dining table held an assortment of trays and dishes filled with . . . stuff. Some of it appeared to be edible, but he couldn't be sure.

Catherine smiled and made a ta-da gesture. "Behold, the Wilson-Hamilton engagement-party buffet. Well, not the whole buffet. Just a few things Carl's mother will be watching like a hawk."

Joe stepped up for a closer look and identified what he could. Several tins of slimy caviar, ranging in color from golden brown to deep gray. Triangles of that mushy kind of cheese he hated. A heap of muffins that, swear to God, looked blue. A bowl of pasta shaped like tiny bow ties and mixed with . . . hell if he knew. A partially sliced thing resembling a Stuckey's pecan log, only pecans weren't black that he knew of.

Not a cinnamon roll in sight.

"I give up," he said. "Animal, vegetable or mineral?"

She shot him a wry look but hovered over the table obligingly. "Here we have fish roe, not to be confused with that smallest tin of tiny gray sturgeon eggs, which is the only true caviar. Over there is Camembert cheese. Do you like corn bread?'' She waited for his nod. "Then you'll love those blue-corn muffins in the basket. Wonderful with the farfel-and-porcini salad."

"Huh?"

"Pasta and mushrooms," she clarified before moving on. "Oh, and the caterer's big on sushi this season. I sliced a bit of this *tekka makki* already."

He was afraid to ask.

Her eyes twinkled. "Chopped raw tuna rolled in rice and seaweed."

"Remind me to stop for a Big Mac on the way to the party," he said, ridiculously pleased when that got a laugh. She had a nice laugh, he decided. It sort of floated, like the way she moved.

She assumed a serious-teacher expression. "The sophisticated gourmet goes for quality, not quantity. Charlotte Wilson judges a person's status by what he selects from her table. Carl and I opted for a self-serve buffet, instead of a formal dinner. Still, there's plenty that might trip you up."

Hiding a prick of irritation, he studied a marble-topped table against one wall that looked like it might be antique. He bet Pretty Boy would know.

Catherine placed a gentle hand on his forearm. "When you realized I wasn't familiar with the sport of baseball, what did you think of me?"

Her question caught Joe by surprise. Shifting gears, he remembered his reaction to her mistaking the Aeros for the Astros. "I thought you were visiting our planet from another solar system."

"But did you think less of me?" she persisted "Be honest."

"No." He adopted the grave tone and expression of his wife's shrink. "I felt extreme sorrow for your misfortune. Pity for your ignorance. But I didn't think less of you."

"Exactly. These next few weeks we'll be reviewing a lot of information—most of it trivial. If I have to worry about ruffling your feathers, we won't cover nearly as much ground." She squeezed his arm briefly. "Believe it or not, we're on the same team."

Team. More important than individuals. Deserving of unquestioning loyalty and commitment. The concept had been drilled into his head until it was a permanent part of his creed.

He covered her soft pale hand with his own callused palm, thinking two more different teammates couldn't exist. "Hey, teamwork I understand. I'll do my best to learn the rules of the game, Catherine."

"That's good enough for me," she said, her smile brilliant with confidence. Releasing his arm, she set about filling a plate with tidbits of food.

Joe's sudden queasy feeling had nothing to do with slimy fish eggs. Catherine might believe in him now. But it was only a matter of time before she learned the sorry truth.

Joe Tucker's best was never good enough.

CHAPTER FIVE

ALLIE STRAPPED on her bulky catcher's gear a lot more quickly than two days ago, when nervousness had made her clumsy. Instead of dropping her off the first day of camp and leaving, Joe had stuck around to check things out. He'd only seen her play a few times in the past and she'd gotten better since then. Still, she'd been pretty freaked.

She shouldn't have worried, though. He'd been funny, nice to the other kids and proud of the way she'd improved. It'd been one of those perfect times that made up for a lot of crap over the years.

Tightening the buckle of her chest pad, she sighed. If he didn't have that society stuff to learn, maybe he'd stick around for every practice. But even she could see that Catherine wasn't the type to put up with all his excuses.

Not like Gram, who grumbled a lot but melted at the first sign of Joe's smile. Or the women he'd dated, who left a million phone messages that never got returned. No, Catherine was different.

Sheesh, she'd gotten Joe to live with two cats—and he *hated* cats.

Allie hadn't figured out what that meant exactly, but she was impressed all the same. Enough so to stick around for a month and see what developed.

Slamming her locker door shut, she grabbed her mitt from the bench and followed a few stragglers outside. Dew sparkled, the sky was as blue as it got, and the air was nice and cool. Her favorite time of day.

She shaded her eyes and scanned the playing fields. Kids stood talking or goofing around with equipment, waiting for the coaches to show up. Her gaze backtracked to a tall blond boy juggling three baseballs for a group of peewee campers.

Tommy Burton.

Her breathing sped up. Her stomach dipped worse than when she rode Greezed Lightnin' at Astroworld. Bending over, she pretended to adjust the straps of her shin guards while she drew a deep breath. Then another. Better. She straightened and walked toward the senior girls' softball field, wishing Tommy would look at her, knowing she'd puke for sure if he did.

He hadn't said hi to her yesterday. But then, she hadn't said anything to him, either, since they'd met. He probably thought she was a total retard.

Two months ago, she and Joe'd been walking past apartment 34C when Tommy'd burst out the door. He'd recognized her dad right off, which was unusual enough to make Joe feel flattered. Listening to them talk, she'd sifted out the important details. Tommy was fourteen, new to the apartment complex and a big fan of baseball. He had eyes the color of bluebonnets a smile that made her heart pound and an upcoming summer job at the nearby YMCA.

A month later she'd asked Joe's permission to register for the Y's summer softball camp—the same program she'd said was for nerds last summer. He hadn't even asked why she'd changed her mind. Totally clueless. She wondered when he'd notice she wasn't a little kid anymore.

"Hey, Tucker, get the lead out!"

Her gaze snapped toward the voice. Coach Harrison stood near third base, his knuckles propped on each side of his beer belly, a whistle resting against the T-shirt slogan, "Y? Because we *like* you." He looked more puzzled than mad.

She glanced around the field. Holly rolled her eyes from the pitcher's mound, impatient to warm up. The other "red" team members stood in their starting positions, all heads turned her way.

Embarrassed, Allie jogged to home plate. "Sorry," she yelled with a quick wave.

"You got that right," a sarcastic voice mumbled, drifting from the direction of the "blue" team dugout. Giggles followed.

Up yours, Sarah, Allie thought, sinking into an easy catcher's squat. It wasn't enough that Tommy's girlfriend was attending softball camp, or that Sarah not only wore a C cup, but filled it without padding. Oh, no. For some reason, the popular girl had decided to pick on Allie, too.

Pulling down her face mask, Allie relaxed a little as her world narrowed to the view between metal bars. Familiar yet exciting. More important than any single person could be, no matter how blond, blue-eyed or handsome.

She lifted her mitt and punched a fist into the sweet spot. "Okay, Holly, put 'er right down the middle. You can do it."

The ball smacked into leather with a satisfying thud. She threw it back without rising.

Catch, throw. Catch, throw. The rhythm seized her, blocking out everything else. No boy to attract. No father to impress. No girl to ignore. In this one area at least, she felt totally at ease with her body, totally confident in her skill.

Warm-ups ended and the game started, adding new rhythms. The swing of a bat. The slashing hands of the umpire. The pinball action of a double play. Allie moved with the beat, enjoying herself more than she'd expected. These girls weren't as experienced or skilled as her All-City League team, but they really got into it. With more practice, a few of them would be able to hold their own against the best. Sarah wasn't one of them.

She ran like a girl, caught like she'd just painted her nails and threw like a shot-putter. It was so totally obvious she'd only registered in softball camp to be near Tommy. But her spazoid coordination didn't seem to bother her—or the other girls. They fought for her attention, even when it usually came in the form of rude cut-downs.

Coach Harrison was actually a pretty decent coach, treating both teams and every player the same. "This is a practice game," he reminded them. "We're here to work on basics and concentrate on technique, not worry about winning."

Behind his back, each team had picked a secret captain to lead the players to victory. Sarah now had another reason to give Allie a hard time—and vice versa.

By the seventh inning, the sun had burned off the dew and Allie was sweating bullets under all her padding. The red team was leading by three, but Holly's pitching had run out of steam.

Allie centered her mitt over the diamond and chanted, "C'mon, Holly, easy out, easy out."

The batter swung, catching a piece of the curve ball and popping it high.

Allie's adrenaline surged. She flipped off her mask and ran, her gaze locking on target, her legs pumping hard. Harder. She gritted her teeth, put everything she had into the leap and reached high.

Her shoulder slammed into chain link. She slid down the bumpy wire and hit the ground rump first.

But the softball nestled snugly in her mitt.

"Way to hustle!" Coach Harrison yelled from near first base. Cheers erupted from her fellow teammates on the field.

Grinning, she stood up and brushed the dirt from her shorts.

"Showoff," a voice hissed from behind.

Allie whirled around. The blue team dugout was right beyond the fence. Most girls avoided her eyes. Three didn't. Sarah and the two brunettes on either side of her—Pam and... what's-her-name.

"Think you're hot stuff because your dad was in the major leagues?" Sarah said, glancing at her two sneering friends for confirmation. "Well, if he was so great, how come when I asked my father, he didn't even remember a player named Joe Tucker?"

Allie spit through the fence and held Sarah's gaze. "Because morons run in your family?"

Gasps and a few snickers broke out.

Sarah's face reddened. "Why you... you..."

"I rest my case."

"Burly girl!" Sarah exploded, the slur on Allie's femininity prompting giggles from her sidekicks. "For your information my father is a full partner at one of the biggest law firms in Houston. *And* he has his own research assistant who'll do whatever he asks. Like look up information on a has-been major-league baseball player."

"Is there a problem, girls?" Coach Harrison yelled from first base.

Sarah ignored him. "Your father was quite a character, wasn't he, burly girl? Breaking curfew. Pulling practical jokes. Getting suspended for fighting." She glanced slyly at what's-her-name. "Joe Tucker played all right—just not much baseball."

Allie lurched forward and curled her right-hand fingers through the chain-link fence. A balloon of hatred swelled in her chest. "My dad broke into the major leagues after only two years in the minors. He batted .311 his first season—.328 his second. If Tory Jackson hadn't landed a cheap shot to Joe's knees when he slid into home, he would've clinched the league's highest batting average his third year out—"

"Play ball!" the umpire called loudly.

"Even with injuries," Allie continued, "he managed to stay on the team roster and play through pain that would've probably *killed* your wuss father. You gotta problem with me, that's fine. You scrape up the guts to come around this side of the fence and we'll settle it here and now. But don't you dare bad-mouth my dad again, understand?"

Nobody on the bench moved a muscle. Allie rattled the chain link. "Understand?"

"What's all this about, girls?" Coach Harrison demanded, gripping Allie's shoulder from behind.

Relief flooded Sarah's face. "She ought to be kicked out of camp, Coach. I mean, she could have a gun in her locker for all we know." She nudged Pam in the ribs. "Tell him what happened, Pam. How she threatened me and picked a fight and everything."

"Drop it, Sarah," a young male voice said firmly.

Every head turned.

Tommy Burton stood outside the far right dugout fence staring directly at Sarah.

She paled but recovered quickly, sending him that sickening fake smile Allie hated. "Tommy! What are you doing here?"

"I had a ten-minute break and thought I'd say hi."

"Well, why didn't you, silly?"

He gave her an odd look. "You seemed pretty busy to me."

Coach Harrison lifted his hand from Allie's shoulder and scratched his head. "You know what happened here, son?"

Bluebonnet eyes bypassed the older man and focused on Allie. "Yes, sir."

She was suddenly aware of her mashed and sweaty hair, the dust turning to mud on her skin, the bulky pads making her a burly girl in appearance, if not in fact.

Coach Harrison blew out his breath. "Well? So what happened?"

Allie watched Tommy's internal struggle between his desire to tell the truth and his reluctance to get Sarah in trouble. It was a no-win situation.

"I lost my temper and got out of line," Allie said. "Sorry, Coach. It won't happen again." The look she sent Sarah said it'd better *not,* or there'd be trouble.

"Are you okay with that, Sarah?" Coach Harrison asked.

Sarah glanced at Tommy, who avoided her eyes, then gave a sullen shrug. "I guess so."

"Good, good. In the future, Tommy, I'd appreciate your taking a break somewhere inside the building please. I want these girls paying attention to their game—not you."

Tommy smiled sheepishly. "I'll do that, sir."

"Okay then, how 'bout we finish this game now? The ump's got your mask, Allie."

Nodding, she couldn't resist a last peek from under her lashes at Tommy. He stared back as if seeing her for the first time. And he kept staring, she knew, all the while she walked toward home plate, looking about as feminine as a Teenage Mutant Ninja Turtle.

She barely managed not to puke.

THE BRONCO SWUNG into the last parking space outside Laurette Stimson Gallery. A good sign, Catherine hoped. The more crowded the gallery was, the less likely they were to be approached. She unbuckled her seat belt and turned to Joe.

"Okay, remember the rules. Keep your mind open and your mouth closed, and we'll finish in plenty of time to pick up Allie from the Y."

Wrist draped over the steering wheel, he shrugged his broad shoulders. "Relax, Catherine. You won't even know I'm there."

I wish. She glanced at the gallery's chrome-and-brass front door, at the Mercedes parked to her right, at the huge oak trees shading the museum district of Houston—anywhere but at this well-groomed stranger wearing dark slacks and a crisp white dress shirt.

"If someone comes up to us," she said, removing her sunglasses and nearly stabbing herself in the eye, "let me do the talking."

"Yeah, I got the message."

"Just stand there with a thoughtful expression on your face and we'll be fine."

"What gives, Catherine? Why are you so nervous?" He seemed a little miffed.

You're too attractive. Too... unexpected. "I told you, Laurette is Father's good friend. He'll be impressed at the party if you mention visiting her gallery. Especially if you talk intelligently about the current artist's work."

"Which you don't think I'll do."

"Did I say that?" She raised a brow at his darkening expression. "No, I did not. Don't palm your insecurities off on me, Joe. I've got enough of my own."

He perked up slightly. "No kiddin'? Like what?"

"Like..." She caught his speculative gleam. "Oh, no, you don't. I'm not spilling my guts for someone I haven't paid to listen."

"Okay already—" he patted her arm briefly "—so I'll take your money. What are friends for?"

Her huff was half laughter.

"I thought so. You don't have any."

Shoving her glasses into their case, she frowned. "We've been through all this before. If I had any money, I wouldn't—"

"What I meant was you don't have any insecurities," he clarified. "Guess I'd be confident, too, if I were a witch."

Her mouth opened and closed. She must have heard wrong. Even he couldn't be that outrageous. Still...

"Did you just call me a witch?"

"Actually Earl did first, after you beat him at pool. He said you put a— Hey, don't look like that. I told him you're a *good* witch."

Incredible. And painful. *"You think I'm a witch?"*

She shook her head, remembering Carl's "constructive" criticisms of her predominantly somber wardrobe, her straight black hair, the dark shadows beneath her eyes after a long day of research. He'd given her the name of his mother's beauty salon and suggested she make an appointment before the wedding.

Joe's rumbling chuckles penetrated her daze. "Catherine, Catherine," he said, his dark eyes filled with gentle amusement. "I was only teasing. You've got to stop taking yourself so seriously. Life's too short to risk spending it with an ulcer."

Fumbling for her purse on the floor, she hoisted the heavy leather bag onto her lap. "Calling me a witch three months before I have to walk down an aisle in front of hundreds of staring people is *not* the way to prevent my getting an ulcer." She rummaged jerkily through the bag's contents, withdrew a promotional pamphlet and tossed it onto his lap. "Look this over. It's a review of the artist's work."

"Catherine—"

"Read it," she ordered. "Then I'll give you a tour of the gallery."

He scanned the copy a moment and grimaced. "Can't I just donate a kidney, instead? Somebody must need one today."

In spite of her bruised ego, she bit back a smile. "'Fraid not. Quit stalling and let's go."

She unlatched her door and started to slide out, sighing when his large hand suddenly gripped her upper arm. Now what? She glanced back over her shoulder and met his eyes.

They were dark with urgency, mesmerizing in their intensity. "You'll be a beautiful bride, Catherine."

Her heartbeat stopped, then hammered loudly in the absolute quiet. For one sweet moment pleasure bloomed in her chest.

"Everyone watching you walk down that aisle will be blown away," he assured her.

Common sense returned in a rush. "I'll try to slow down my broomstick," she said wryly.

His shout of laughter broke the tension. Hopping down to the asphalt, she slammed her door shut and walked to stand beneath the gallery awning. Close call, there. Too close. Flirting was as natural to this man as breathing, a textbook reaction against the threat of serious commitment. Responding to his undeniable charisma was unprofessional. And very stupid.

He was a means to an end, she reminded herself, watching him lock the Bronco and pocket his keys. Carl might not fill a shirt quite so impressively, or walk with quite the same athletic swagger, or make her feel more alive the closer he approached... Oh Lord, she was doing it again. Catherine tore her gaze away.

Carl offered everything she wanted. Her own home. Her own career. A chance to be the kind of mother she herself had always wanted. One who would make her children proud and be there for them every day.

If he didn't make her heart pound, at least he would never break it. And instinct told her Joe could. *If* she let him.

Joining her at the entrance, he opened the massive door and touched the small of her back. She scooted forward to escape those long fingers and plunged into a small reception area. Track lights beamed on a contemporary glass-brick counter topped with polished black marble.

Catherine headed for the guest book lying open next to a Mont Blanc pen. "Laurette must be thrilled with this show's success," she said in a hushed churchgoing voice. Signing both their names with a flourish, she stepped away from the counter and gestured for Joe to follow.

Ceiling window panels filled the main gallery with soft diffused light, aided by bleached wood floors and white walls. Doreen Walden's paintings hung at strategic intervals, enhanced with spotlighting. Grabbing Joe's elbow, Catherine slipped among the twenty or so well-heeled art patrons circling the room.

She paused in front of a tall canvas titled *Welcome*. Painted in a sketchy cartoonlike style, the images startled or shocked. A blankly staring pig's head mounted on a wall. A naked woman hanging upside down from a doorway, her sagging breasts dripping blood. A child playing with her dolls on the floor, oblivious to her surroundings.

Joe leaned close to her ear. "Welcome to what?" he murmured, stirring the hair at her nape. "Hell?"

Suppressing a shiver of awareness, she frowned. "Doreen is working through a conflict with her mother in these paintings. She's welcoming us to her world."

He grunted noncommittally and followed her to the next canvas. This one was titled *Family Tree,* and depicted a buxom tree-woman rooted to the carpet and wearing a blue evening gown. She held a serrated knife in one branchlike hand; the other had been cut off, the stump dripping blood. A newborn baby cried from a crib in the background.

"Doreen is one sick puppy," Joe rumbled in Catherine's ear, sending another delicious thrill racing down her spine.

The blond-haired woman standing next to them obviously overheard and sent Joe a withering glare. He answered with a slow lopsided grin, his rugged face tanned and starkly masculine in the pristine white setting.

The blonde's fingers fluttered to her Vidal Sassoon hair, her Paloma Picasso necklace, her Dr. Rosenthal tummy tuck. Her glare melted into a soft smile, and Joe's eyelids lowered a fraction.

Catherine watched in growing disgust. Why didn't they just drop to the floor and do the deed? Laurette could slap a title on them and call it performance art.

Tugging on Joe's elbow, she dragged him to the next painting and fought the urge to scratch something. Preferably the blonde's face—but Joe's was an acceptable substitute. She stared blindly at a pair of shriveled breasts on the canvas until the elegant couple sharing the view moved on.

"Must you be so obvious?" she hissed.

He didn't pretend to misunderstand. "It's more efficient that way. You oughtta try it sometime on Pretty Boy and see if he thaws."

"For your information, Carl is a very warm person."

"Warm? Hell, the man probably pisses icicles."

"Shh! Honestly. Must you be so vulgar?"

"Must you be such a prude?"

"Keep your mind open and your mouth closed. Those were the rules, remember?"

"Yeah, I remember. The thing is, doll, rules are meant to be broken."

She arched a brow. "Seen one too many James Dean movies, have we?"

"Enough to know a good exit line when I hear one." He whirled to leave.

She pulled back on his arm so that they faced each other squarely. "Running away is easy for you, isn't it?"

He scowled pointedly down at her hand. "Not always."

"I think it's become a habit," she said, speaking to the flare of panic in his eyes. "Why dig in your heels and tough it out when you can avoid conflict altogether?"

He reached for her restraining hand and unpeeled each finger. "Don't analyze me, Catherine. That's not a part of our deal." His voice was low. Deadly. "In case you haven't noticed, we're causing quite a scene. Now, you may want to stand here and compete with Doreen for attention, but I'd just as soon leave the sensationalism to her."

Catherine grew aware of her surroundings. Some of the gallery patrons seemed amused, others offended, but not a one of them looked at the paintings.

She smiled weakly and turned back to Joe. "I think that's enough art appreciation for today, don't you?"

He bared his teeth in a cold smile. "Avoiding conflict, are we?"

Before she could muster a scathing answer, a blur of motion swept into the main gallery and stopped, condensing into a silver-haired woman in a flowing white caftan.

Laurette Stimson wrinkled her stately brow. "Heavens, is there a problem here?"

Good manners prevailed and people turned toward the walls. Catherine silently groaned as inquisitive black eyes darted from her to Joe.

"Ca-a-atherine," Laurette said, extending her palms and walking forward. She clasped Catherine's fingers and pecked the air near both her cheeks. "How nice to see you. And where is that gorgeous fiancé of yours?"

Catherine extricated her hands and checked her wristwatch. Three o'clock. Carl never deviated from his schedule. Never. "He's playing tennis at his club," she said, sensing Joe's smirk and flushing against her will.

She admired Carl's discipline, his commitment to both business and personal responsibilities—all desirable qualities in a husband and father. So why did they suddenly seem inflexible and boring?

"I'm sorry Carl couldn't make the show. But who is this handsome devil with you?" Laurette tilted her head at Joe, her black eyes gleaming—an exotic cockatoo inspecting the choice morsel tossed into her cage.

Joe stretched out his hand and clasped hers. "Joe Tucker. It's a pleasure to meet the owner of such an *important* gallery."

He couldn't have spoken more flattering words. The businesswoman preened. "What do you think of the show, Mr. Tucker?"

"Joe," he corrected, flashing that lady-killer grin.

Laurette nodded, her color high. Apparently feminine hormones of any age responded to Joe's bag of tricks.

"So tell me, Joe, how do you feel about Doreen Walden's work?"

"I like Catherine's work better."

Oh, God, Catherine thought, a confusing mixture of embarrassment and pleasure holding her mute. Her "sofa art" couldn't measure up to Laurette's standards.

"Really?" Laurette's tone was a bit cooler. "Catherine who? Perhaps I know her."

"You couldn't possibly," Catherine blurted, earning two startled glances. "I mean, it's highly unlikely, since she doesn't network in the art community or exhibit her work. She moved recently to...the outback." Two pairs of eyes blinked. "Australia," she added, sinking deeper and deeper.

"Hmm. Well, aboriginal art has inspired some powerful work in contemporary art. Have her send me some slides when she's ready to show and I'll take a look at them." Brightening, Laurette turned to Joe again. "You still haven't told me your reaction to the show today."

"We've really got to run, Laurette," Catherine said. "We'll be late for—"

"Come now, Catherine, a few more minutes won't matter. I've been polling men's viewpoints on Doreen's 'mother' period, and I'm interested in Joe's opinion."

With pained resignation, Catherine watched Joe study the closest paintings and assume the thoughtful expression she'd suggested.

"It's obvious this artist experienced a lot of trauma as a child," he said slowly, as if deliberating each word.

Poor Joe. She hoped this wouldn't set back their training schedule.

"I'd guess these paintings are her attempt to escape from her past, to cut the branch from the tree, so to speak. And yet they transcend the mere cathartic." He met Laurette's keen gaze head-on. "By sharing such brutal and uncensored images, she's fused the personal and the political—without being didactic. It makes for some poignant statements about specific neglect. And a dramatic comment on abuse in general."

Laurette's eyes brightened with unmistakable respect. She smiled and patted his arm. "Well put, Joe! You come back and visit anytime. You're exactly the kind of patron I like circulating in my gallery. Perceptiveness like yours is good for sales."

Joe cleared his throat and looked anxious to get away.

"Oh, and, Catherine. Be sure to give your father my best," Laurette murmured, moving at last toward her other patrons.

Nodding absently, Catherine stared at Joe, who avoided her eyes and took off as if released from class by a schoolroom bell.

Following his tall figure outside, she waited as he unlocked the passenger door and helped her into the Bronco. There was only one explanation for Joe's astounding answer—the gallery's promotional literature. The minute he slammed her door shut, she scooped the pamphlet up from the floor and frantically skimmed the copy. Then skimmed it again.

The driver's door opened and she stuffed the brochure into her purse. Joe settled behind the wheel, glanced at his wristwatch and cast her a hesitant look.

"There's a good hour to kill before camp lets out. Would you mind if I stopped by my apartment and picked up a few things Allie and I need?"

"Huh?" She had trouble concentrating.

"My old apartment. Norman is supposed to have a box packed and ready to pick up. It should only take a minute."

"Oh. Fine," she mumbled, drifting back into her jumbled thoughts.

If he hadn't parroted the reviewer's opinion, that meant Joe's words had come from a rich vocabulary and complex intellect she hadn't known he possessed. It seemed that the more she learned about her "unsophisticated" student, the more there was to discover.

And, dangerous or not, she intended to do some exploring.

CHAPTER SIX

THE DRIVE to his apartment building was conspicuously quiet. Joe gripped the steering wheel and wished Catherine would say something. Do something besides send him those probing little glances that made him feel like a damn lab monkey.

His intellectual mumbo jumbo at the gallery had obviously shocked her—which shouldn't have surprised him. He'd learned long ago that most people saw only what they expected to see.

And yet, he'd somehow hoped Catherine would look deeper. Discover what no one else had since Mrs. Henkel, his Littleton High School English teacher, who had challenged and shamed him into trying out for the lead role in *Romeo and Juliet*.

"You must exercise your mind as well as your body," the Shakespearean scholar had told him. Over and over and over. Until at some point he'd not only believed her, he'd also actually enjoyed the mental workouts she gave him. His grades had gone up steadily in every subject.

But nobody—least of all Joe himself—had expected his SAT scores to kick valedictorian butt. Man, had Mrs. Henkel been pumped! She'd even made a special trip out to the house to talk with his parents.

Adjusting the rearview mirror, Joe caught sight of his scowling reflection and blew out a breath. No sense beating that dead horse again.

"Why didn't you go to college?" Catherine asked out of the blue.

Damn, he was beginning to think she really was a witch. Forcing his features to relax, he shrugged. "I got drafted straight into the minor leagues after graduation."

"Let me rephrase the question. Why did you *choose* not to attend college? I mean, you must have been offered athletic scholarships. Academic ones, too, if you used the brain you were born with, instead of the one people like me assumed you had."

He shot her a startled glance.

"I'm sorry I fell for the dumb-jock stereotype, Joe."

Gratification blazed through him, as hot and fierce as sexual release. He'd spent a good part of his life apologizing to other people. Being on the receiving end felt great.

"No reason you shouldn't've fallen for it. I fit the image closely enough." Maybe too closely, he realized now. He'd almost forgotten it was an act.

"True. Which makes me wonder why you'd want to seem less intelligent than you are."

His goodwill vanished. "So only people who use fancy words are intelligent, is that it?"

"Obviously not, or I would have seen through your smoke screen right away."

Her rueful expression surprised him. He remembered their first conversation at The Pig's Gut. She'd apologized then, too, for assuming that guests at her engagement party would have more sophisticated interests than baseball. He'd never met a woman who owned up to her mistakes as readily as Catherine. Hell, he couldn't think of a man who did, either. For the first time in sixteen years he found himself wanting to explain his actions to another person.

Eyes straight ahead, he cleared his throat. "When I got those scholarship offers, I was a kid, ya know? Cocky and impatient. Four years seemed like a century to wait for my shot at The Show."

"The Show?"

"Yeah, The Show—the major leagues. I never even considered what I'd do after I got too old to play baseball."

"What about your parents? Didn't they realize the benefits of your having a college degree to fall back on?"

Joe choked back a snort. The gap between her WASP upbringing and his own blue-collar roots had never seemed so huge. He maneuvered the Bronco onto Highway 59 before answering.

"In the Tucker family, and Littleton in general, college was for rich people. Other people. Guys went straight from high school into an entry-level job at one of the refineries. I was damn lucky to have the option to play baseball."

"But you could have played and attended college, too. I find it hard to believe you weren't even tempted."

Yeah, he'd been tempted. But in the end, he'd loved his father more. "You gotta remember, nobody in my class was headed for college, except maybe a few geeks. Parents didn't pound on their kids to make good grades in school. It just wasn't important."

"Hmm."

This was why he never had "discussions." They only stirred up emotions better left alone.

"So what was?"

"What was what?"

"If a good education wasn't important, what was?"

That was easy. "Sports."

She waited a heartbeat. "And...?"

He couldn't expect a Connecticut blueblood to understand. "No ands. People in Littleton—especially *guy* people—ate, drank and breathed local high-school sports. Still do, for that matter, same as in every small Texas town. My dad was no exception."

"He must have been very proud when you made the draft."

"Yeah, he was." Joe smiled at the understatement. "The day we got word, he took me to The Pig's Gut. Bought a beer for everyone there, climbed on a chair and made a toast to me."

"Really?" Her voice lifted in delight—and what could've been longing. "Do you remember what he said?"

"Like it was yesterday." Joe raised an imaginary beer and deepened his voice. "Over the lips, past the gums, look out major leagues, here we come!"

But fate had stopped one of them cold. He lowered his hand, his reminiscent grin fading.

"Here *we* come?" Catherine asked. "Isn't that taking fatherly pride a little far?"

Joe rode out a wave of irritation. "You don't know how much he loved baseball. Hell, he coached every Little League and senior league team I was on. He never missed a high-school game, practiced with me for hours and hours after a long day at the garage. Made me tough enough, consistent enough, good enough to play with the big boys. It was me out there on the AstroTurf wearing a major-league uniform. But it was my dad's dream that got me there.''

''Your *dad's* dream?''

He cast her a dark look. ''Give it a rest, Catherine. His dream, my dream, our dream—what difference does it make?''

''Hmm.''

The sound set his teeth on edge. All she needed was a notepad, pencil and couch. God, just like his wife's shrink. Stirring up old resentments, acting like he could change what couldn't be changed. He let the silence stretch, growing tenser by the second.

The Loop 610 South entrance sign suddenly loomed ahead. Steering into the proper lane, he reduced his speed on the elevated curve. Accelerated on the down-ramp. Kept his eyes peeled for cops as he drove through the Bellaire speed trap.

What the hell kind of answer was ''hmm''? Was she watching him again with that detached look he hated? Unable to stand it, he pretended to check his right side-view mirror.

Catherine sat staring trancelike out the passenger window, her low ponytail exposing part of her neck. His gaze riveted on that vulnerable spot—and irritation became something fierce and purely masculine. He wanted to swoop down and leave his mark on that pale curve of skin. He wanted it so much he could barely drag his gaze back to the freeway.

Lord have mercy.

He was a leg man, for God's sake. Breasts rated a close second. But necks were for supporting a pretty face, not giving a guy a semi. This whole bet thing was making him crazy. If he weren't careful, she'd slap him in a padded room and file the key under "Dracula Complex."

He sensed rather than saw Catherine shift to face the windshield.

"Hmm," she half sighed.

"Hmm *what*, dammit!"

She lurched against her seat belt, then pressed a hand to her chest. Her green eyes took on the look of a hissing cat's. "What on earth is wrong with you?"

He hadn't meant to scare her. Hadn't known his question would come out as a shout. Hell, before meeting Catherine, women had actually complained about his easygoing indifference.

Massaging the faint throb of a headache, he glanced at the Astrodome out his left window. "Sorry. Guess I'm getting tired of being analyzed, that's all."

"Excuse me?"

Like she didn't know what he meant. "Those little 'hmm' sounds you keep making. Any minute I expect you to say, 'Veddy interestink.'" His German accent stank, but by the sound of her outraged sputter, she got the picture.

"That's absurd. And paranoid. I'm not analyzing you, Joe, but I'll tell you one thing—somebody sure as heck should!"

Grinding his teeth, he glanced up at the rapidly approaching exit sign—his exit sign—and swerved sharply toward the off-ramp. The tires squealed. The Bronco earned its name. Once he was on residential streets en route to his apartment, he risked looking at his passenger. If her eyes had hissed before, they practically snarled now.

"Go ahead, Catherine, get it out of your system. I wouldn't want you to bust a vein on my account."

Her face grew alarmingly red. "I take back everything I said earlier. You are a dumb jock. An exceptionally stupid dumb jock. In fact, compared with you, dumb jocks are regular nuclear physicists!"

A bark of laughter escaped him. "You might wanna work on your couch-side manner, doll. Either that, or resign yourself to throwing Tupperware parties the rest of your life."

The sound of her agitated breathing filled the enclosed space. He glanced over, distracted by the rapid rise and fall of her white shirt pocket. There wasn't much under there, but what there was had a damn nice shape.

"You know what I think?" she asked, her voice shrill enough to shatter glass. "I'll tell you what I think. I think *you're* the one who resigned yourself to throwing Tupperware parties."

He snapped to wary attention.

"Figuratively speaking," she added. "You resigned yourself to giving up college and playing baseball for a father you loved and respected. A father who, by himself, had neither the athletic talent nor the opportunity to escape Littleton—"

"You don't know what—"

"A father who discovered," she interrupted loudly, "that by living vicariously through his son, he could achieve his own personal dream. Even if that dream wasn't shared."

Joe's heart had started racing at the first hint of her conclusion. He drove now on automatic pilot, turning left into the entrance of a large apartment complex called Timber Trails. Crawling over concrete bumps he normally hit at teeth-jarring speed, he followed the winding driveway to building D and swung into a parking space.

How had Catherine guessed he'd wanted to go to college? No one but Mrs. Henkel had known about his hesitant desire, born during his senior year, to keep learning something besides baseball strategy, to maybe even help other kids learn, too. Mrs. Henkel had thought he'd make a wonderful teacher and had gone to his house as a personal favor to crusade for acceptance of a scholarship.

Big Joe had laughed in her face. And God help him, Joe had avoided that wonderful old lady's disappointed gaze and agreed with his dad.

"When did he die, Joe?"

He blinked twice and scrubbed his face in both palms.

"Your father, I mean."

Lowering his hands, he stared at the dashboard and laughed bitterly. "Two months before the Astros called me up from their farm in Tucson, Mom found him underneath Ed Parker's Buick with a wrench still clutched in his hand. Massive coronary, the doctors said."

"Oh, Joe." Her voice wrapped him in a hug.

"Two friggin' months, Catherine. Seeing me play major-league baseball was all he ever wanted, all either of us ever worked for. Fat lotta difference it made. We're all just pawns in the end."

"You don't mean that."

"The hell I don't! This minute, this very second we're living right now, is the only truth there is. The commercial was right. You've gotta grab all the gusto from life you can—*when* you can—because the best planning in the world won't change fate."

"So you don't plan for the future," she said, her expression thoughtful. "I guess that means you won't ever buy a house, won't get married again, won't save for Allie's college—"

"Leave my daughter out of this."

"Okay. Let's talk about your aversion to marriage."

"Let's not."

"Allie needs a mother."

"Allie *has* a father, dammit! A broken-down has-been who's doing his sorry best to start a new career and take decent care of her. I sure as hell don't want or need the burden of a wife on top of that."

"Oh, that's right. Why build a happy family when fate could turn on you and ruin everything?" Her neutral mask dissolved into disgust. "That's a coward's way of thinking. It puts the burden of responsibility for your actions on some nebulous scapegoat."

"Wrong, Sigmund. That's a realist's way of thinking. But you go on scheduling every trip to the john if it makes you feel more in control. I won't burst your bubble."

He didn't know what he'd expected. Anger probably. For damn sure not the gentle compassion softening her features.

"I got sidetracked from the real issue here. We were talking about your father."

Joe sighed. When she latched on to a subject, it would take the Jaws of Life to pry her loose. "What about him?"

"You blame fate that he died disappointed, mere months before getting to see you play in the major leagues. But did you ever think that his choice of dream—not fate—was the real culprit? That if he'd chosen a goal that hadn't relied on your skills, but on his own, Big Joe would have died content?"

"Catherine. I'm a dumb jock. Speak English."

A smile tugged at her mouth. "In plain English, I mean that working toward a goal—and developing our personal strengths along the way—is very rewarding. Often more rewarding than attaining the goal itself."

Choices. He'd made so many bad ones. He supposed Big Joe could have, too. "So if Dad had wanted, say, to be the best mechanic in Littleton, you think he might've died happy?"

"I think...that it's something to think about."

Was it ever. The possibility that Joe might not've been responsible for his father dying unfulfilled shifted the ground beneath him. From the look of Catherine's widening eyes, she must feel the same. No, she was watching something. He followed her gaze to his apartment living-room window.

The drapes were drawing open in jerky fitful increments, revealing his agent, Norman, as bald and pink as a newborn baby.

And just as naked.

CATHERINE SAT on the edge of a worn corduroy recliner and cocked her ear toward the hallway. Fortunately the walls were thin.

"Dammit, Norman," Joe bellowed from the bedroom. "This is a family apartment complex. Next time you open the drapes, at least have the decency to wear a trench coat!''

"Mumble, mumble, Doris mumble.''

"I don't care if she made you wear a friggin' tuxedo in the bathtub, that doesn't give you the right to parade around *here* buck naked. From now on, take your shower sooner. Like before dawn.''

"Mumble, mumble.''

"Then why aren't you— Aw jeez, Norman, you've been like that since seven? Allie and I have to *sit* on this furniture when you leave!''

"Doris mumble, mumble, Doris mumble, mumble, mumble.''

"So call her up. Tell her you're a miserable naked slob without her. But first come out and apologize to Catherine— No, no, not like *that*. Have some dignity, man.'' A door opened. "When you leave this bedroom there'd better not be any skin showing except on that thick skull of yours,'' Joe warned, his voice louder without the muffling effect of walls.

Slam!

Flinching, Catherine grabbed a magazine from the rack by her chair and whipped it open onto her lap. Seconds later Joe stalked into the den.

"God,'' he muttered, shaking his head. "Sorry you had to hear that.''

"Hear what?''

His expression said, *Gimme a break*.

"No, really, I was so interested in this article I didn't hear a thing.''

He moved closer and peered down. "I see what you mean. Can I read that when you're finished?''

She followed his gaze and felt her facial muscles freeze. The only print visible on the lurid photo spread listed Miss Candy Cane's Top Ten Turn-ons.

Catherine slapped the magazine shut and crammed it back into the rack, her face heating at the sound of Joe's rich baritone laugh. She glared at his pointing finger and he laughed harder—wonderful full-bodied whoops—then plopped down on the arm of her chair as if his legs wouldn't support him.

"Your mouth," he managed finally, gripping the recliner headrest with one hand and nudging her arm with the other. "It's all shriveled up. Like you just sucked on a lemon." A fresh burst of laughter trailed over her head.

Unaccountably hurt, she went on the offensive. "You should be ashamed of yourself, Joe Tucker, leaving that smut lying around where Allie can find it."

Sobering, he wiped the last trace of moisture and twinkle from his eyes. "Excuse me, Miss Holier-than-Thou, but that must be Norman's magazine, 'cause it sure as hell ain't mine. And as for Allie finding 'that smut,' I'd a whole lot rather she look at pictures of a normal naked woman than at one of Doreen's sicko paintings you call art."

He had an excellent point, damn him. She sniffed and folded her hands in her lap. "Your idea of a normal naked woman is exactly why unnecessary elective surgery and eating disorders are so prevalent today."

"Oh, bite me, Catherine." He sounded more weary than angry.

"I would, but my mouth is too shriveled to do enough damage."

His surprised chuckle rumbled near her ear. "If only I'd had a camera."

Staring at her clasped hands, she felt a smile tug at her lips. "I'm surprised you noticed my mouth at all with Miss Candy Cane staring up at you."

"Who, the model in the magazine?"

"Do you know a lot of women named Candy Cane?"

"Let's just say I know the type. Great bodies, little-girl pouts, graduates of How to Be Sexy 101. Trust me, your face is much more interesting."

"I'd rather be sexy."

It took a moment for Catherine to realize she'd spoken the thought out loud. Horrified, she scrambled to stand up. A heavy male hand pushed down firmly on her shoulder.

"You are sexy."

Her gaze snapped up. If he was making fun of her, she couldn't tell from his serious brown eyes. She smiled a perfunctory thank-you, patted his hand once and started to rise for the second time.

He pushed her back down again. "You are sexy," he repeated. "Hasn't Carl told you that?"

She stared at her sensible navy shoes peeking from beneath her sensible navy slacks—embarrassed for herself, for Carl, for this basically kind man who had the instincts of a gentleman, if not the polish.

"Why would he lie?" she asked softly.

Warm fingers cupped her chin and lifted. His brows formed a bank of dark thunderclouds. "Pretty Boy is a jerk."

"Don't say that. He's been totally honest with me since we met. I don't need for him to tell me

I'm ... sexy." She willed herself not to blush and failed. "I wouldn't believe him if he did."

The anger died in Joe's steady gaze. "Then believe me."

She yearned to, with a plain woman's fierce passion. "I can't, Joe. You said yourself you're a realist."

Instead of releasing her chin and letting them both escape, he grinned. The same slow "I like what I see and I know what to do with it" grin he'd bestowed on that disapproving socialite in the art gallery.

No wonder the woman had puddled at his feet.

"Damn right I'm a realist. And the honest fact is there's not a woman on this planet who isn't sexy in some way. Could be her smile. Or the curve of her hip. Or maybe just the way she moves her hands. Hell, I had a sixty-year-old English teacher in high school who could've worked for a 900 phone service her voice was so hot."

His thumb rubbed lazy circles on Catherine's skin, wreaking havoc with her pulse.

"I wasn't lying to you, doll. But I can see I'll have to convince you better. Now, where should I start?"

"By letting go of my chin." Her voice came out husky and weak, not at all like her own.

"Uh-uh. We're in the middle of a lesson here, Teach." He tipped her face this way and that as if studying one of her Mardi Gras masks.

She felt poised on the brink of discovery. Excited and scared. Trapped in his gentle grip, she was free to examine him openly at close range.

Her gaze roved over the aggressive square jaw, the bumpy ridge of his nose, the shaggy dark hair, thick brows and hard planes of his cheeks. Not handsome by sophisticated standards, but uncompromisingly masculine. Sexy in a way no Pretty Boy could match.

Her mind jerked guiltily.

"You ever been to Colorado in the summer?"

She struggled to switch gears. Fortunately he didn't wait for her reply.

"Once during a three-game series in Denver, I skipped practice and headed for the mountains. Smelling that air, hiking those trails until sunset was worth getting fined when I got back." His faraway expression cleared.

Her breath caught and hung suspended. She couldn't look away from his hypnotic dark gaze.

"Your eyes, Catherine, remind me of aspen leaves in the sun—all shivery green and full of sass. They look at a man and cut right through the bull. Mysterious, I guess you'd call 'em." His tone grew intimate. "And sexy."

When his fingers splayed up from her chin onto her cheek, her breath made up for lost time, growing shallow and fast.

"Your skin reminds me of Snow White's," he crooned in that whisper-in-the-dark voice. "I had a crush on her as a little kid. Guess she ruined me for women who fry themselves on beaches and in tanning booths." He brushed her cheek lightly with the backs of his knuckles, then the pads of his fingers, as if she were fragile and precious. "Your skin is like white satin. Soft. Smooth." He traced a path down to her neck. "Sexy."

Catherine sat spellbound, no more able to resist his entrancing words than a child could resist a fairy tale. At the first touch on her throat, she tilted her head back.

"Ah, yes," he said on a masculine sigh, enclosing her throat from ear to ear. "Your neck, Catherine..."

The sound Joe made in his chest sent spirals of heat to places long dormant in her body. She waited, her pulse a frantic staccato throb beneath his fingertips.

When he removed his hand from her throat, she trapped a moan of disappointment.

When his mouth replaced his hand, she released a moan of pleasure.

He smiled against her skin and nuzzled deep, his raspy beard a welcome irritation. Her eyes closed as his teeth nipped gently, the pressure exquisite and knowing. He soothed his bites with a warm wet tongue, heightening the moist heat between her legs.

She turned her head slowly as he basted and scorched his way across her neck. Her affection-starved soul absorbed the sensations thirstily. More alive than ever before in her life, she reached up and threaded her fingers through his thick hair.

"Catherine," he murmured.

"Joe," she whispered.

"Holy Moses!" a voice exclaimed.

Her eyelids popped open. She pulled back at the same time Joe jerked upright. They both blinked at the bald man with twinkling blue eyes who stood watching them from the hallway. As instructed, Norman had covered most of his pink skin with a long-sleeved shirt and trousers.

"Sorry to interrupt," he said, sounding anything but sorry. "You kind of caught me by surprise."

His timely appearance had been a blessing, Catherine assured herself, for reasons too complicated to sort out now. Although the image of Carl's face was pretty darn clear in her confused mind.

Since Joe still seemed a bit shell-shocked, she smoothed her slacks, rose shakily from the chair and hoped her neck didn't look as ravaged as it felt.

"You must be Norman," she said, walking forward and extending her palm.

The older man met her halfway and shook her hand. "And you must be the shrink. Sorry, but Joe didn't mention your name."

"Catherine," she offered dryly, the last remnant of fantasy wearing off. "It's a pleasure to meet you. How are you enjoying your sabbatical?"

His round face crumpled like a fallen soufflé. "I miss my wife."

She hid her rush of sympathy behind a no-nonsense look. "Then what are you doing here in Houston, instead of Dallas where you can tell her in person?"

He ran stubby fingers over his shiny dome—a habit from more bountiful days, she suspected—then dropped his arm in defeat.

"Doris doesn't want to see or talk to me. She kicked me out of the house and changed the locks." His gaze met hers, his blue eyes stark with misery. "She's filing for divorce as soon as our lawyer gets back from Hawaii, and I don't know what to do."

"Do you love her, Norman?"

One hand slowly rose to twist the ring on his left finger. "I never knew how much."

"Then the first thing to do is pretend I'm Doris." She smiled gently, took his arm and led him to the dinette table. "I'll make us some coffee. We'll sit. You can tell Doris how you feel and maybe get a handle on what went wrong. We'll figure out where to go from there. How about it?"

A spark of hope lit in his eyes, filling her with satisfaction and a strong sense of purpose.

When the front door opened and closed, neither one of them paid attention.

CHAPTER SEVEN

FIFTY MILES AWAY Mary Lou dressed carefully for the man who'd crept into her heart and refused to leave. Tonight couldn't get here soon enough. All she had to do was get through this day, she reminded herself. Then all her longings would be over.

She backed away from her full-length reflection and grimaced. Desperate circumstances called for desperate measures.

Her grubby sneakers, frayed jeans and long-tailed denim shirt with grease stains trailing down the front were the oldest clothes she owned. Reaching for her battered straw fishing hat, she crammed it low on her head. Perfect. With her thick black braid trailing halfway down her back and virtually no makeup helping her cheat, she looked as different from the woman John had taken to dinner six nights ago as she could manage.

Shutting her closet door, she headed for the small apartment kitchen and packed an ice chest with Diet Cokes—John's favorite. He drank too many, he'd admitted once. Today he'd be forced to try the caffeine-free variety.

Two loud knocks made her heart surge. *Just get through this day.* She repeated her mantra silently as she walked to the door and pulled it open.

"Hi there." John's gaze traveled from the crown of her ratty hat to the hole in her sneaker toe, obvious delight warming his brown eyes. "You look adorable."

Her insides melted. God, this was going to be hard. "I look like Apple Annie and you know it, but thanks. Would you mind carrying an ice chest to the car for me?"

"Of course not."

"It's in the kitchen." She stepped aside and he swept past, smelling of breezy cologne and looking virile in khaki shorts, navy crewneck shirt and canvas boat shoes.

With a brief but interested glance around her neat apartment—she'd met him at the restaurant the other night—he hefted the chest and turned back around. She tried not to stare at his bunched biceps and flat belly as he crossed the threshold, but he was an exceptionally handsome man in the prime of his life, and she was human. Her gaze fed hungrily on his lean body all the way to the Jaguar.

Once inside, he faced her with a smile. "Okay, how do I get there?"

Two days ago she'd come up with the plan to invite him along on her monthly trek to the old Denton homestead a short drive from town. She rattled off directions now and sank into butter-soft leather with a defeated sigh.

Ironically John was in high spirits. "This would be a great day to be out on the lake. Hot. Sunny. Good stiff breeze. Do you like to sail?"

"I've never been sailing."

"Then you haven't lived. There's nothing more exhilarating in the world than skimming over the water with the wind in your face. I keep a catamaran at Lake Conroe.''

''How nice for you.''

His hands on the wheel tightened, then relaxed. ''Yes, it is. I take her out every chance I get, which isn't often enough. Maybe on your next day off we could drive up together.''

Idle talk, as if they had a lifetime of adventures ahead of them, instead of only two-hour business meetings once a month. *If* he didn't fire her, that is.

''It's not that far,'' he continued as if she'd responded. ''A bottle of wine, a beautiful sunset and you on my boat—'' he heaved an exaggerated sigh ''—I'd be one happy man.''

The knife in her heart twisted. ''Stop.''

His startled glance turned grim. ''Stop what?''

Her misery and pent-up frustration spilled out. ''This fantasy. These invitations. Why are you pursuing me, John? Boredom, defiance of convention—why?'' She turned her head.

''Do you really think so little of me?''

Impossible as it seemed, he sounded wounded. She bit back her passionate protest and felt his probing gaze.

''My God, you doubt yourself, don't you? But that's ridiculous. I've been looking all my life for a woman like you.''

She rolled her eyes. ''Now *that's* ridiculous.''

''Dammit, Mary Lou, you're being the worst kind of reverse snob! My wife cared more about how many times she made the best-dressed list than she did about me. That's what money and social standing can do to ordinary human beings.''

As if she didn't know exactly. She would've laughed if her vocal cords had been functioning.

His knuckles whitened on the wheel. "If it hadn't been for my daughter, I would've bailed out long ago. Marla would've fought me for custody out of pure spite, and I couldn't put Beth through that."

What would he think about a mother who hadn't seen her daughter in thirty years? The answer had her shifting on the leather seat.

"But what about later?" Mary Lou managed. "Say, when Beth was in high school."

"By that time I was married to my business concerns. Beth was the one who talked me into getting a divorce, actually. When she left for college, she wanted to know that I had a chance for happiness, that I wouldn't bury myself even deeper in work than I had before. So I asked her mother for my freedom and paid a considerable fortune to gain it." His tanned jaw clenched once. Twice.

She waited, knowing there was more.

"Let me tell you something about freedom, Mary Lou. The media are full of statistics about the unbalanced ratio of single women to eligible men. But no one ever talks about the pit-bull aggressiveness of these same poor women in pursuit of a financially successful man.

"I went from flattered to disgusted within two months. The thing was, nothing I said or did seemed to affect their attitude. Nice or not, as long as I could still offer security I was a valuable commodity. It really shook my self-confidence."

John Chandler, insecure? But he had the world at his feet.

He cast her a hooded look. "And then I bought a struggling truck-stop business and hired a beautiful completely disinterested woman to manage it for me."

Her traitorous heart soared. She forced herself to look away so she could think straight. "I was a challenge to you after those other women, that's all."

"No, you were a breath of fresh air. Warm. Unpretentious. Listening to me—really listening—as if I were a man, instead of a bank account. You honestly didn't seem impressed with my money or anything beyond how I treated you and the staff."

She didn't know what to say. Fortunately something about the landscape penetrated her dazed thoughts. "The county road to my place is coming up," she warned.

John slowed the car, then turned right at her direction. A red dirt road ribboned ahead, bounded on both sides by a barbed-wire fence and rolling green fields dotted with live oaks.

"It's beautiful land, Mary Lou."

"Yes." But it wasn't hers. She dreaded the moment he saw the Denton homestead.

John drove slowly down the unpaved road, the Jaguar's tires kicking up red clouds of dust and quartz gravel. Something thunked on the car's low underbelly and made him wince.

"We should've taken my car," Mary Lou said on a moan.

The fact that he didn't argue increased her misery. Three miles and nine flinches later, a sagging aluminum gate appeared on the right.

"Slow down—that's the entrance. Wait a minute and I'll unlock the gate."

Wondering why she'd ever thought this was a good idea, she was out of the Jaguar before it stopped rolling. The bicycle chain and padlock should clue him in that security wasn't too critical. She set the combination to Catherine's birth date, numbers Mary Lou would never forget, then unwrapped the chain and opened the gate.

Hopping back into the car, she pointed at two ruts in the parched yellow grass leading up a hill to a stand of oaks. "That'll take us to the house. I've cleared the broken beer bottles and such as best I could. But stay in the ruts to be safe."

To his credit, he didn't hesitate to drive onward. She stared dully out the window at the passing scrub brush, prickly pear and trash trees choking out whatever grass had once survived. Her daddy used to make a token effort to clear the acreage during his infrequent dry spells. But with both her parents dead going on seven years, nature had a stranglehold on the land that Mary Lou had neither the time nor money to fight.

The Jaguar jounced through the ruts, topped the hill and stopped. A cluster of live oaks spread majestic branches over the weather-beaten shack she'd lived in for eighteen years.

"Welcome to the Denton homestead," she said woodenly.

Unable to bear his silence, she got out of the car and walked toward the sagging front porch. Mr. Jenkins at the hardware store had given Mama six gallons of paint when Mary Lou was about ten. Someone hadn't liked the color once it was mixed up. Mary Lou had thought it was beautiful.

She stopped and studied the aqua blue dandruff speckling the silver wood. The tin roof had long since rusted through in patches. Every windowpane had been used for target practice by kids sighting in their rifles. To the right of the house, set back a discreet distance, a small structure leaned on the verge of collapse.

Footsteps crunched behind her and she hugged her stomach. "Until I started school, I thought everyone had an outhouse. The teacher had to show me how to flush the toilet and use the faucets. Her face..." Mary Lou would never forget the mingled pity and morbid fascination on that woman's face. It was an expression she saw often in the following years. "Her face made me feel ashamed, and I didn't know why. But I learned soon enough that I was white trash."

Turning, she looked up into John's grave eyes. "It was worse when I found out Daddy had sold off a farmhouse and nine hundred acres chunk by chunk to buy his booze. Mama finally put her foot down when all that was left was this old sharecropper's shack. That was before she gave up and started drinking, too."

"Poor baby..."

"That's right, I was poor—dirt poor—but I was smart, too. I studied the way people talked and ate and dressed, and copied the things I thought would make me fit in. By the time I got to high school, my drama teacher couldn't believe I hadn't taken private acting lessons. I never told her that, in a way, I had." The bittersweet memory led to thoughts of New York, and Lawrence. And the divorce trial records easily obtained by anyone wishing to investigate her past.

She adjusted her straw hat the better to see John's eyes. "Don't you understand? The Mary Lou Denton you know is an act. *This*—" she gestured at the squalid surroundings "—is who I am. What I am. Sooner or later your family and friends would find out, John."

He reached up and gently removed her hat, then cupped her face between his hands. "Who cares?"

Who cares? "I do. And so do you, deep down. God, the tabloids would have a field day if they got wind of your dating a woman like me."

"An intelligent, beautiful—"

"Truck-stop manager, who also happens to be your employee, who also happens to come from the lowest rung of society."

"Mary Lou, sweetheart—" he firmed his hold, his expression so tender her chest ached "—all that means is that you were smart enough, tough enough and courageous enough to rise above what life handed you. If anything, I admire you more now than before." His eyes darkened subtly. "All that counts is how we feel about each other. All that matters is this."

He lowered his head and took her mouth in a searing, possessive kiss. His tongue found hers and he groaned, the sound so rich with masculine satisfaction it stirred her deeply. She moved closer, threading her fingers through his beautiful hair, loving its silky texture.

Their bodies bumped, shifted, melded intimately. His hands splayed over her hips and pulled, showing her his desire more clearly than words. Her moan seemed to excite him more, and the kiss intensified. She was burning, flaming...

Mary Lou flung her head back and gasped for air. "Stop."

His lips were on her throat. "Not until you agree to have dinner with me again," he murmured against her skin.

Her laugh was half sob. "I can't."

He trailed soft kisses below her ear, over her drowsing eyelids, down her cheek. "You can," he whispered fiercely, claiming her mouth once more.

A long time later, she did.

"...SO WHICH would you prefer, darling?"

Catherine had no idea. Her attention had wandered five minutes ago, an all-too-common occurrence in the week since Joe had kissed her neck—and one of the reasons she'd asked Carl over tonight.

"Umm...whichever *you* prefer." She peeked across the living-room sofa to gauge his response.

Wearing Italian loafers, baggy wheat-colored trousers and a black silk T-shirt, he looked like a model for *GQ*. An extremely irritated model.

"You look very handsome tonight," she added, hoping to distract him with his favorite subject.

Surprisingly, his frown only deepened. He propped his empty wineglass on one thigh and tapped the crystal rim with his index finger. The fine gold hairs on the back of his manicured fingers glinted in the lamplight.

It was a nice hand, she told herself. A perfectly good hand, even if his fingers were...well, stubby. At least, they were short compared to—

"Catherine!"

Her gaze shot up to meet his. "Yes, Carl?"

He tap-tap-tapped his glass.

She smiled weakly. "Would you like a refill on your wine?"

"I'd like you to answer my question." His gray eyes were frosty.

Never again would she make fun of game-show contestants. "Could you repeat the question please?"

He shook his head in righteous disgust. "I *asked* if you prefer to honeymoon in Acapulco or St. Martin, but obviously you have something more important on your mind. Care to tell me about it?"

Well, you see, darling, another man made me want to tear his clothes off recently, and I was wondering if you could top that.

Stalling, she sipped her white wine and remembered Charlotte Wilson's earlier phone call. "If you must know, Carl," Catherine said now, "I'm upset about our engagement party." She matched Carl frown for frown. "I thought you and I had agreed it should be an intimate, casual affair."

"We did. So what's the problem?"

"The problem is your mother mailed out almost two hundred invitations to a cocktail party yesterday."

The tension seeped out of his perfect features. "Is that all you've been worried about?"

"All? Think of the expense! Not to mention the planning and logistics of serving that many people in a private home." And the increased chances of someone recognizing Joe's true identity.

Carl set his glass on the cherry coffee table, placed her own beside it and took both her hands in his. "Between the two of them, my parents have a huge circle of friends and business associates. And since you refuse to let them help with the wedding costs—" he placed two fingers against her parting lips "—don't argue, I'm not opening that can of worms again. I'm simply pointing out that this is their only chance to show you off to people who might not be invited to the wedding."

She arched her brow. "Come on, Carl, show me off? Why don't we just include a copy of my family tree in a wedding announcement and save all this fuss and money?"

"It's too late. The invitations have already gone out."

She saw the moment he realized his mistake.

"Catherine, I didn't—"

"It's okay," she interrupted, torn between laughter and sadness. "Your inheritance is safe. You've never lied to me about your reason for proposing, and honesty is more than many marriages start out with. But Carl—" she bit her lower lip, then plunged ahead "—we need to settle something before our engagement goes any farther."

He pulled back, wariness evident in every taut line of his body. "That sounds ominous."

"Ominous, no. Serious, yes."

"Is it about starting a family?" He looked genuinely worried now. His inheritance depended on producing a grandchild.

"No. Well, sort of," she amended.

"Is it about working after the children are born?"

"No." Oh, damn. "Well, sort of."

His brow smoothed. He flashed the smile that had raised $1,500 for Richmond College at a bachelor auction four months ago. The winning bidder had introduced Carl, her prize "dinner date," to Catherine of the Connecticut Hamiltons—and the rest, as they say, was history.

"I've got it," he said happily. "You've decided to call off our bet and stay home to raise the children."

"No!" She reached for her glass of chardonnay and took a fortifying sip before turning to face him again. "It's not about your inheritance, or the bet, or what you and I want individually. It's about *us*, Carl, and the reality of our living together. Making children together."

She could tell by his puzzled expression she would have to spell it out. "What if we're not physically compatible? What if we can't stand making love? To each other, I mean."

She wasn't a virgin. But she'd never responded to anyone—including her fiancé—as she had to Joe. So far Carl had shown no inclination to test their compatibility beyond kissing her good-night after their dates. Was she doomed to a passionless marriage? Suddenly she had to know.

Comprehension dawned on his face and, with it, a gentle smile. For the second time that evening he set her wineglass on the coffee table and took both her hands in his.

"Catherine, darling, I didn't realize you were such an innocent. There are things you can do, ways to please me... Well, when the time is right, I'll show you what I mean and it'll be fine. Really."

"You'll show me ways to please you," she repeated.

"Of course I will. I'm not an oaf." He squeezed her fingers. "Now, don't waste another minute worrying about satisfying me in bed, is that understood?"

"Okay." She jerked her hands from his grasp. "I'll worry about *you* satisfying *me*. Because quite frankly, I'm not at all sure you can."

His look of shock might have been funny another time. Right now it roused the grateful spinster in her to fury.

Catherine jumped up and strode back and forth in front of the large bay window. "Of all the selfish, insensitive, *oafish* remarks I have ever heard—and as Lawrence Hamilton's daughter, I've heard plenty—your comments win the Pulitzer, Carl."

She whirled toward the sofa and set her hands on her waist. "You'll show me how to please you? I shouldn't worry about satisfying you? Ha! I could reduce you to a quivering mass of begging testosterone if I put my mind to it. Because you know what, buster? I am sexy."

The statement echoed in the silence. Her bravado faltered.

And suddenly Joe's voice was in her head, making her believe the words, infusing her with sultry confidence as she walked forward. The sleeveless coral silk jumpsuit she wore clung to her figure in a way Carl apparently found fascinating. The spinster inside her grew bolder.

"My eyes are like aspen leaves in the wind," she informed him in a chesty voice, batting her lashes for emphasis. "My skin—" she ran her fingertips from her wrist up her bare arm, then lifted a coy shoulder "—is as soft and smooth as Snow White's." No wait, you couldn't feel a cartoon. "And...white satin," she added, memory of a crooning description sending a shiver up her flesh. She reached the sofa and looked down into eyes that had warmed up considerably past frosty.

"My neck is . . ." Uh-oh. Joe hadn't gotten around to describing her neck. But his groan had spoken volumes. "My neck is like a Botticelli painting, as graceful as Venus rising from the sea," she improvised, figuring this was her show and she could write the lines to suit herself.

In one fluid movement, she sat in Carl's lap and threaded her fingers through his precision-cut blond hair. "I can please you, Carl." Astoundingly, the proof pressed hard beneath her thighs. "Now let's see what you can do for me."

And darned if he didn't seem eager to try.

His enthusiastic kiss should have pleased her greatly. It was wet and hot and accompanied by roving hands seeking her bare skin in a feverish frenzy. It had all the genuine passion missing from his kisses in the past, plus the advantage of her being primed and ready—no, *aching* to be set aflame.

But instead of wanting to tear his clothes off, she felt an insistent urge to keep her jumpsuit buttoned tight. His teeth nipped her neck too hard, his hands stroked her skin too roughly. His hair was too short and silky, his shoulders too narrow.

She pushed against his chest and said, "Stop."

The action only seemed to arouse him more. He pressed her closer and captured her mouth in another bruising kiss. When his fingers jerked her first button free, he moved his lips to the exposed skin and she began struggling in earnest.

"Carl, stop!"

"Get your hands off her," a steely voice ordered, "before I shove your ass straight through your teeth."

ONE SHOULDER against the living-room door frame, Joe watched Catherine's face register intense relief. She scrambled up from Carl's lap and fumbled to fasten her top button. Obviously her protest hadn't been an act.

Joe's anger turned ugly. He stared long and hard at Pretty Boy.

Blanching, Carl rose from the sofa and adjusted his clothing. "How dare you break into this house and disturb our privacy! Catherine, call 911."

She darted a nervous look at Joe. "I don't really think that's necessary—"

"Of course it's necessary. If you won't report him to the authorities, I will."

"Yeah? You and what army?" Joe asked insolently.

"Ah, spoken like a true Pig's Gut gentleman."

Joe came off the door frame so fast the other man didn't have time to step back. Toe-to-toe with Catherine's gentleman fiancé, he leaned down and thrust out his jaw. "Until you learn what the word 'stop' means, I'd be careful what I called other people if I were you."

Carl glared up balefully. "Fine. I'll wait until after you make a complete fool of yourself at the engagement party."

"You're gonna be pukin' crow the next morning, so save your breath—and your allowance pennies. Catherine wants a big corner office in Greenway Plaza for her practice."

"You just stay over the garage where you belong and I'll take care of Catherine's needs."

"From the look of things when I came in, you weren't takin' care of anyone but your little buddy Dick there."

"Why, you . . . insufferable swine!"

Joe blinked, then propped one hand at his waist. "Why, you *meanie,* you," he said, stamping his foot.

Carl's apoplectic sputter released Joe's wolfish grin. He was starting to have fun.

"Boys, boys!" Catherine said, pulling the two of them apart with surprising strength. "I can't believe what I'm hearing. We're not on a school playground. Grow up and let's discuss this rationally." She folded her arms and eyed Joe narrowly. "Exactly how *did* you get inside my house?"

It took all of his advanced experience to hold a poker face. He shrugged. "The back kitchen door was open." That much was true, anyway. "When you didn't answer my knock, I came in to make sure you were okay and heard you telling this joker to get his paws off you."

Carl audibly ground his teeth. "That is *not* what she said."

"What would it take for you to get the message, pal—a goddamn singing telegram?"

"Boys!"

Joe turned to Catherine and grew still. Her color was high, her eyes full of shivery green sass. Her agitated breathing drew his attention to small plump breasts encased in scalloped lace, if he read the silk embossing correctly. And he was a master at deciphering what hid beneath a woman's clothing. When he slowly raised his gaze, her cheeks had grown pinker.

His muscles tensed as she seemed about to call his
bluff.

"Next time, knock louder," she said wryly, bending over to pick up two wineglasses from the coffee
table. "I think I could use a refill. Would
you . . . gentlemen care to join me?"

Without waiting for an answer, she headed for the
kitchen. Carl sent Joe a poisonous glance before following.

Expelling a relieved breath, Joe stared at the empty
doorway. The truth of his pathetic behavior embarrassed and confused him.

He'd seen Carl drive up an hour ago and had gone
damn near crazy wondering what the two of them
were up to. Telling Allie he needed to borrow a book
from Catherine, he'd crept around the house and
struck pay dirt at the living-room bay window. The
sight of her slinking forward like some Marilyn
Monroe reincarnation, then sitting in Pretty Boy's lap
and twining her fingers in his hair . . . well, he'd almost smashed his fist through the window.

Instead, he'd charged through the back door and
heard her say the magic word—"Stop."

Joe didn't want to think about what his murderous reaction meant.

"Joe?" Catherine called in a "get your butt in
here" tone.

Rumpling his hair, he thrust his hands in the back
pockets of his jeans and walked to the kitchen. Catherine and Carl sat at the breakfast table sipping wine.
A third full glass sat in front of a chrome-and-cane-
back chair angled conspicuously away from the table.

Joe flipped the seat around and sat in a straddle, enjoying Pretty Boy's contemptuous sneer.

"I'd like to clear the air here and now," Catherine began.

Lifting his glass, Joe gave the contents a long noisy sniff.

"You two are behaving like children and it's got to stop."

Joe swirled his wine next, licking the rivulets that spilled over the brim as if they were drips from an ice-cream cone.

"I want you to shake hands and agree to a truce until the engagement party is over." Her voice sounded tight and strained. "Joe? Carl? Which one of you is gentleman enough to make the first move?"

Holding Carl's disgusted gaze, Joe raised his glass to his lips, threw back his head and downed the wine like a shot of tequila. Then he wiped his mouth on his T-shirt sleeve and risked a glance at Catherine.

She was not amused.

Sighing, he set his glass down and reached across the table at the same time Carl did. Their gazes locked with their hands. The shake was prolonged and just short of painful.

"Weights?" Joe asked, impressed against his will.

"No, tennis. Batting?" Carl asked.

"No, weights. But I play a little tennis, too."

He recognized the competitive spark of interest in Carl's eyes and accepted the unspoken challenge. They were both smiling when their hands parted.

"Well, then, see?" Catherine said brightly. "That wasn't so bad, was it? Now you can go your separate ways with no hard feelings."

Carl met Joe's gaze. "I'm a member of Seven Lakes Country Club. I could probably get a court for around noon tomorrow."

"Grass or clay?"

"Clay. Top-notch shape, too."

"You're going to play tennis together?" Catherine asked, her tone incredulous.

Joe flashed her a grin and turned back to Carl. "My racket needs restringing. I doubt if I can get it done by noon."

"Borrow one of mine. The Yonex is a little long for me—it ought to be just right for you."

"Thanks, I might take you up on that."

"You're borrowing a racket from Carl?" she squeaked.

Joe would never in a million years understand the workings of a woman's mind. "You wanted us to shake hands and make up, but you don't want us to play a friendly game of tennis?"

She opened and closed her mouth, then lifted her chin. "What about Allie? Tomorrow's Saturday, remember? There's no camp."

Oh, hell. He'd promised to spend the entire day with his daughter. And Sunday was the carnival fund-raiser for Allie's fall softball league. So much for showing Pretty Boy the difference between amateur and pro athletes.

"Bring her along," Carl suggested. "There's a lake for swimming and canoeing, an Olympic-size pool, a rec room in the clubhouse—plenty to keep her entertained. You come, too, Catherine. We'll all have a late lunch and make an afternoon of it."

Joe smiled genuinely for the first time that night. He hadn't known how he would occupy Allie all day. This was a perfect solution.

"Sounds great, Carl. Thanks for the invitation." He turned to Catherine. "So? What d'ya say?"

She looked from one man to the other and shook her head. "I will never, as long as I live, understand the way men think."

CHAPTER EIGHT

CATHERINE FLIPPED UP the collar of her ankle-length beach robe and tugged down the brim of her floppy straw hat. Even protected by sunglasses, sunscreen and the branches of a huge oak tree, she glanced with loathing at the high noon sun.

Only gunslingers and fools braved the most lethal rays of the afternoon. Carl and Joe were dueling it out on a broiling court somewhere behind Seven Lakes Country Club. And unless they had Colt .45s tucked in their tennis shorts, that pretty much pegged them in her book.

Earlier she'd taken Allie to the clubhouse rec room, filled with laughing young people. The girl had peeked inside, her expression both wistful and scared, then quickly withdrawn and asked to see the lake. Although Catherine had never really liked lakes and oceans—she much preferred the unlimited visibility in a swimming pool—she'd understood and obliged Allie's unease.

She herself had stood on the outskirts of charmed circles all her life. Schoolmates whispering with heads together. Families swinging clasped hands. Lovers cuddling close and stealing kisses. Always the odd person out, always alone. It didn't take a Ph.D. to figure out why creating a strong family unit of her own was so important to her.

Studying Allie now from under her hat brim, Catherine suppressed a smile. If she'd looked like *that* at age twelve, she wouldn't have stayed alone for long.

Wearing a sunflower-print bikini, Allie lay sprawled on a towel with her head propped on one hand in an unconsciously sensual pose. Her shorts, T-shirt and sandals were stacked neatly by her feet.

"I like your suit," Catherine said. "Is it new?"

The girl blushed, her body stiffening. "Gram bought it for me right before she left. This is the first time I've worn it."

Catherine couldn't wait to see Joe's face when he saw his little girl now. "Are you sure you don't want to sit by the pool, honey?"

"Yeah. The lake's real pretty."

Following Allie's gaze to the rippling blue surface, Catherine acknowledged its beauty. But Lord only knew what vile creatures swam underneath out of sight.

Three empty canoes sat on the shore half in, half out of the lapping water. The long pier was deserted. The floating dock, about fifty yards from the pier, was not. Three teenage boys horsed around on the rocking plank boards, making a lot of noise and casting frequent glances toward the tree. Catherine had no illusions about who they were looking at.

"When do you think they'll be through with their match?" Allie asked, referring to Carl and her father.

"Not before one of them wins or collapses from heat stroke. No, I take that back. Your father would play on his knees if he had to."

Allie giggled and sat up, then slanted a look of shy admiration at Catherine. "How come you're not gaga over Joe? I mean, he can't sweet-talk you into doing what he wants like he does with other women."

Remembering her melting response to his claim that she was sexy, her secret thrill at his almost jealous interference last night, Catherine was suddenly grateful she wore sunglasses.

"He acts...different with you," Allie continued. "Like he actually cares if he screws up."

Catherine chose her next words carefully. "I've found that people tend to live up to others' expectations of them, good or bad. If he acts differently with me, I suppose it's because I expect him to act responsibly, whereas other people expect him to screw up." She let that sink in as they both stared at the lake.

"I didn't always expect him to screw up," Allie said finally. "But after a while, after so many broken promises, it got to where—" She stopped, her voice thick with emotion. "It got harder and harder to believe him, ya know?"

Catherine leaned forward and stroked the girl's silky cap of hair. "I know, sweetheart, I know." And she did. A girl's hero worship for her father could only withstand so much neglect before it died of malnourishment.

"Maybe if my mother had lived, he'd be different," Allie continued, hugging her shins and resting her cheek on her kneecaps. "But she died when I was born. From complications—whatever that means. Gram wasn't very thrilled about getting stuck with me. She'd already raised her family."

Obviously those were very familiar words. Catherine's own mother hadn't wanted her, and even her

psychology training hadn't prevented feelings of in-
adequacy and guilt. She battled her irritation at
Gram's insensitivity.

"Did you ever want your dad to remarry? He must
have had chances. You said yourself most women are
gaga over him."

"Oh, Joe'll never get married."

So confident. So final. "You can't know that for
sure."

"Well, that's what he said, anyway. That taking
care of me is more than enough responsibility for
him. That a wife would only tie him down more."

Familiar stuff. Catherine's outrage swelled and
died. "Your father would never tell you that. What
happened? Did you overhear him talking to someone else? Your Gram maybe?"

Despite Allie's attempt to shrug, she looked small
and forlorn and guilty.

"Ah, sweetheart, I know that must have hurt. But
you've got to remember that no one is perfect. Not
me, not you—no one. We all have reasons for acting
as we do, and I'm pretty sure I know why responsibility is so hard for your dad."

Quietly, gaining conviction as she voiced her theory, she told Allie about Big Joe imposing his dream
on a young man with other aspirations. How his
death convinced Joe that planning and commitment
were futile and led to pain. And that it was up to those
who loved him to demonstrate how accepting responsibility leads to self-respect.

She lifted Allie's chin and stared into thoughtful
brown eyes wise beyond their years. "I know this is
heavy stuff to be laying on a twelve-year-old. But
you're very mature, Allie, very special. Believe in

your dad just a little while longer, and I know you won't be sorry. Will you do that?''

Catherine could sense the careful consideration of her request. This girl never made promises lightly.

"All right, Catherine, I guess I can hang in there a little longer." Her golden skin flushed. "Thanks."

And suddenly the eyes that had been so wise seconds ago grew vulnerable and hungry for something Catherine had waited a lifetime to give.

She never knew who moved first, only that the hug they shared was long and mutually fierce.

Hoots and whistles from the water broke them apart. Pulling back, Catherine smiled mistily and gestured to the trio of teenage boys. "They've been trying to get you to notice them since we got here."

Allie glanced at the floating dock, then plucked shyly at her towel. "Yeah, right."

"Yes, right. Let's face it—you're wearing a bikini. It's a scientific fact that bikinis regress the male brain to preschool levels of maturity. Just look at them showing off."

Allie gazed over at the dock. One boy promptly shoved another into the water, then grappled with the remaining occupant for sole possession of the island and, presumably, Allie's attention.

She looked intrigued. "You really think that's all for *me?*"

"Smile and wave to them."

After a startled glance at Catherine, the girl lifted her arm, smiled and swayed her palm like a beauty queen.

The two wrestlers froze in place. The third boy—who was clambering back onto the raft—saw his opportunity, grabbed their ankles and jerked. His buddies hit the water hard while he stood up and waved at Allie.

She lowered her arm, met Catherine's I-told-you-so gaze and broke into a replica of her father's cocky grin.

"Cool," she said smugly.

Catherine laughed and shook her head, feeling a bit guilty for launching a weapon like Allie on unsuspecting mankind.

All three boys were back on the floating dock, shouting and shoving and waving. The tallest and most athletic of the bunch began diving off the side. The others tried to compete. Back dives. Front flips. Cannonballs. The square platform rocked violently as they grew rowdier and more reckless.

Allie watched the performance with obvious delight, but Catherine didn't like the uncontrolled quality of it all. She stood up and gathered her towel.

"I think it's time we leave and let them settle down. Come on, Allie."

The girl raised a pleading face. "Just a few more minutes? Please?"

Catherine sighed, hating to spoil the party, then turned to frown at the three teenagers. They stood poised, their backs to the water and toes hugging the edge of the platform as if waiting for a cue. All three suddenly arched up into backflips, sending up a triple geyser of water on landing.

"That was so cool! Did you see it, Catherine?"

She had, and something wasn't right.

Allie waved at the surfacing heads and whistled loudly, receiving huge answering grins. On two faces.

Catherine searched the water for the third face, the boy whose feet had slipped on take off. *Oh, no.* A cold dread stole through her limbs, making her as sluggish as a reptile in winter. Her thoughts raced in contrast.

"Catherine, are you okay?"

By this time, the tallest boy was peering anxiously around the platform.

Oh-no-oh-no-oh-no-oh-no.

"What's wrong? Answer me."

But Catherine was too focused on a spot just beyond the platform, the place where a vibrant boy had disappeared. She prayed the water was clear. And please God, not too deep.

JOE HELD his racket at the ready and swayed on the balls of his feet. The motions were futile but, hey, a man had his pride. He'd go down fighting.

Across the net, Pretty Boy tossed the ball high, arced back his racket and followed through in a poetry of motion that had dazzled Joe for the first six or so serves. Now he focused grimly on a small section of clay court, knowing the missile was coming. Knowing it would be ugly.

The green blur hit just inside the fault line and spun straight into Joe's swinging racket. The impact thudded, instead of thwacked, but at this point, screw technique. The ball sailed back over the net, and that was all that counted. It wasn't another ace.

Pretty Boy's serve was not just good. It was damn near unconscious.

Now Joe had a shot at winning the point, and he *wanted* it. More than a beautiful woman, more than a pile of money—more than a World Series championship ring, goddammit. And he *went* for it. With aggressive volleys, solid backhands—gut-wrenching forehand drives, goddammit.

And the little twerp drove everything right back down Joe's throat.

Heat shimmered up from the clay. Sweat dripped like rain from his nose and chin. His knees hurt like hell and he knew he'd pay later. Backpedaling to the baseline to return a lob, he concentrated on the ball and pretended it was Pretty Boy's head.

Six feet four inches of royally pissed-off athlete went into his overhead smash. He'd never hit a ball— any kind of ball—so hard in his life, not even for a home run. *Take that!* he thought seconds before something smacked him in the forehead.

Staggering, he watched Carl vault the net and jog forward.

"Are you all right?"

Joe's focus cleared. He looked up at the cloudless sky. "Did a meteor fall or something?"

"I'm afraid my return caught you off guard. Sorry about that. You want to rest a minute before the next set?"

To give the guy credit, he was trying to look concerned. But he'd just whipped a pro athlete's butt. Well, ex-pro. Of another sport. Using a borrowed racket. After major surgery. Still, if it'd been Joe, he'd be rubbing his opponent's face in it.

He probed the knot swelling at his temple and snorted. "What I want is to end this torture before you maim something vital. How about letting me buy you a beer in the locker room?"

Carl look startled, then disproportionately pleased. "Only if you let me get the second one. By the way, that last return of yours was a helluva good smash."

"Obviously not good enough. Where'd you learn to play like that, anyway?"

"Princeton had an excellent program. I've kept at it ever since. The pro here has helped a lot. I could probably set up a private lesson for you if you're interested."

"Nah. It's bad for my knees—and worse for my ego." He grinned ruefully, giving the victor his due.

"You actually played very well. With a little work on returning serves, I wouldn't want a repeat match." Sweaty, rumpled and clearly a decent sport on the tennis court, this Carl was a whole lot easier to stomach than Pretty Boy.

They collected balls, zipped up rackets and packed up nylon bags as they talked, then headed for the clubhouse at an easy stroll. Joe felt a lance of pain in his left knee with every step. He really was an idiot sometimes.

At the crowded outdoor pool, they searched the area for Allie and Catherine, wanting to discuss lunch plans. Bathing beauties galore, but no Snow White and a little pal dwarf. What had they done while he'd been making a fool of himself on the court? Neither one of them had shown much enthusiasm for coming here. He'd clinched their cooperation by offering to give up his match if they *really* didn't want to lounge in idle luxury for an hour or two.

For the first time, he felt a twinge of guilt at his selfishness.

"Maybe they're in the rec room," Carl said after it was obvious the two weren't at the pool.

"Why don't you look there while I check out the lake?" Joe couldn't picture Catherine exerting herself in a canoe, but Allie was another story. "I'll meet you in the locker room in ten minutes."

Nodding, Carl headed off on his mission. Joe got his bearings and followed a mulched path leading to, according to the trail sign, "Lake Paradise. Swim and Canoe at Your Own Risk." Carl had said the clubhouse sat near the only natural lake in the community. The remaining six were glorified stock tanks placed throughout the golf course as hazards.

Joe glimpsed a bit of lake, broke through a grove of trees and spotted two figures on shore. Catherine was dressed like a good Muslim wife, Allie like a— Good Lord! Was that *Allie?*

He stalked forward, the lecture he'd given Norman replaying in his mind. How could Catherine have allowed his daughter to expose herself like that? He frowned at the tall, shrouded woman and stopped in his tracks, his senses on red alert.

Catherine stood unnaturally still, her focus riveted on the lake.

She turned and spoke sharply, the next instant shucking sandals, robe, hat and glasses, then running toward the pier. Slim and sleek in a one-piece black swimsuit, she hit the boards at full stride and never slowed down. Stunned, he watched her launch herself from the pier in a flat racing dive and cut through the water with powerful strokes.

And at last he noticed the dock about fifty yards from the pier. The one where two teenage boys were diving and disappearing for long stretches at a time, then surfacing and diving again.

Oh-no-oh-no-oh-no-oh-no.

THE LAKE WAS COLD and foreign—completely unlike her heated lap pool. Time was her enemy. She felt it ticking with each stroke of her arm. Building with the fatigue of her muscles. She kicked harder, faster, and reached the dock.

One boy surfaced, his ragged breath mixed with sobs. Another head bobbed up beside him. "Mark's gone, Danny. Oh, shit, he's gone."

No time to comfort them. No time for fear. She swam around the floating platform, took a deep breath and dove.

Murky, not clear. She shuddered and searched for the boy's unconscious body. Would he sink straight down or drift? She didn't know. Her lungs hurt. It was deep, dammit. She used precious energy driving for the bottom. Yuck! Silt and slime and prickly plants. She swept it with her arm and pushed up for the surface, her lungs burning. Panic. A frantic last surge.

Air! So sweet. Yet something the boy didn't have. She drew in a deep breath and dove.

The current swayed the reeds. There! A shadow—no, a school of small fish. Another sweep of the bottom, and another. *Ouch!* She clutched her finger and kicked to the surface.

Air! Sweeter than before. She glanced at the cut slicing her finger, drew a ragged breath and dove.

Where are you, Mark? You are *not* gone. You are *not* going to die. She swept the bottom three times, converting her fear to anger. If she'd come face-to-face with the shark from *Jaws* just then, she would have drawn first blood. Oh, God, her lungs were on fire. She wasn't going to make it.

She broke the surface, dragging in great gasping gulps of air. Dizzy, trembling with exhaustion, she cursed the lake, the boy, the fate that Joe believed would prevail. The fate she would *by God* have a hand in forming. She took a deep shuddering breath. And dove.

She was swimming blind now, past the point of focusing. Her ears roared. Her oxygen-deprived body screamed in agony. She hadn't known you could cry while holding your breath underwater. Poor Mark. He didn't deserve this. She swept her arm over the lake bottom and bumped something solid... slick... *human.*

Groping over the boy's skin, she clutched a handful of hair and pushed awkwardly off the bottom. So weak. So far away. Reaching inside herself, she tapped a hidden reservoir of strength and kicked desperately toward the surface.

They spewed into fresh air and gasped. No, she gasped. The boy was completely still. A thin red cut on his forehead told its own story. Her strength gave out. She felt him slipping from her arms. She grabbed frantically for a handhold.

"I've got him, Catherine. Let go."

Joe.

She sagged in relief, swallowed water and coughed violently. Through blurry vision, she saw Joe swim to the floating platform and hoist the boy, then himself, up onto it. She heard him ask the two hovering friends if they knew CPR. His curse sent Catherine sidestroking to the platform.

"Help me up," she said hoarsely.

Strong hands grabbed her wrists and plucked her from the water. The boy lay stretched on his back. He looked pale. Asleep. Dead. Kneeling down, she gently turned him over and sent up a prayer. When the trickle of water from his mouth stopped, she rolled him face up, tilted back his head and listened for breathing. Nothing, dammit.

She lowered her mouth to his. Two quick breaths, then she walked her fingers down his chest, braced her overlapping hands against cold flesh and pushed for fifteen simulated heartbeats.

"Help's coming," she thought she heard Joe say.

She ignored him, her concentration on the boy.

Stop to see his reaction. Breathe into his mouth. Push-push-push-push... The nightmare continued. Worse than before, because the sun was shining, the oxygen was there for his taking. She worked rhythmically, robotically, hearing the sound of quiet crying but unable to waste her precious energy on emotion.

The crying grew louder. A siren wailed in the distance. She worked steadily. Push-push-push-push. Stop to see his reaction. Breathe into his mouth. Push-push-push-push...

You are not going to die. Stop to see his reaction. *You are going to live.* Breathe into his mouth. *You are going to sit up and wave to Allie.* Push-push-push-push— Oh!

The boy made a gurgling sound. Water erupted from his mouth in a beautiful purging vomit. She turned him gently on his side and let God and nature take over. He retched and gasped and coughed and *breathed,* and suddenly Catherine was sobbing while the others broke into cheers.

Joe's arms came around her then. Hard and strong and sheltering. She buried her face in his soggy shirt and sobbed harder.

"Shh, Catherine. Honey. He's going to be all right. You saved his life." He held her and stroked her hair while the paramedics paddled out to the floating dock and treated the boy, then cleaned and bandaged her finger.

"Does your cut hurt so much?" Joe asked her, looking worried and frustrated when that prompted fresh tears.

He didn't understand her need to cry, but he let her do it in the safety of his arms. Then he tucked her in a blanket, lifted her into a canoe and held her close while one of the boys paddled them to shore. When her legs wouldn't support her, he scooped her up, carried her a quarter mile to the parked Bronco and settled her inside. And after he buckled her seat belt, after he told Allie to hop in and Carl to follow in his car, he gently kissed the top of Catherine's head.

No, he didn't understand. And because he didn't— yet comforted her, anyway—nothing would ever be the same.

SOMETHING HAD CHANGED.

Joe had ignored it while heating a can of soup in the kitchen of the garage apartment, then sending Allie to the main house with a tray. He'd suppressed it when Carl's luxury car had remained parked in the driveway until seventeen minutes past nine o'clock and the lights in the distant upstairs windows had blinked off promptly at ten-thirty. He'd even managed to ignore it while hustling Allie into her bedtime routine and reading the newest *Sports Illustrated* before switching off the lamp.

But now, staring at the ceiling from his sofa bed, he couldn't hold back the images crowding his mind. They marched forward one by one and demanded to be seen.

Catherine, the snobbish socialite, elbowing into The Pig's Gut crowd and beating the reigning pool champ.

Catherine, the pompous shrink, recognizing Norman's pain and starting his healing process.

Catherine, the uptight prude, melting at Joe's touch with a responsiveness that heated his blood.

Catherine, the hothouse flower, saving a boy's life with gritty courage and amazing stamina, yet downplaying her role to a television news reporter who was early on the scene.

With each vivid memory another preconception bit the dust. The woman that emerged firm in his mind was an intriguing blend of strength and vulnerability, passion and caution. When she'd cried in his arms earlier today...God. He'd only felt that fiercely protective of one other female. Yet his awareness of Catherine's sleek body was a long way from fatherly affection.

Of all the stinking luck, he was attracted to a woman who was engaged to marry someone richer, someone handsomer, someone more responsible. Someone else. As Allie would say, it sucked big-time. He knew damn well he would be a better lover for Catherine than Pretty Boy. But a husband? Not in this lifetime.

And there was the answer he'd been searching for, the "something" that had "changed."

Three weeks ago he would've shown Catherine exactly how sexy he thought she was, to hell with what happened later. After all, "later" was just another word for "fate." But now . . .

Now he wondered about her future with Carl. The guy was from her world. He could give her everything—including the counseling practice she wanted. And anyone with half a brain could see her talents were wasted doing research.

Suddenly Allie stirred in her sleep on the roll-away bed across the room. Romeo meowed once in protest from his usual sleeping spot at her feet. The tomcat adored Allie and barely tolerated Joe's presence. The feeling was mutual. Give him a true-blue Fido any day.

A jet shadow leapt from the darkness onto Joe's bed. Juliet walked daintily up his sheet-covered body to settle Sphinx-like on his chest. She broke into a rumbling purr and began kneading.

"Okay, okay. You're the exception," Joe murmured, absently rubbing her ears.

Her purring was hypnotic. On a rising tide of drowsiness, his mind drifted, snagging a sensation here, an image there. Smooth wet skin. Fiery green eyes. Sleek curves in a T-back swim suit. *I picked a helluva time to develop a conscience.*

It was his last clear thought before sleep took him under.

CHAPTER NINE

CATHERINE OPENED her eyes Sunday morning to bright sunlight and nagging pain. She started to stretch and gasped. When had a Mack truck driven over her bed? It hurt even to squint.

Reaching for her second pillow, she plopped it over her face. Better. No, just darker. She couldn't breathe. Flinging the pillow to the floor, she waited for her heartbeat to slow. Obviously sore muscles weren't the only side effects from yesterday's rescue. She wouldn't be taking up scuba diving anytime soon.

Despite her physical and mental trauma, she felt oddly content. A little less... hollow than usual.

It was all that attention, of course. A Channel 13 live-action reporter had taped interviews with her and Mark's teenage friends, who'd called her "awesome." The story had made the six- and ten-o'clock news. The boy's parents had also phoned last night to thank her profusely. Then Carl had stayed and talked until she'd pleaded exhaustion and gone upstairs.

His parting kiss had been heated and tender. No doubt that was where this warm feeling came from. Probably. Maybe.

Maybe not.

She sat up and met her rueful gaze in the dresser mirror. "All right, Doctor, you're attracted to Joe. He offered you comfort and you took it. Period. Keep things professional and you'll have nothing to be ashamed of.''

Her eyes darkened in memory. Of shaggy wet hair dripping into short thick lashes, muscular arms lifting her with ease, a hard masculine jaw inches away from her lips— No!

Saying the word aloud, she threw back her covers and headed for a hot shower. She'd devoted her entire life to becoming what her mother was not. Well educated. Refined. Restrained. A source of pride to Lawrence Hamilton and the family name. She had no intention of adding "a good time for Joe Tucker" to the list.

These restless stirrings Joe produced were the result of freedom from her father's critical eye, she assured herself. If she cut herself some slack—within reason—her disturbing dissatisfaction would pass. Of course it would.

Ten minutes later, her sore muscles and conscience eased, she rummaged through her wardrobe. Too dark, too old, too boring— Ah! She smiled and pulled out a sleeveless mock turtleneck in vivid cherry red, pairing it with fitted white shorts and flat white sandals. Another fifteen minutes went toward painting her toenails to match the clinging knit. Her terminally straight black hair was always a problem, but she dragged on a tortoiseshell headband and hoped for the best.

"Mirror, mirror, on the wall," she murmured, turning for a last look at her reflection.

Not Snow White by any means. But not bad, either. Maybe she'd been wrong to think loose clothing made her look less skinny. The form-fitting turtleneck and shorts revealed what curves she did have, and even she had to admit her legs weren't terrible. Daily laps in the pool had really paid off.

She hummed all the way to the kitchen and was pouring a bowl of stale cereal when a knock set her pulse leaping.

Professionalism, she reminded herself, smoothing her shorts before opening the door wide. Her initial disappointment dissolved into genuine pleasure.

"Hi," Allie said, her gaze anxious and appealing. She held a foil-wrapped plate in her hands. "How are you feeling?"

"A little sore. But other than that, just fine. Come on in." Smiling, Catherine stepped aside and caught a whiff of bacon as the girl passed. Her mouth watered. "Is that what I think it is?"

Allie set the plate on the kitchen table and peeled back the foil, exposing scrambled eggs, bacon and toast. "I hope you haven't eaten yet. I made a huge breakfast—too much for us to finish—so I kept this warm until Joe finally saw you moving around down here. Are you hungry?"

Joe had seen her moving around? He'd watched and *waited* for her to move around?

"Catherine?"

"Hmm? Oh...yes! I'm starving. And that looks ten times better than the cold cereal I was going to have."

Allie smiled shyly. "You looked so tired last night I didn't think you'd feel much like cooking this morning. Are you sure you're okay?"

Catherine realized her own post-rescue behavior must have seemed almost as frightening as the accident itself. "I feel great. Really. Especially with a hot breakfast to dig into. This is one of the nicest things anyone has ever done for me." First the soup and now this. "Thank you, honey."

She opened her arms and Allie stepped into them eagerly. A cup-runneth-over emotion swelled Catherine's chest, even stronger than the day before. She rested her chin on top of the girl's silky dark hair and thought, *This is what I've been missing in life. This is what I want.*

"Joe made the bacon," Allie confessed, her voice both muffled and sheepish.

Chuckling, Catherine squeezed tight, then pulled back. "Is that a warning?"

"Well, he didn't burn nearly as many pieces as he usually does, and we ate all of those. We saved the good ones for you."

In Catherine's whole life, nobody had ever saved the good pieces for her. The pressure in her chest increased. Blinking rapidly, she turned to gather utensils and pour two glasses of orange juice. When everything was on the table, she motioned for Allie to join her.

"Be sure and thank your dad for me," Catherine said once they were both seated.

"You can thank him yourself. I mean, I hope you can. Later, at my fund-raising carnival."

Catherine stopped chewing. Fund-raising carnival?

"My fall softball league has a carnival every summer to raise money. The principal of Washington Elementary has a kid in the league, so we get to use a school building this year, instead of a softball field. I'm working at the Face Painting booth."

Ah. Catherine swallowed her eggs and smiled. "You paint a pretty mean teddy bear—so your dad told me," she added at Allie's curious look.

"Yeah, well, he told *me* I shouldn't ask you to go with us because you need to rest. But you don't look tired. And you said you feel fine." Her big brown eyes pleaded for Catherine to accept the convoluted invitation.

Lord, it would be hard enough to maintain a professional attitude during her regular lessons with Joe. Spending time with him outside the boundaries of necessity would be extremely foolish.

She sighed. "Allie—"

"Hey, no problem. Most of the booths there will be stupid anyway. You know, little-kid stuff. I wouldn't go, either, if I didn't have to." Allie's quick gulp of orange juice wasn't quite fast enough to hide the tremble of her bottom lip. She lowered her glass and grew fascinated with the refrigerator.

Catherine put down her fork. "What time should I be ready?"

Allie's head whipped around. Wary hope lit her eyes. "It's no big deal. Really. You don't have to go if you don't want to."

"Honey, I can't think of anything I'd rather do than spend the afternoon with you. Really."

Allie broke into an irrepressible grin. "Cool."

Catherine hoped so. But considering the heat Joe generated in her lately, she had her doubts.

JOE PAUSED beside the Beanbag Toss and checked his watch. Only fifteen minutes left in Allie and Catherine's shift. He might as well head back to the cafeteria. He started forward just as his internal radar bleeped. *Hel-lo.* From the strength of the signal, she had to be close. . . .

There. Behind the Lollipop Tree. A redhead on the low side of thirty, he guessed.

"Want some candy, little boy?" she asked, raising her voice above the shrieks, giggles and chatter of a zillion kids. Her blue eyes gleamed with more than mischief.

Apparently the prizes hidden in lollipop wrappers weren't the only enticements she offered. He looked her over with a practiced eye. Very attractive. Very built. Very willing. A combination sure to warm the interest of any breathing male.

"Sorry, doll. Gotta watch my weight." He patted his belly for emphasis.

"Mm-mm-mm," she murmured, all but smacking her lips as she eyed his stomach and every other part of his anatomy. "You look fine to me. Sure there's nothing here you want?"

He shook his head with false regret. If his smile was a little forced, he didn't think she noticed.

Just then two little girls ran up to the Lollipop Tree. When the redhead turned to help them, Joe moved into the passing flow of hall traffic and didn't stop until he turned a corner. Flipping off his Astros cap, he squeezed the bridge of his nose.

He'd just met a centerfold lookalike and been turned off. It didn't take a nuclear physicist to figure out why. The reason was simple. Dumb-jock simple.

He resettled his cap and swallowed a curse. Maybe if Catherine hadn't opened her front door earlier wearing those shorts and tight turtleneck . . .

His traitorous memory conjured up every incredible detail. Perfect palm-size breasts, a waist he could span with both hands—and Lord have mercy—those legs! He'd seen them yesterday, of course, but crisis and Catherine's need for comfort had overridden his normal lechery. No such luck today.

He'd damn near stepped on his tongue following those legs out to the Bronco. Long and shapely and alabaster smooth, they were the gams Snow White hid beneath her velvet skirts from horny little dwarfs.

The next couple of weeks were going to be pure hell.

Moving back into the carnival traffic, Joe passed the Cakewalk, Ring Toss and Fishing Pond before regaining a semblance of calm. He'd gotten through worse things in his life than frustrated lust. All he had to do was follow Catherine's cue and be a perfect gentleman. Then after the party she'd marry her Pretty Boy, he'd pursue his broadcasting career and buxom redheads, and they'd both live happily ever after. Piece of cake.

Feeling a little better, he noted several painted chubby cheeks bobbing past. A butterfly. Two dancing teddy bears. A gruesome puckered scar—he whirled around and glimpsed the back of a tall boy's head. What the...?

Shrugging, he continued toward the cafeteria, checking out face paintings as he went. A bright rainbow. A cheerful daisy. The name "Laurie" with a smiley face dotting the letter *i*. A hideous wound dripping blood—he reached out and grabbed the passing boy's arm.

The kid's hair was buzzed close except for a thatch of three-foot-long ponytail at his nape. One earlobe bristled with metal.

"Who painted your face?" Joe asked.

"Let go'a me, man."

Joe held the kid's gaze until his pimply sneer faded.

"The b-babe in the Face Painting booth."

"*Which* babe?"

"The older one."

The older one, huh? Releasing the teenager's arm, Joe moved off at a fast clip.

Word had spread about the new attraction at the Face Painting booth. The line of customers stretched clear out the cafeteria door. Slouching teen boys shuffled right along next to their younger siblings. Trust Catherine to bring the two natural enemies together.

Pushing his way into the cafeteria, Joe leaned against a back wall where he had a clear view of the artists over the Bake Sale table. Allie was handling the cutesy stuff while Catherine specialized in gross-out. Their techniques were as different as their designs.

Catherine mixed and painted with confidence. Allie's movements were deliberate, her shoulders hunched and tense. Watching his daughter's oh-so-careful brush strokes, he felt a familiar constriction in his chest. She was always so damn serious.

It scared him, this need of hers to do things well, to please others. To please him. As if he would love her more, would be what she needed him to be if only she could please him *enough*. Allie's mother, Vicky, had been like that, too.

Joe stiffened and pushed off from the wall, searching for... he didn't know what. Allie's coach maybe. Someone who could take her and Catherine home after the carnival. He made it all the way out the door before what Catherine had told him at the art gallery came back to taunt him.

Running away is easy for you, isn't it?

He stopped and blew out a breath.

Why dig in your heels and tough it out when you can avoid conflict altogether?

Damn, things had been simpler before he'd met Catherine! Rubbing his neck, he turned around and walked back into the cafeteria.

Allie was painting the finishing touches on a red teddy bear as he approached the rear of the Face Painting booth. Neither she nor Catherine noticed him, since they both sat facing the opposite direction.

His daughter applied a last dab, cocked her head, then tweaked her canvas's freckled nose. "There you go, Megan. Try not to touch your cheek for a few minutes. It's still a little wet."

"Can I th'ee it now?" the gap-toothed youngster pleaded.

"Sure you can." Allie picked up a hand mirror and faced it toward the child. "But whatever you do, don't smile. Oh, no—too late!" She pointed in mock dismay to the little girl's right dimple. "See what you did? You gave him a belly button."

Megan giggled, her dimple giving the painted bear a perfect "innie." Joe found himself thinking what a wonderful big sister Allie would've made if things had been different. Without analyzing why, he turned to Catherine.

He had a good view of the back of her head and her customer's face. Like the kid he'd grabbed earlier, this boy's hair was buzzed close except for a single lock of hair—located not at his nape—but just above his forehead. Army-boot knockoffs, strategically

ripped jeans and a black T-shirt completed the nine-
ties' version of tough-guy chic.

Styles might've changed over the years, but one
thing hadn't and never would. The kid's eyes were
groping everything they touched.

"I'm almost finished, Travis," Catherine said,
grasping the teenager's chin and leaning close to add
a dribble of blood down his cheek. "Hold still now.
There!" She leaned back and dropped her brush into
a jar of water. "I think that's my best one yet."

Travis stared at her and blinked. Having experienced that same lobotomy stupor himself, Joe figured Catherine must be smiling.

She began cleaning her brush for the next customer. "Thanks for donating to the fund. And be
sure to tell your friends to stop by our booth."

"Yeah, sure," Travis mumbled, finally getting the
hint and standing up. He moved off in a daze as two
women bustled into the booth, apologizing for being
late for their shift.

Joe waited through the changing of the guard and
two customer demonstrations before stepping closer
to the booth.

"Yo, Allie, Catherine! Nobody likes a back-seat
painter. Come on out and let those women do their
jobs."

Four faces turned. Two of them broke into identical beaming smiles, making him very glad he'd decided to stay. Allie and Catherine slipped out of the
booth.

"So what would you ladies like to do first?" he
asked, sandwiched between them as they headed for
the door. "Eat? Check out the games? There's a

stuffed elephant at the Bottle Throw with your name on it, Allie.''

He felt a slight tug on his right arm and looked down into hesitant dark eyes.

"I, um, kind of told Holly and Jessica I'd meet 'em at the Dunking booth, Joe. A bunch of us are gonna try and drown Coach Moxley.''

"Okay, then, the Dunking booth it is. I wouldn't mind taking a shot at the coach myself.''

He felt a slight tug on his left arm and looked down into direct green eyes.

"I think Allie made plans to be with her friends *alone,*" Catherine explained. He came to a stop.

Allie was his pal. She loved doing the carnival thing with him—didn't she? Frowning, he turned to his daughter.

"It's okay, Joe. I didn't say I'd meet them there for sure. Let's go on to the Bottle Throw. I want to. Really.''

She *didn't* want to, he could tell. But she didn't want to disappoint him, either. Just as he'd never wanted to disappoint his father.

Shaken by the insight, he retreated to familiar territory. "Who beat Babe Ruth's 1935 record of 714 home runs? Winner gets to sink Coach Moxley—alone." It was a baby question; one she could answer in her sleep.

Allie searched his eyes as if debating his sincerity.

He shrugged. "Guess I'd better warm up my throwing arm—"

"Hank Aaron, April 1974, fourth inning of the Braves' home opener against the Dodgers. Piece'a cake."

Joe forced a grin and checked his watch. "Meet us back here at six o'clock on the nose, hotshot." He dug out a five-dollar bill from his pocket, slapped it into her palm and curled her fingers tight. "Come find me if you need more money."

She seemed to hover on the brink of protest, then stuffed the cash into her jean-shorts pocket. "Thanks, Joe. For letting me go, I mean."

They both knew she referred to more than the Dunking booth. He nodded and shooed her off, experiencing a pang of loss so piercing it gouged a hole in his chest.

He wasn't the center of Allie's universe anymore. She was growing up, choosing her friends over him when once there would've been no contest. When had this happened? And God help him, what would he do without his little pal?

"Allie hasn't left the nest, Joe," Catherine said, demonstrating that uncanny ability of hers to read his mind. "She has a lot of test flights ahead. And she needs you there to catch her if she falls."

Like he'd saved Vicky? "I'm a lousy catcher, Catherine."

"That's bull!" She moved up toe-to-toe and flung her head back. "Who was voted the International League's Catcher of the Year his second season in the minors? Who called two no-hitters his rookie year with the Astros? Who was plagued by injuries but had 'an arm like a cannon' throughout his career? Winner gets a free ticket to any game at the carnival."

Joe couldn't have been more surprised if she'd spit in his face.

"Bzzz! Time's up. The answer is Joe Tucker, a very *good* catcher by anyone's standards. And I'd trust you to be my safety net anytime."

Her fierce green eyes compelled him to believe, to absorb some of the feminine strength she offered so generously to anyone who was confused or hurting. If a woman like *this* believed in him . . .

The empty hole in Joe's chest filled with a mixture of wonder and tentative hope. He suddenly felt like leaping tall buildings in a single bound, slaying fire-breathing dragons with a magic sword, sweeping the Bake Sale table clear of goodies and sampling the sweetness of Catherine.

Instead, he lifted his elbow with as much respect as he could infuse into the gesture. "Looks like I owe you a free game."

Smiling, she accepted his arm and strolled by his side through the cafeteria. Her small hand made him intensely aware of his greater height and strength, his inherent obligation to protect her. There was an age-old sense of rightness to this gentlemen stuff that transcended snobbish rules.

"Do you by any chance like stuffed elephants?" he asked on impulse.

Her startled glance turned mischievous. "About as much as I like stodgy Democrats."

He chuckled, remembering how he'd once thought her humorless. "Feel like checking out the Bottle Throw first?"

"No way. I'm not wasting my free ticket on something that requires skill." She seemed to consider her options a moment. "I know, take me to the Lollipop Tree. If I don't win a prize, at least I'll get to keep the candy."

Joe silently groaned. Fair was fair. But with luck, he could divert her to another booth along the way.

"THAT MAN IS LEANING OVER again, Mommy."

"Hush, Angel, and put your hook back in the pond."

"But he can reach it better'n me. No fair!"

Grinding his teeth, Joe straightened. The angelic blond whiner couldn't have been more than four or five. She clutched a cane pole in one hand and a small teddy bear in the other. Slanting him a resentful look, she stuck out her tongue, then dangled her line over the multicolored bath toys bobbing in the kiddie pool.

He concentrated once more on The Fish, the one that would win the prize he'd spotted on his way to the Bottle Throw. The one that'd looked so easy to catch fifteen minutes ago.

But snagging a metal ring protruding from *any* of the floating backs—much less The Fish's pale blue one—was not a piece of cake. Every missed swipe was another ticket down the toilet, and so far he'd flushed the bowl nine times.

"Why don't we go on to the Bottle Throw?" Catherine suggested, her words slurred around the lollipop in her mouth. Standing at his side, she balanced a half-eaten bag of popcorn, a balloon poodle and a wrapped chocolate cake in her arms.

"In a minute." Ten was his lucky number. This was it. He could feel it in his bones.

"Mom-my, he's hogging the blue fishy. That's the one *I* was gonna catch. No fair!" The little girl edged close to Joe and pressed against his side. A pudgy elbow jabbed his hip. "*My* fishy."

The booth attendant, a girl about Allie's age, frowned at her small rowdy customer. "No touching, or I'll have to ask you to leave."

The mother rushed forward and pulled her struggling child from Joe's side. "Now, honey, we don't touch or talk to strangers. Look, there's a yellow fishy by your hook. It wins a pretty red necklace. You'd like that, wouldn't you?"

"I don't want a red necklace. I want a *green* necklace. No fair!"

The attendant dug into a box by her feet and came up holding a plastic green necklace. The mother looked pitifully grateful, the child petulant but unsure what she should complain about next.

Joe turned back to the pool and steadied his hook over his rocking plastic target. Almost . . . just a fraction to the right . . . bingo!

An errant fishhook swung over and hit his line, jerking his hook from The Fish's ringed back. He glared down in time to see Angel smirk.

Ignoring her mother's embarrassed gasp, he held the child's triumphant blue gaze. "Do you like your teddy bear, Angel?"

Something in his tone must've warned her, because she hugged it tighter as she nodded.

"Then keep your hook away from my blue fishy. Do you understand?"

This time her mother gasped in outrage, but Angel seemed to get the picture. She nodded solemnly and dangled her hook as far away from his as possible.

The booth attendant gave him a secret thumbs-up signal. "You want to keep trying, mister?"

Catherine spit her lollipop stick into a nearby trash can and nudged her knee against him for lack of a free hand. "This is ridiculous. Let's go try the Bottle Throw. Please."

Joe looked longingly up the hallway toward the line of men and boys waiting to hurl baseballs at a stack of bottles. He might not throw like a cannon anymore, but he could still nail what he aimed at twenty out of twenty times.

"In a minute," he promised, shoving another ticket toward the attendant.

Angel's hook made a pass at the yellow fish and missed. "No fa-a-air," she wailed as her mother dragged her away. The child's replacement hooked a green fish on his first try, earning a piggy bank as his reward.

Joe grimly handed another ticket to the attendant.

The new angler beside him missed once, sorted through a pocketful of empty candy wrappers for her last ticket and landed a pink fish and inflatable beach ball for her trouble. Joe avoided the attendant's eyes and forked over another ticket.

He'd gone way past irritation to a declaration of war. Sweat beaded his brow. Determination clenched his jaw. He was going to catch that mother Fish if he had to use every last ticket out of his original chain of thirty—which was a distinct possibility at the rate he was going.

Maneuvering his hook closer to the rocking blue bath toy, he silently coached himself. Finesse, not brute strength; savoir faire, not arrogance. He dipped his line, lifted gently and gaped at The Fish dangling from his hook dripping water into the pond.

"All right!" the attendant yelled, lifting her hand for a high five.

He put down his pole and slapped her palm weakly.

Grinning, she reached behind her and plucked the blue fish prize from a shelf. "Boy, did you ever earn this, mister. Congratulations."

"Thanks." He took the prize and moved away from the booth, gazing down at a twelve-inch plastic Snow White. Her clothes were poorly made, her features painted on. The impulse that had driven him to bypass a perfectly good stuffed animal for the doll seemed silly now.

"She's much better than an elephant," Catherine said, her ESP no longer surprising him.

"You think?" He could swear Snow White's painted laugh was directed at him. "I could've gone to Wal-Mart and saved myself a bundle."

Catherine shifted the items in her arms and shook her head. "A store-bought doll wouldn't be nearly as special as this one. Not many fathers would go to so much trouble, Joe. Allie will be thrilled."

Her wistful expression fisted his free hand. Man, would he like a few minutes alone in a dark alley with Dr. Lawrence Hamilton. Forcing his fingers to relax, he took the cake from her arms and held out his prize.

"It's for you."

Her eyes widened. "But... you worked so hard."

Self-conscious as hell, he thrust the doll closer. "Take it, Catherine. Allie hates dolls."

Her bag of popcorn and balloon poodle dropped unnoticed to the floor. "Oh, Joe," she breathed, reaching for the prize as if the cheap plastic were bone china, the thin cotton dress plush velvet. She pressed the doll to her heart.

Damnation. Did no man in Catherine's life appreciate how extraordinary she was? He mentally consigned Carl into that dark alley with Dr. Hamilton.

"Thank you, Joe," she whispered, her smile wobbly and tender.

Some shred of self-preservation kept him from pulling her into his arms. Clearing the huskiness from his throat, he glanced at his watch.

"Guess we'd better head back to the cafeteria. Allie will be there soon."

For the second time that day Joe fled from a woman without looking back. Only this time, he forced every step.

CHAPTER TEN

CATHERINE FROWNED at Joe as they walked side by side through the Galleria mall. He'd been uncooperative for three days—ever since the Fish Pond incident to be exact—and she was fast losing patience.

Breaking through a cluster of women dressed in saris, she pulled him through and headed toward an up escalator. "This is an investment in your future as much as mine, you know. You need new clothes for job interviews."

Sometime during the past week it had become as important to groom him for his own broadcasting career as it was for her engagement party. She'd spent hours tutoring him in basic grammar, delighting in his quick progress. When she'd worried about his Texas drawl, he'd assumed Cary Grant's suave accent with uncanny accuracy. Too bad Joe hadn't mastered the actor's suave manners as well.

"Don't you agree?" she persisted.

Joe responded with a grunt. Shoulders hunched, hands shoved deep in his jeans pockets, he trudged beside her with dragged-by-wild-horses enthusiasm.

"You'd think I was making you scrub toilets, for heaven's sake. What is it about shopping you hate so much?"

"You got an hour?"

"Do I *have* an hour," she corrected. "And no, I don't have time to waste and neither do you, unless you plan on losing the bet before you even open your mouth at the party." She'd checked out his meager wardrobe the day before. This trip was a necessity.

"Thanks for your confidence."

She rolled her eyes and hitched up her shoulder-bag strap. "I didn't mean that as an insult and you know it."

Not trusting herself to say more, she surged ahead of him into the crowd, wishing she'd never gone to that damn carnival.

All her life she'd worked hard to justify her very existence. Her father's rare praise, her Ph.D., even her engagement to Carl had been earned through model Hamilton behavior or scholarship.

Yet Joe had given her the Snow White doll with no expectation of gain. That in itself had made his gift special. His added implication that she was a desirable woman made the plastic doll a cherished treasure. At least, she *had* cherished it until he'd turned surly to keep her at arm's length.

Well, she'd gotten his message loud and clear. She no longer attached undue significance to the doll. He had Allie and his career to worry about. She was engaged to another man. She'd be Carl's ball and chain—not Joe's. He could relax.

Slowing her steps, Catherine fell back beside Joe, unwilling to explore her sudden desperation to win the bet and lock in a demanding career.

"Maybe you're taking this clothes thing too personally. You're Cary Grant, remember? You've been cast in the role of Sebastian Doherty, a socially prominent Easterner visiting Houston on business, and you're attending a party full of prospective customers. We're here to find you a costume that fits his character. It's as simple as that.''

"Sebastian." The word might have been skunk spray, from Joe's expression and tone. "Why the hell can't this guy have a normal name?''

Catherine bit her cheek until the urge to maim passed. "Normal is a relative term. The name Skeeter may have a certain *je ne sais quoi* at a pool table, but Charlotte Wilson's buffet table is quite another story.''

They tailgated the heels of two men arguing about where to eat lunch, then passed on the inside lane. The escalator loomed ahead.

"Trust me on this, Joe. Sebastian is a powerful name. It means 'revered' in Greek.''

He snorted. "It means 'pretentious ass' in Texan.''

"Ah, but Father is a *Connecticut* Hamilton. He respects pretentious asses—watch your feet." She grabbed his forearm and steadied the transfer of size-twelve sneakers onto size-ten escalator steps.

He gripped the rubber banister and twisted around. "My navy sport coat is pretentious," he insisted, his jaw daring her to disagree.

An image of shiny elbows and too-wide lapels flashed in her mind. How to put this tactfully? "It's not made of silk, linen, wool or tweed. Father would spot that across a crowded room and dismiss you as an insignificant stranger.''

He lifted a sardonic brow. "Some enchanted evening.''

After a startled glance, she chuckled. "Exactly. Now, I think we'll shop for your coat and trousers first and move on from there.''

"What do you mean, move on from there? What else is left to do?"

Oops. "Oh, this and that. Relax. I promise it'll be better than scrubbing toilets— Watch your feet."

They lurched off the escalator and she prodded him to the right. This was her favorite part of the upscale Houston mall. Glitzy storefronts encircled a large ice-skating rink in three tiers. Shoppers on the upper levels could look over the inside railing for a bird's-eye view of the rink.

She cast a wistful peek down at the whirling skaters before guiding Joe into the flow of international shoppers. "The store I'm taking you to has a wonderful selection of Armani suits. And, of course, all the top American labels."

He scowled and picked up his pace.

"Any necessary alterations will be finished in plenty of time for the party." She hop-skipped to keep up with his long strides. "Carl says they serve the best cappuccino this side of Seattle. Who knows, Joe? You might even enjoy yourself."

"And the pope might marry Madonna. Gawd. Spare me the Pollyanna crap and just get me in and out of there fast," he ordered, the verbal equivalent of throwing ice water in her face.

Recoiling, she gazed in frigid silence straight ahead and matched him step for wooden step. Shoppers chattered around them. The piped in chorus of "It's a Small World" wafted up from the skating rink. She sensed him looking at her but only lifted her nose higher.

"Catherine . . ."

He couldn't say it, the coward.

"Catherine . . ."

Pitiful. He could just forget it now.

"Catherine, I'm sorry," he said at last, as if each word squeezed his testicles.

She kept walking. No more jumping through hoops for rude bastards.

"I said I'm sorry," he repeated more loudly.

Well, goody for him. He could take his apology and stuff it where—

He grabbed her elbow and pulled her to a stop at the atrium railing. "Dammit, Catherine, I said I was sorry. Did you hear me?"

She met his eyes coolly. "Pollyanna was paralyzed, not deaf. Now please let go of my arm."

His grip slackened along with his jaw. After a moment he seemed to find his voice. "Pollyanna wasn't paralyzed."

"She most certainly was. She fell from a tree trying to reach a doll she'd won at the town carnival's Fishing Pond booth. Her legs were paralyzed. As I recall, Pollyanna got really bitchy after that." Catherine gave him a pointed look. "A person can only take so much abuse, you know."

He speared fingers through his hair, loosening a spill of dark strands down his forehead. Chagrin twisted his rugged features. "I *am* sorry, Catherine. My only excuse is that I haven't been sleeping too good."

"Too well," she corrected, for the first time noticing the shadows under his eyes, the lines of weariness bracketing his mouth. She felt a niggle of alarm. "Why haven't you been sleeping? Is your knee still hurting you?"

He averted his eyes.

"I should have stopped you from playing that tennis match. Or at least made you go for a follow-up exam." Without conscious thought, she lifted her fingers and brushed back the hair from his forehead.

His hand shot up with rattlesnake speed and captured her wrist. Gasping, she stared into eyes shifting with browns and golds in a kaleidoscope of turmoil.

"Save your tender concern for Pretty Boy," he warned. "I don't want it, and I sure as hell don't need more complications in my life."

Mortified, she tried to twist out of his grip and succeeded only in hurting her wrist. She stopped struggling and focused on a stunning red cocktail dress in the window display behind him. The alluring blond mannequin was everything she'd never be.

"Let me go," she demanded, hating the slight quaver in her voice.

The sound he made seethed with frustration. Or disgust.

If he didn't let her go, she would cry. "Please," she whispered.

"Dammit, woman, it's not my knee keeping me awake at night." The sensual growl in his hushed baritone brought her gaze up.

There was no mistaking his meaning. Masculine fantasies woven in the darkness were reflected in his heavy-lidded eyes. She stared in wonder and felt her bones melt. His gaze flared with satisfaction and lowered to her mouth. For one suspended heartbeat, all noise and motion ceased as he slowly lowered his head.

Someone whizzed past, bumping Catherine's hip and breaking Joe's hold on her wrist.

"Daniel, come here!" A young mother grabbed her runaway toddler and cast an apologetic look over her shoulder. "Sorry."

Catherine nodded and managed a weak smile.

Joe whirled around and leaned his forearms on the wrought-iron railing. Thin white cotton tightened across his broad back; soft denim hugged his muscular catcher's legs. He looked powerful, frustrated and intensely masculine.

Her breath seeped out in a shaky sigh. She felt flushed and swollen in areas that had no business swelling in a public mall. Oh, God, what now?

What about Carl? What about Joe's aversion to "complications"? What about Allie's need to have her dad's full attention and her own need to establish a career outside her father's shadow? What about the children she wanted so desperately?

Her questions flew wildly, smacking hidden obstacles like birds against a windowpane.

"Don't worry," Joe muttered, staring down at the skating rink below. "I'm not going to do anything to screw up your engagement—or the bet. I'll be a perfect gentleman."

Catherine opened and closed her mouth, knowing silence would serve her best. At the moment her jumbled thoughts were not those of a perfect lady.

ACROSS TOWN in the gymnasium at the Y, Allie sat cross-legged on the varnished wood floor with three of her camp buddies: Kim, a tall curvy blonde with great bat speed; Emily, a petite brunette who could field a bad hop quicker than a kitten on a frog; and Holly, who fell somewhere in between blond and brunette, tall and petite—but whose whirlwind pitches made her anything but average.

Most of the camp ate lunch outside under the trees, which was why Allie had sneaked into the gym. She wasn't feeling so hot. Plus, she was sick to death of watching Sarah hang all over Tommy.

Finishing her last bite of sandwich, Allie hugged the bloated ache in her lower abdomen that had gotten worse every hour. "Aw, ma-a-a-n, I *hate* getting my period."

Kim, the oldest of the three, looked properly sympathetic. "Maybe it's a false alarm. Sometimes I get cramps and nothing happens. I'm still pretty irregular."

"Me, too. Mom says it's the Taylor-women curse," Emily volunteered.

Holly pulled apart an Oreo and licked the center without comment.

Allie sighed. She'd gotten her first period the day after her twelfth birthday. She'd be thirteen next month. "Nah, I'm due anytime." She made a face. "Like I don't wear enough pads behind home plate as it is."

"Yu-u-uck!" Kim dropped her half-eaten sandwich onto a square of paper towel.

Emily giggled. "You can always let Mr. Tampon make a real woman of you."

Just the thought made Allie shudder. She'd probably be a virgin till she died.

Holly dusted cookie crumbs off her palms and hugged her bony knees. "My mom's thinking about taking me to the doctor if I don't start soon. Why do I have to be such a freak?"

"Be glad you don't have to mess with it yet," Kim said, removing a plump peach from her bag.

Allie nodded agreement and stared into space. "Y'all ever wonder why boys have it so easy? I mean, think about it. Girls lose blood on a regular basis. We grow these ... *things* on our chests that control our popularity with boys." She shared a look of mutual resentment all around before continuing the list. "We suffer horrible pain having babies—"

"Don't forget pap smears," Kim interrupted, drawing three pairs of curious eyes. "You don't know about those?" She said it like Gram had once asked Joe, "You don't know about Harry's cancer?"

Like Gram, Kim proceeded to tell what she knew in a hushed tone, describing skimpy paper gowns and cold metal stirrups and probing rubber gloves until Harry's chemotherapy sounded like a piece of cake. Allie drifted with the others into stunned silence, pondering the injustice of it all.

"Betcha can't make the basket from this distance sitting down," Holly suddenly challenged, eyeing the hoop a good twenty feet away.

"A dollar says I can."

"You're on, Tucker."

Allie grinned, secretly thanking Joe for buying mushy apples on his last grocery run. She'd taken one bite and flung it back into her bag, uneaten. Crumpling the weighted lunch bag for a one-handed push shot, she drew a bead on the basketball hoop, coiled her muscles and released the trash in a sailing arc.

Paper dropped through net without a swish.

"Two points!" she crowed, dodging the cookie Holly threw at her head. Looking for a weapon, Al-

lie snatched the peach on its way to Kim's open
mouth and hurled it at Holly.

Holly shrieked and ducked the overthrown fruit,
then grabbed a potato chip from Emily and sailed it
into Allie's nose.

And the war was on.

There'd be extra laps around the bases as punishment and an awful mess to clean up, but not one of
them hesitated to join the front-line action. Bread
crust, pickles, corn chips, grapes—the air flurried
with food missiles until each lunch sack was empty.

Laughing so hard she drooled, slipping on smushed
fruit and crunched chips, Allie began throwing stuff
that had fallen to the floor. A piece of bologna
slapped her in the cheek and stuck. Emily pointed her
finger and hooted.

Allie unpeeled the meat from her skin and spun in
a circle, searching for something large enough to wipe
the glee from Emily's face. There, by the stacked
bleachers! Kim's half-eaten peach, just oozing slimy
pulp. Lunging forward, Allie scooped up the fruit and
grinned. She'd fire the last shot and rule!

Still in a crouch, she turned on the balls of her feet
and watched the three girls scatter with panicked
yelps. Emily threw up her hands and dashed for the
double doors—a bid to steal base.

"I don't *think* so," Allie yelled, winding back her
arm just as the doors opened from the outside. Emily slipped out and Sarah Sokol walked in. But the
"ball" had already been released.

Hard.

It smacked Sarah right between her size-C cups and
clung there, squished and drippy, before plopping to
the floor. Her shocked blue eyes looked down at the

orange splat on her chest and lifted up much narrower than before.

"You little bitch!" she yelled, her fair complexion turning red. "You did that on purpose."

"Hey," Allie protested, "I thought you were—"

"Did you see what she did, Tommy? I told you she was dangerous, but you wouldn't believe me."

With dawning horror, Allie realized that the tall blond boy stood watching the scene from the door.

"She throws as hard as a boy." Sarah's chest, the one fate had sprinkled with fairy dust, magically expanded and angled toward the door. "I'll probably have a huge bruise."

"Oh, puh-leeze," Holly muttered, moving up next to Allie.

Sarah's head snapped around. "You shut up! You're as butch as *she* is. You're all a big joke, the way you act like every play, every game, is so-o-o important. Just wait'll Coach sees this gym. We'll see what he thinks about his pets then."

Allie saw Tommy's bluebonnet gaze scan the gross mess on the floor and lift to the corn chips in Kim's hair, the pickle slice on Holly's shoulder, the . . . Oh, God, was there something on her cheek? She touched her skin and silently groaned when her fingertips came away yellow. Mustard, from the bologna Emily had thrown.

Wishing the floor would swallow her whole, Allie realized Kim had moved up to her left side.

"And what'll you say when Coach asks what business you two had going into an empty gym?" Kim asked slyly.

Allie's gaze collided with Tommy's. Of course. He'd brought Sarah here to make out. The truth was there in his eyes, along with...embarrassment? No way. If he knew how much Allie hurt right now, he'd laugh. Or worse, feel sorry for her.

Sarah tossed her golden hair. "I'll tell him we heard you animals tearing up the gym and came in to check it out." She plucked at her stained T-shirt. "Once he sees this, your ass is grass, Tucker."

How could someone so pretty smile so ugly?

"Keep workin' at it," Sarah added. "And you might even grow up to be a bigger loser than your dad."

Allie'd never gotten so mad so fast in her life. Years of sprinting for pop flies went into her race for Sarah. The blonde never had a chance, although she squeaked and skittered ratlike toward Tommy.

Allie grasped the back of Sarah's T-shirt, yanked the girl close and spun her around, then gripped her wrist in an unbreakable hold. "I warned you never to bad-mouth my dad again, didn't I, Sarah?"

Sarah cast a pleading look at Tommy. "Help me, please."

"You know what happens to girls who don't know how to talk nice or keep their lying mouths shut?" Allie held the other girl's wide gaze, easily restraining her weak tugs. "They get their mouths plugged up, that's what."

Still holding Sarah's wrist, she bent down, scooped up the mangled peach and shoved it into Sarah's gaping mouth.

The girl sputtered and pitched her head, spitting out the fruit and screeching out her rage. Allie stood back and grinned.

"What's going on here?" a deep voice asked from the doorway.

Coach Harrison walked into the gym, followed by Emily and Tommy. Sarah teared up instantly, looking pitiful and abused with orange mush all over her face and the skin on her wrist glowing red.

Allie met her friends' sympathetic eyes and knew a grass ass was the least of her worries.

"Well? I'm waiting for an answer. Why is Sarah crying?"

Allie's throat closed up. Heat flooded her cheeks. She'd acted like a bully, the butch Sarah had accused her of being. But the one thing Allie had never been in her life was a coward.

"Coach," she rasped. Clearing her throat, she tried again. "Coach, I—"

"Sarah slipped on the floor and fell on a peach, Coach Harris. She'll be fine in a few minutes." Tommy's beautiful blue eyes never wavered from the older man's skeptical gaze.

Sarah began making choking noises, as if unable to gasp out a protest past her crying.

"C'mon, Sarah, let's go get your face cleaned up. Then we'll come back and help straighten up this mess," he promised, sending Allie an apologetic glance that made her heart pound. Draping an arm around Sarah's shoulders, he led her rather forcefully out the door.

When Allie turned back to face the coach, the look on his face warned of serious punishment. It probably didn't help her case any that she couldn't stop smiling.

JOE SHIFTED his pinched neck against the sink basin of Etienne's Hair Salon and winced. Instantly the tepid spray of water against his hair stopped.

"Is that too hot, sir?"

He cracked open his eyelids. The shampoo girl's silver blond buzz cut made her look damn near bald. Her dark eyes, cigarette burns in a white sheet of a face, peered down with friendly concern.

"It's fine," he assured the hovering face. "Has anyone ever mentioned how much you look like—" Instinct stopped him short. She probably wouldn't appreciate being compared to Casper.

"Sinead O'Connor?" she supplied helpfully.

Thank you, Lord. "Yeah, that's the one. I guess you hear that a lot, huh?"

She nodded with cute Casper shyness and started the water again. He drew a relieved breath, stinging his nose and fumigating his brain cells in the process.

No wonder the employees in this place looked dead. Whatever hair products they sniffed each day should be locked up with cans of spray paint. Neon art, black and silver walls and blaring alternative rock music gave the salon a futuristic feel. He should've put his foot down and gone to Harvey's Barbershop.

"If you don't mind my saying so, Mr. Tucker, you seem awfully tense. Try and relax. Watch a little MTV." She waved a dripping hand at a tilted monitor mounted on the wall. "Who knows? You might even enjoy yourself." Unaware she'd repeated Catherine's earlier words, the girl looked into his suddenly narrowed glare and squeaked.

Water flooded his ear canal. He jerked away, wrenching his neck in the guillotine basin.

She dabbed his ear with a towel and blushed a becoming flesh tone. "I'm s-so sorry."

"Don't worry about it, doll. I won't melt."

Giving her his best smile, he let his eyes drift shut on her dazed expression and plotted revenge against Catherine, the real culprit of this entire disastrous afternoon.

Enjoy himself, ha!

The diabolical woman had led him into a hushed boutique reeking of leather, scented candles and that fancy coffee served in thimble cups. She'd explained her mission to Friedrich, the sales assistant from hell, who accepted the challenge with fanatical determination.

Joe grimaced, remembering endless changing of clothes. Constant tugging of pleats, cuffs and lapels on his person. Humiliating discussions of his "swarthy" complexion next to colors named after various fruits. And to top it off, a final bill that, even split fifty-fifty with Catherine, was more than he normally spent on clothes in an entire year.

He'd suffered through it all with stoic resignation, his hair shirt for revealing his lustful urges to Catherine. But forcing him into this—this *salon*, for cripe's sake—was by God the final degradation! He sure as hell wasn't paying for half of this torture, no siree.

Blunt fingertips massaged shampoo against his scalp in soothing circles, then moved down to his neck. A pleasant citrus smell clouded the sink. His rigid muscles relaxed.

"I knew you'd enjoy Mary's shampoo," a familiar voice crowed, blasting his eyes wide open.

Catherine sat in the black vinyl chair next to him wearing a smug smile and those white shorts from the carnival, the ones that showed off her long curvy legs.

Her loose black T-shirt had molded close each time she'd reached toward a high clothes rack.

When Mary began rinsing the shampoo from his hair, he gratefully closed his eyes.

"Bet you wouldn't have gotten a free massage from that old barber you go to in Littleton," Catherine said.

"You're right. Harvey would've given me a shave and a haircut, the sports channel and a look at the latest centerfold—all for only twelve bucks, thank you very much. What's this place costing you?"

"Humph. Disgusting."

"Well, if it's so damn expensive—no offense, Mary—what did you bring me here for?"

"I didn't mean that the *cost* is disgusting. I meant that gawking at a centerfold in a barbershop is disgusting. Actually, juvenile is the better word. Why do grown men do that?"

He thought a minute. "Because we can?"

Water flooded his ear canal.

He glared up at Mary, who, far from apologizing, nudged him upright and proceeded to test the root strength of his hair with a dry towel.

"Why do women get so bent out of shape at men admiring their bodies?" he grumbled. "It's a compliment."

"A compliment?" Catherine's eyes glinted dangerously.

You are one dumb jock, Tucker.

"For the record, Joe, women don't get bent out of shape when men admire our bodies. In fact, there's nothing we like better. It's when you drool over siliconed, liposuctioned, fuzzy-focused, air-brushed photographs that we get a little crazy. Our natural bodies can't possibly live up to those unnatural standards.''

"Nobody's asking you to." Personally he preferred soft yielding flesh over nippled grapefruits hands down—so to speak.

"Right," Mary muttered, draping the towel over his shoulders and tugging a comb none too gently through his hair. "That's why twenty extra pounds kept me home Saturday nights, while guys just as overweight as me had steady girlfriends."

Her bitterness startled him, since her black smocked figure was petite and trim. "Well, you obviously did something about your weight. You look great."

"Yeah, I did something." She finished combing his hair and exchanged an enigmatic look with Catherine, trapping Joe between currents of emotion he didn't understand.

"Did you make an appointment yet?" Catherine asked.

The young woman bleakly shook her head.

"He's expecting your call. He'll work out a fee schedule you can handle."

"I'm...scared."

Catherine rose swiftly, rounded the chair and enfolded the younger woman in her arms. Her thigh pressed against Joe's knee, channeling her compassion and strength to him as surely as it did to Mary.

"You can beat this thing, Mary. Tell you what, why don't we go into the back office and make that call together?"

"Right now?"

"Right now. The first step. How about it?"

Joe felt Catherine's thigh tense as the silence stretched.

"All right," Mary relented. "But you have to talk to him first."

"Deal." Catherine pulled away, her smile a rising sun in the artificial landscape. She took Mary's arm and walked a few steps before stopping to look over her shoulder.

"Oh, Joe? Robert said to send you to his chair when Mary was through. It's the third station from the front entrance, remember? Trust him. You won't be sorry." On that cryptic note, she led Mary through a door beyond the last sink.

Deep in thought, Joe got up and wandered into the main salon, barely noticing the admiring glances from beneath curlers and snipping scissors throughout the room. He found the right chair and sank into a casual sprawl, nodding at the approaching man Catherine had introduced earlier as Robert.

Tall and pale, wearing baggy black trousers and a muscle-molding gray T-shirt that belied his indolent manner, Robert nodded back. His black ponytail was longer than Catherine's.

"All set to get started?" he asked.

Joe hesitated, then decided what the hell. "Can I ask you a personal question, Robert?"

The hairdresser's world-weary gaze traveled from Joe's crossed sneakers to his shaggy hair, gaining interest along the way. "Ooh, those are my favorite kind."

CHAPTER ELEVEN

JOE HELD Robert's gaze, sending an unoffended but firm message to forget that line of thinking.

The hairdresser sighed and pulled a square of silver fabric from the bottom drawer of his station. Shaking out the folds, he whirled the cape with matador grace over Joe's chest and shoulders and fastened it behind his neck. "What's the question?"

"Do you know what's wrong with Mary? Medically speaking, that is."

"Why do you care?"

"Catherine is worried about her. That makes me care."

After a long measuring look, Robert said, "Mary is bulimic. Not that anyone around here knew it. When she started losing weight about six months ago, we all wanted a copy of the diet she was on." He ran ten fingers through Joe's thick dark hair, lifting the varying lengths with an expression of growing horror. "Who cuts your hair, dear? Weed Eaters R Us?"

"Harvey's Barbershop."

Rolling his eyes, Robert plucked a comb and scissors from his top drawer and set to work. "When Catherine was here for her last appointment, I walked in on her trying to convince Mary to start therapy. You could've knocked me over with a sneeze, but apparently Catherine had spotted the signs of bulimia right off."

"She got Mary to make some kind of appointment today," Joe admitted. "I guess it was for counseling."

Robert smiled, comb suspended, and shook his head. "That lady is something else. She's helped half the employees at Etienne's work through personal problems at one time or another. That's why this bet you've got going is so great. We all have a list of clients to send Catherine once her practice is open."

Damn, did anyone *not* know about this secret bet? Joe glanced to his right at a row of caped customers and the stylists attending them. Gazes skittered away. Scissors and blow dryers suddenly swarmed above heads.

"Oh, don't worry about us spilling the beans. We wouldn't dream of ruining Catherine's big chance. No one deserves a break more than her—" Robert pushed Joe's shoulder with two fingertips "—but I guess you know that. You're helping her more than anyone."

"Yeah, I'm helping," Joe mumbled.

Helping to confuse her, stirring up embers her fiancé hadn't touched with a five-inch pole. Six inches, tops. Still, she seemed content enough with her upcoming marriage.

So why was he playing with fire? Because, like looking at a centerfold, he *could*?

He faced his actions head-on, not liking what he saw. Such behavior was not only disgusting and juvenile, it was selfish as hell. Catherine was the one who'd get burned in the long run. And she deserved better. She deserved her big chance.

A fine mist of liquid hit Joe's face.

He sucked in his breath and glared at the plastic spray bottle inches from his nose. "Dammit, man, are the employees in this place licensed to use water weapons?"

"Temper, temper," Robert scolded as he set the bottle down and picked up comb and scissors. "You were daydreaming, and Catherine asked me to give you the inside scoop on a few VIPs who'll be at the party. They're clients of Etienne's Hair Salon."

"Masochists, are they?"

"I should be so lucky. No, I'm afraid they're pretty tame, but they do have their little quirks."

"Anything I could use in a social conversation?"

"Probably. But let's get one thing clear, big guy. I don't mind your using information to play a harmless role. But if I find out you've hurt one of my clients or Catherine, *especially* Catherine—" he pointed the scissor tips at Joe's torso "—then your liver is shish kebab."

Joe looked into cold gray eyes and was glad Catherine had this guy on her team. "I understand."

"Good." Robert flashed a wicked grin and began the rhythmic comb-snip, comb-snip of his trade. "Now then, let's start with Mrs. Brad Prewitt, of Prewitt Oil and Gas. Her first name is Laura, and she's absolutely gaga about her show dog. Treats it better than she does Brad, from what I can tell. Just let her know you're canine friendly and she'll love you forever."

"No sweat. I like dogs." Wagging tails. Paws on shoulders. Playful woofs. "What breed is it?"

"A miniature poodle. White. Fits in her purse. It has some fancy name, but Laura calls it Puff."

Trembling bodies. Painted toenails. Shrill yaps.

The snipping stopped. "Now, now, Puff is a dog. You said you liked dogs."

"Marshmallows with legs don't qualify."

"Oh, *spare* me your threatened manhood and pay attention to the guest list." The scissors chattered back into action, spitting alarming quantities of hair in all directions. "Mrs. Michael Kendall, of Kendall Electronics, will be there, bunions and all. Martha's having orthopedic surgery a week after the party. She'll probably be cranky as hell standing around in high heels, so I'd avoid her if I were you. Or invite her to sit."

Sounded like a good plan to Joe.

"Now Mrs. Dusty Black—her husband is general manager of a top radio station in Houston. Anyway, Dawn's a real gem. She's chairing a November ball benefiting hospice facilities for AIDS patients. Imply you'll sponsor a table and she'll claim you as her first cousin." Robert paused and shook his head. "Trash that thought, I wouldn't want you to mislead her about something that important."

He tapped his bottom lip, then smiled. "I know. Mrs. Frank Anderson, of Anderson, Miller and White. Christy's a little paranoid since her husband was kidnapped a year ago and ransomed for two million dollars—"

"Lord have mercy!"

"Oh, they hardly missed the money, but both of them are security fanatics now. Christy's a black belt in karate and a crack shot with a pistol. I bought her Beretta when she moved up to a .357 Magnum."

Joe secretly added Mrs. Frank Anderson to his list of guests to avoid. As he listened to three more client profiles, his amazement grew. The things these women revealed! During twenty years of sitting in Harvey's chair, the most intimate thing Joe had ever revealed was a nasty case of athlete's foot—and then only to explain his constant scratching.

He finally held up his hand. "Wait a minute. Shouldn't I be learning about the husbands, as well as the wives?"

"You know, I thought that very same thing when Catherine said for me to focus on the women only. But now that you actually look civilized, I can't say I disagree with her strategy." Robert whisked Joe's face and shoulders with a towel and motioned to the bulb-framed mirror ahead. "Take a look."

Joe had been avoiding doing just that for the past ten minutes. When he saw his ears for the first time since grade school, they turned bright red.

"Catherine, love, what do you think!" Robert exclaimed as she approached from behind. "Am I not a genius?"

Stunned green eyes met Joe's own shaken gaze in the mirror. This was worse than the nightmare where he'd gone to Mrs. Henkel's English class naked.

"I went for the tragic-poet look," Robert gushed on. "It suits him, don't you think? He could land a commercial for Obsession perfume in a heartbeat. *God,* I'm good."

Joe squeezed his eyes shut. When he opened them, Catherine was still staring at him.

"Give me your gun," he ordered Robert, not sure who would get the first bullet.

Huffing, the hairdresser swiveled Joe's chair toward the salon and yelled, "Is this a great look for him, or what?"

All activity ceased. Twenty pairs of eyes pinned back Joe's wings and held up a magnifying glass. Ignoring the shouts of approval, he slowly raised his gaze to Robert. *Right between your eyes, buddy.*

Catherine moved up behind Joe's chair and turned it toward the mirror. "You're overreacting. If you'll calm down and look at yourself objectively, you'll see it's perfect for Sebastian Doherty."

Joe glared at himself in mutinous silence. The shaggy waves over his neck and ears were gone, trimmed close to expose rims of tender white skin. The hair on his crown had fullness, his bangs were fuller still. It was a calculated haircut. A male model's haircut.

"I look like Pretty Boy," he said with a sneer.

Catherine made an odd sound. "Believe me. You do not look pretty."

For some reason that hurt. His mood grew blacker. "It's too damn short and stiff. It looks like it wouldn't move in a hurricane."

"Oh, for heaven's sake." She reached up, threaded her fingers through his hair and rumpled the hell out of it. "There! It moves, Joe. And it's not the least bit stiff."

Maybe not, but something else was getting stiffer by the second. The innocent touch of her hands had sent his blood surging the opposite direction. He doubted Catherine would notice, but he bet ol' gray eyes over there would be smirking soon. A diversion, that was what he needed.

"So, Robert, aren't you cutting Catherine's hair today, too? After all, she'll be the center of attention at her engagement party."

They both seemed startled by his question. She touched her simple ponytail in a defensive gesture. "My hair doesn't need cutting."

A little different when it's you're own scalp, eh, doll? "Oh, I dunno. I'll bet Robert's been dying to try something new on you."

"Yes. Oh, yes!" the hairdresser picked up the cue. "I've been trying to update her cut for years, but she won't let me change a thing. Joe's right, Catherine, everyone will be looking at the bride-to-be. You've just got to let me do this for you. It'll be my engagement present. Please don't say no."

Catherine turned to Joe with a die-you-mangy-dog glare.

He shrugged and grinned, feeling better than he had all day. "C'mon, Catherine, trust him. You won't be sorry."

"I CAN'T GET OVER the change," Carl repeated, following Catherine into the kitchen. "You look fantastic! So...chic."

This was the first time she'd seen him since getting her hair cut two days ago. His effusive praise should have pleased her. Instead, it made her feel as if she'd removed unsightly warts from her nose. "Would you mind dropping the subject?"

"But you look so—"

"Different. We've already established that." She set the wine bottle he carried next to three others on the table. "I'm glad you approve."

"You don't sound glad. What's wrong?"

She eyed the tray of empty wineglasses and sighed. "Nothing, Carl. Thanks for the bottle of wine. I wish you could share it with us." She'd *counted* on him sharing it.

He gripped her shoulders and spun her around, his thumbs rubbing her bare upper arms. "You can always reschedule the lesson for another time."

Irritation crackled to life. "You're the one who canceled at the last minute! I can't just turn Joe away at the door."

"Why not?" His fingers dug possessively into her skin. "I don't like the idea of your being alone with him."

She raised a brow. "A little late out of the holster, aren't you, Carl? I've worked alone with the man for three weeks." His ardent stare goaded her on. "If Joe hasn't tried to jump my bones by now, he's not going to do it because of a stupid haircut! He's not that shallow." Her jab went right by him. If anything, he looked even more besotted.

"You're beautiful when you're angry," he said, as serious as a grade-B movie.

She choked back a laugh. Another voice whispered in her mind seconds before Carl pulled her close for a kiss.

Your eyes remind me of aspen leaves in the sun.

Her body softened in memory. Carl deepened the kiss, his lips hot and insistent, his arousal equally so. When he finally pulled back, his gray eyes glittered with an expression she'd seen once before. Only then an entire busy mall had faded to another dimension, and now she found herself wondering if the chardonnay was properly chilled.

"Why don't I call Mother and tell her to hold dinner while you make excuses to Joe?" he suggested, pressing the small of her back until their bellies mated. "I think it's time we found out how compatible we are, don't you, darling?"

"Right now?"

"Sooner than now." He rotated his hips and groaned.

Panic mingled with anger. "You've managed to resist me this long. I think you can manage a little longer."

"But I *can't*. You weren't like this then."

She wrenched out of his arms and hugged her sudden chill. "I'm the same person I've always been, Carl. A pair of scissors didn't change me."

Two knocks sounded in the charged silence. The kitchen door opened and closed on its own.

Catherine's gaze never wavered from Carl's. "I'd like you to leave now please."

"You don't understand. It's not just your hair that's different. It's your clothes, too—"

She whirled away but he grabbed her arm, forcing her to look at him. "You smile more often, Catherine, and you seem younger. Happier. You *have* changed, dammit. And I won't apologize for admitting I'm glad." With his tanned cheeks flushed and his jaw thrust out, he looked boyish and more sincere than she'd ever seen him.

For the first time in weeks she felt a curl of hope regarding their upcoming marriage.

"That wax in your brain plugging your ears?" Joe's voice cracked whiplike between them.

Carl released her arm and they both turned.

"I distinctly heard her ask you to leave, Wilson." Arms folded, his backside propped against the wooden door, Joe seemed relaxed and indifferent— until she noticed the bulge of his jaw.

Beside her, Carl radiated hostility. "You interfering bastard! I'll be eternally grateful when you are out of my life and Catherine's house once and for all."

Joe puckered his lips and made a kissing motion.

Carl lurched forward. Catherine snatched a fistful of knit shirt as he passed. The material stretched but held.

"Don't sink to his level, Carl. Go home. Your mother's waiting."

Joe's guffaw galvanized the smaller man. He broke from Catherine's hold and charged ahead. She closed her eyes and winced at the unmistakable thud-thud-thud of fists on flesh. Poor Carl. She would kill Joe for this.

Silence pried her eyes open.

Her fiancé stood breathing heavily, his hands clenched. Joe sat slumped on the floor, blood trickling from his nose.

"Stand up and fight, you coward!" Carl challenged.

If Catherine hadn't rushed forward, she might have missed the deadly glint in Joe's hooded eyes. The warning stopped her cold and drove Carl back one step. The next instant she wondered if she'd imagined his lethal expression.

"I'm a lover, not a fighter," he said, dabbing at his nose with the end of his Rockets T-shirt. A grin flirted with his mouth. "You didn't learn that at any Ivy League school."

Carl obviously didn't know whether to be flattered or offended. "There's a little poison ivy at every school—even Princeton. I ran across my share."

Catherine threw up her hands and walked to the table. "I need a drink."

Four wine bottles sat in a row. She set about un-corking each one, ignoring the talk behind her of hooks and undercuts and Tyson's latest match. The evening was a joke. She'd set up this wine-tasting les-son thinking Carl would join in, then the two of them would go out to dinner afterward. Instead, he'd brought an apology with his 1991 Georis Carmel Valley Merlot.

He'd completely forgotten that his parents were expecting him for dinner, he'd said, and he mustn't disappoint them at this stage in the game. Meaning, before he'd provided an heir of course. Interesting that they hadn't invited the heir's future mother to dinner, as well.

Catherine pushed down the corkscrew levers and popped open a 1993 Sonoma chardonnay. Arms closed around her midriff from behind.

Carl nuzzled below her ear and murmured, "I've got to run, darling. I'll make it up to you this week-end. We'll settle that . . . issue we were discussing ear-lier, hmm?"

An urgently pressing issue, from the feel of things.

Aware of Joe watching them, she unwrapped Carl's arms and turned. "Do tell Charlotte and Jeffrey I'm sorry I couldn't make it."

Her fiancé had the grace to look guilty. "I'll get theater tickets. We'll go to Tony's afterward for a light supper."

She was acutely aware of Joe standing up and walking to the sink. He turned on the faucet and made splashing noises.

Carl lifted one hand and brushed back her new bangs. "Wear something red, why don't you? It suits you." His gaze drifted over her sleeveless scarlet shirt and slim white jeans, his eyes turning smoky with admiration.

It was impossible not to feel flattered. Still, the last thing she wanted was a clinch at the front door. "Go on now or you'll be late. Bye-bye."

He cast a sullen glance toward the sink.

Joe paused in the midst of patting his nose with a paper towel and wiggled the fingers of his free hand. "Ta-ta."

Scowling, Carl bussed Catherine's cheek. "I'll call you," he promised.

She nodded and shooed him off, waiting until the front door opened and closed before turning back to the third unopened bottle. Suddenly she was all thumbs.

"This cabernet sauvignon is Father's favorite wine. Charlotte ordered several bottles for the party. We'll start with it while your palate is still clean."

Odd how she knew exactly where Joe was even with her back turned. He was approaching from her right. Damn, the corkscrew was going in crooked. "Father will have already approved the first glass, so we don't need to fool with the sniffing ceremony. But it would really make points if you could compare tasting notes."

She pushed down the corkscrew levers then pulled. Nothing. She pulled again.

"What are tasting notes?" His question rumbled next to her ear.

The cork thwopped out. Her hand flew up, her knuckles ramming hard into his face. "Oh!"

He cupped his nose with both hands and swore.

She dropped the corkscrew and grabbed his wrists. "I'm so *sorry.* Did I hurt you?"

The eyes above his knuckle registered disbelief.

She tugged at his wrists. "Let me see."

"Promise you won't hit me?" His muffled voice sounded suspicious.

"Not as long as you behave. Now quit being ridiculous and put your hands down."

He did, revealing red swelling and a renewed trickle of blood. She bit her lower lip.

"That bad, huh? You and Pretty Boy have some humdinger spats ahead of you." He started to smile and winced. "My money's in your corner."

She hurried to the freezer, wrapped several ice cubes in a dish towel and returned to the table. "Sit," she ordered, pulling out a chair.

He sat, one tooled-leather ankle over the opposite knee. Denim pulled taut in places she struggled not to notice. Lifting his chin with two of her fingers, she positioned the bundled ice against his nose. "Give me your hand."

It came up large and beautifully formed, made for cradling a woman's hip or a baby's head. Foolish thought. So foolish. She pressed his fingers against the cloth and hoped he couldn't feel her slight tremble.

"Stay still," she commanded, removing her own hand.

His slitted eyes gleamed. "When do I get a Milk-Bone?"

"Not until you speak, Rover." She drew out a second chair and made herself comfortable. "Why did you stand there and let Carl do this to you?"

His propped ankle slipped off his knee. He braced his boots wide. "What do you mean?"

Any doubt she'd possessed vanished at his defensive body language. She leaned over and patted his rock-hard thigh. "You're a nice man, Joe Tucker. But I promise not to tell Carl."

They exchanged a long look, his wariness relaxing into a warm and comfortable silence, an acceptance that nudged up the corners of her mouth. She realized that among all the men she'd known, past or present, Joe was the first she considered a true friend.

"Want some wine now?" she asked softly.

He lowered the ice pack and probed his nose. "As long as I don't have to sniff it."

ALLIE TIED the laces of her scuffed rental ice skates and rose from the bench, wishing she'd never agreed to come. But Joe'd had some wine thing to go to at Catherine's, and Holly had sounded like an infomercial over the phone....

Her mother would drop them off at the Sharpstown rink and pick them up *hours* later. Holly would pay all fees out of her baby-sitting money. No, dorkhead, she didn't want to ask someone from her own school. Yes, she would teach Allie how to skate. The place would be packed with kids—at least half of them boys! Wearing jeans was...fine. No really, it was. But Holly could bring some of her extra practice clothes for Allie to wear if she liked.

And Allie had said okay. Not only that, she'd changed into her friend's clothes at the garage apartment before leaving.

Eyeing the skaters whizzing past now, she wanted to turn around and walk home. Oh, there were lots of kids here all right, most of them close to her age.

And most of them were wearing jeans.

The few dressed like her spun and leapt and hot-dogged like the expert she wasn't. "I'll get you for this, Holly. You won't know where or how or when, you'll only know it's coming. And it'll be ba-a-ad."

Holly finished lacing her skates—the snowy white unscuffed skates she'd brought in their own padded case—and glanced up. "Would you quit with the jeans thing already? I wish *I* filled out that dress like you do. You could pass for fifteen."

Allie wiped her palms down her thigh-length flared skirt. "You think?"

In the apartment mirror, she'd liked what the clinging white material had done for her figure. And her hair had seemed glossier, her dark eyes brighter than usual. Even her legs had seemed longer in the short flippy dress and opaque white hose.

She smiled at her sandy-haired friend. "You look nice, too. That color matches your eyes perfectly."

"Maybe. But all the guys will be staring at you," Holly predicted.

Staring at her? "How could you *do* this to me?"

"Would you chill? What is your problem?"

"Me, have a problem? Just because I'm dressed like Nancy Kerrigan and *I've never skated in my life?*"

"I told you, I'm a good teacher. I've taken lessons since I was six." Holly stood and prodded Allie's mincing steps toward the ice.

"Slow down, will ya?" Wobbling worse than if she wore spike heels, Allie watched the younger girl step through a gap in the railing down onto the ice. When she stood in the opening herself, she teetered on the spongy surface. "You go ahead. I think I'll just watch."

Grinning, Holly grabbed Allie's hand and yanked.

Allie's blades hit the ice and slid in opposite directions. Flailing, she managed to catch her friend's arm and rise from a split. Once their noses were on the same level, she looked deep into Holly's laughing blue eyes. "You won't know where—or when. But I'll be your worst nightmare."

"Yeah, yeah, yeah. Do you *see* all these guys? Omigosh—"

"Hi, Holly."

"Hey, Holly."

Holly stared dazedly after the two teenage boys who'd blown by skating low to the ice. "That was Brian and Steve. They're a grade ahead of me and they've *never* talked to me before." She turned and looked at Allie as if she were Glenda, the good witch, materializing from a shimmering ball.

"I didn't do anything," Allie protested.

"Are you kidding? You're good luck. I'd wear you around my neck if I could."

Which was practically what she wound up doing. Only Allie's death grip on her friend, strong ankles and fear of making a fool of herself kept her from falling those first couple of times around the rink. By the third lap she was starting to get the hang of it. By the fifth, she'd mastered the basics and let go of her friend. Alone and laughing out loud, she picked up her speed.

It was like putting her face in front of an airconditioning vent. No, like sticking her head in a refrigerator freezer. Colored spotlights pulsed to the beat of a Mariah Carey song. Kids talked and shrieked and flirted in a revolving merry-go-round on ice.

"How's it goin', Holly?" a boy shouted from behind.

Holly's head swiveled. "Uh, good. It's goin' good, Kevin," she repeated more loudly, waiting until he'd rocketed past before clutching Allie's arm. "If this is a dream, don't wake me up. I've liked him since the third grade."

Allie had caught a glimpse of Kevin's Brad Pitt grin as he passed. "I'm sorry," she said with true sympathy.

"Yeah. Well."

They skated for a while without talking. The sixties' tune of "Johnny Angel" blared from the speakers, bonding them to every girl who'd ever had a hopeless crush on an incredibly fine boy.

When the song ended, Holly pivoted on one blade and skated backward. "So, you're not still mad at me, are you?"

"Nah." The music, the lights, the frosty air so different from the mugginess outside—it was all too magical. "I'm having an okay time."

"I knew you would. You're skating like a pro already."

"It's not that different from in-line skating."

"Is there *any* sport you're not disgustingly good at? I'd hate you, except I've had more guys talk to me tonight than in six years of coming to this rink. They're working up the nerve to meet you, ya know."

Allie blushed. She'd noticed the increasing number of skate-by glances. Their interest amazed and thrilled her. She didn't quite know what to do with the attention, but she could get used to it real easy.

Holly spotted someone across the ice and waved. She lowered her hand and her voice at the same time.

"Becky Dawson. Biggest snob in the whole fresh-man class. She must've seen Kevin say hi to me." Her eyes widened. "Speaking of snobs..."

Allie followed her friend's riveted gaze. Sarah Sokol was stepping onto the ice with Tommy Burton right behind! Allie's right skate nicked her left. She stumbled and would've eaten ice if Holly hadn't grabbed her elbow.

"What are *they* doing here?" Allie wailed.

"Oh, jeez, they're meeting up with Becky. *Perfect*. She's waving Kevin over." Holly whirled around and skated forward again. "I hate her!"

"I hate her worse."

"You hate Becky?"

"No, stupid. I hate Sarah."

"Yeah. Well."

Yeah. Well. Hating hot babes was just as futile as liking incredibly fine guys. Unless...unless you could show them up.

Allie thumped her friend's arm. "I've got it! Has Kevin ever seen you skate, Holly? I mean like that." She flung a hand toward the center of the rink, where Ice Capades wannabes did their thing.

"You mean show off? No way."

"Trust me Holly, if you're good he'll see you and be impressed. I'll bet Becky can't do anything but bat her eyes fast." She let that sink in, then gave Holly a little push. "Go on. Get out there and make him look at you. Really *look* at you for once."

Holly's jaw firmed. She grabbed Allie's wrist and yelled, "C'mon."

Allie didn't have a choice. It was either "c'mon" or be dragged on her stomach across the ice. They wove to the inside fast lane and Holly took off like a speed skater, hanging on to Allie with a pit-bull grip.

She wanted to scream stop. Staring faces flashed by and her pride kicked in. She concentrated on matching Holly's powerful gliding motion and found her own body's rhythm, the coordination that never failed. Then suddenly she was alone.

Holly veered off to the center and started spinning, faster and tighter until she became a human top. Allie grinned and located Kevin far ahead. He was watching! She turned back in time to see her friend's twisting leap. *Go, Holly!*

Filled with a rush of triumph, Allie surged past slower skaters. Cold air stung her cheeks. Her leg muscles burned. She was flying, soaring, invincible...

Her right skate hit something thin and black on the ice. Her body flung forward. She landed with stomach-jarring impact and skidded for at least a year, piling up the makings of a snow cone with her crossed forearms. When she finally stopped, she wished the fall had killed her.

"Are you okay, Allie?" Strong arms helped her to a standing position.

Allie blinked up into Tommy's worried blue eyes. She doubted she'd feel a broken arm right now.

"That was a pretty hard fall you took."

Her face grew hot. "I'm fine, really." Turning, she brushed slivers of ice from her skin and torso and noticed Sarah standing nearby. Her smirk oozing spiteful glee, she patted a thin black rubber skate guard against her thigh.

Remembering the instant of her crash, Allie narrowed her eyes. "Where's your other skate guard, Sarah?"

Sarah looked startled, then she shrugged. And smiled.

Allie's first impulse was to smash something harder than a peach in the girl's face this time. Pure instinct stopped her short. Instead, she faced Tommy again. "She threw her skate guard in front of me so I'd fall."

He shot Sarah a suspicious glance.

"She's lying! I did no such thing!"

"I don't lie," Allie said, recapturing Tommy's gaze. "Funny. I used to think she wasn't good enough for you. But anyone who'd stay with her knowing what she's like . . . well, there's only one reason you'd do that." She saw the flicker of guilt in his eyes and felt her stomach sink. "I guess that means you're good enough for each other."

Pushing into a shaky glide, Allie moved back into the slower lane of skaters. She felt bruised and sad, but not bad about herself. And that was worth something, she guessed.

Holly streaked up in a blur of blue. "Kevin told me you fell. Are you hurt?"

"I'm okay. I hope I didn't ruin your dress, though." A streak of gray slashed down the middle.

"Forget the dress—it'll wash clean. Did you see me out there?"

"Yes. You were awesome, Holly."

"That's what Kevin said. You were right, Allie! It was like he saw me for the first time. We talked for five minutes while Becky just stood there and glared. Do you feel like getting a Coke or something?"

"Not really." Allie noted her friend's crestfallen expression and added, "But you go on ahead."

Holly beamed. "Thanks, Allie, I won't be long."

A flash of blue, and Allie was alone again. She probably should take a break. Her elbows stung. Her knees ached. She finger-brushed her hair and made a face. Ice had melted in the strands.

A tall boy skated up on her left. Dark hair, dark eyes, cute smile. "Hi, you're Holly's friend, aren't you? My name's Brian."

"Hi. My name's—"

"Allie," Tommy finished for her, skating up on her right. "She's a friend of mine, too. At least, I hope she's still a friend." With his blond head tilted down and his vivid blue eyes asking for acceptance, he was her Johnny Angel in the flesh.

"Friends don't abandon the friends they came with," she managed.

"I didn't. Sarah got mad and left with Becky."

"She got mad?"

Tommy grinned, and she thought her heart would burst *Alien*-style out of her chest. "I guess I made her mad," he admitted. "Do you mind if I skate with you awhile?"

She glanced to her left and wondered when Brian had skated off.

"I'd really like to," Tommy added.

"I'd like that, too." She couldn't get much happier than this, Allie thought.

Then Tommy reached for her hand.

CHAPTER TWELVE

RESISTING AN URGE to fuss over Joe's swollen nose, Catherine reached for the bottle of cabernet sauvignon and filled two glasses. "Take a sip."

She watched in unabashed enjoyment as he lifted his glass and swallowed. His new haircut exposed the strong clean line of his jaw and muscular neck, the surprisingly noble flow of his brow and well-formed head. His rugged masculinity seemed somehow intensified by the shorter cut. Just looking at him curled her toes. *Why* couldn't Carl make her feel this way?

He lowered his glass and caught her staring.

"What do you taste?" she asked, startled at the huskiness in her tone.

"Wine."

"Can you be a little more specific?"

He frowned at his glass. "Red wine."

She leaned forward and carefully replugged the bottle of cabernet.

"I'm not being a smart ass, Catherine. I really don't know beans about grapes. I'll just have to memorize what you tell me. Go ahead. Give me some tasting notes." He put down his stemware, sat back and laced his fingers over his stomach.

He was right. She shouldn't expect him to recognize the subtle traits she'd spent years learning to identify. Setting aside the chardonnay cork she'd been about to replug, she lifted her glass toward the light and mimicked her father's lofty expression.

"Moderately deep color, tinged with purple." Lowering the glass, she breathed in a teasing mix of fragrances. "Enticing nose of blackberry and...mint, I think."

She closed her eyes and tipped the rim to her lips, letting the liquid swirl across her tongue and palate. In a serious tasting, she wouldn't swallow. But then, nothing that involved Joe was ever serious.

"Rich velvety flavors. Nutty young oak. Ripe blackberry." She sipped again. "Mmm, lots of underlying vanilla. Superb balance, well-knit and finely resolved. I remember now why this is Father's favorite." She took another healthy sip before opening her eyes.

Joe closed his gaping mouth. "Get outta town. You can tell all that stuff from just a few sips?"

She tried not to preen. "Well, I might have missed something. I'm a little out of practice."

He reached out and filled another empty glass with chardonnay. "Do this one," he ordered, pushing the glass her way.

"Pass me a wafer first." She ate the dry biscuit he offered, then lifted the rapidly fogging glass of chilled white wine. "Pale gold color," she observed, bringing the rim to her nose. "Citric...slightly floral bouquet." She sipped the contents, again closing her eyes to focus her senses on taste alone. "Green apple, with hints of vanilla. Good structure, with balanced acidity." She indulged in another swallow. "Ah, I'm getting lovely lemon tones dominating the finish. Very nice." Opening her eyes, she flushed as Joe saluted her with his glass of cabernet.

"Pretty damn impressive. Useless and pretentious, but impressive. Who taught you this parlor trick?"

"It's useless and pretentious. Who do you think?"

"Your father."

"Go to the head of the class." Returning to her glass of red wine, Catherine savored another sip. "Let's review the cabernet notes again. I want you to remember them."

She settled back and drilled him in earnest, making him repeat her words until she was certain he wouldn't trip up. They moved on to the chardonnay and then the merlot, both of them honoring Carl with a toast for providing the excellent vintage. She felt a delicious thrill of rebellion at swallowing her "tastes," dispensing with wafers altogether and not even bothering to use a fresh glass for each wine.

By the time they sampled the last bottle, a light herbaceous *fumé blanc,* Catherine positively glowed with optimism. Her student had not only mastered the tasting notes, he'd delivered them with good diction, proper English and Sebastian/Cary Grant urbanity. She poured herself a teensy bit more wine and beamed.

"You have a beautiful speaking voice, Joe. Deep. Confident. With your memory for facts and quick wit, you'll make a wonderful sportscaster."

His ears reddened endearingly. He propped the stem base on his thigh and circled the glass rim with one fingertip. "Norman has booked me some time in a studio next Wednesday. I'm going to make a new broadcast demo tape to send out."

"That's great. Then what?"

His hand stilled. "Then I hope to God someone out there takes a chance on hiring a screwup like me."

She peered at his shuttered expression and realized he was serious. "I'd hardly call you a screwup. You made it to The Show. You've raised a lovely girl any man would be proud to call his daughter."

"Yeah. Too bad I haven't made her proud to call me Dad."

At Allie's age, Catherine would have given anything to have a father like Joe. "From what I've seen, you're a wonderful dad."

"You've only *seen* the last three weeks." His mouth twisted. He set his wine on the table as if he'd suddenly lost his taste for it. "Last summer I promised Allie we'd go somewhere special together during her Thanksgiving break. Then a friend of mine won a skiing trip and invited me to go on Thanksgiving weekend. I figured, hey, I'd never get another offer like that. Allie wouldn't mind waiting till her Christmas break to do something."

"That's when you injured your knees?"

He made a sound of disgust. "Eight hours of surgery, three months of rehab. No trip for Allie."

"Accidents happen. Don't be so hard on yourself."

He raised tortured eyes. "I pissed my career down the toilet and hurt my little girl—all because I was too selfish to think about anything but having fun."

"But you're building a new career now. And little girls are resilient. Allie forgave you, didn't she?"

"I guess she did. I hope she did. But for months she wouldn't smile, wouldn't look at me. Or if she did, it was like—" He shot up from his chair and started pacing, as agitated as a caged tiger prodded with a stick.

"It was like what, Joe?"

"Like I'd just drowned her kitten. The same way Vicky used to look at me."

Vicky. The wife he never mentioned. Catherine watched him stride back and forth, wanting to comfort him but sensing there was more. "Why did Vicky look at you that way?"

"Lots of reasons. I was always on the road. I cared about my buddies more than I did her. If she cooked better I would come home for dinner more often. If she was funnier I would laugh like I used to. If she wasn't pregnant I would still love her.... Hell, the more I told her that was ridiculous, the worse she cut herself down and the guiltier I felt." He stopped and plowed his fingers through his hair. "Even the sex went sour after a while, and that's what got us into trouble in the first place."

Catherine ignored an irrational stab of jealousy. She nudged his vacated chair with her toe. "Please sit down. I feel like I'm at Wimbledon."

He gave the chair a disoriented glance, then did as she asked, stretching his long legs out beside her.

"Thank you," she said. "Now finish the story."

"It's not very original. We'd only dated a couple of months when she got pregnant. Vicky swore she hadn't missed a single pill. Maybe she had, maybe she hadn't, but she'd been raised in foster homes and had no family, so I did what I thought was right." He reached for his wineglass and took a deep swallow. "From the beginning, her mood swings scared me. One minute she was Julie Andrews singing on a mountaintop, the next she was giving me *that look*. Or crying. She cried a lot.''

"Did her obstetrician know she was depressed?"

Joe nodded. "He said it wasn't unusual with so many hormonal changes going on. Told her to lay off caffeine, walk every day and take her vitamins. I pretty much tuned out her crying after that. Yeah, I was a real supportive husband.'' He raised his glass and drained the contents, his eyes bleak with self-contempt. "Then I came home one afternoon from a three-day road trip and found her still in bed. I don't think she'd gotten out of it since I left. Her hair was dirty, her eyes were dull—and God, she was so thin."

"What did you do?''

"I cleaned her up and got her to eat, then called her obstetrician and gave him hell. After that, Vicky saw a psychologist every week during her last trimester of pregnancy.''

Ah. The missing link. The reason Joe distrusted "shrinks.'' "What was the doctor's name?''

"Whitmire. Tall, distinguished-looking, fancy office in downtown Tucson.'' From his tone, Joe might have been reading the man's rap sheet. "You know him?''

"No."

"Lucky you. He had Vicky so dependent on him she dreaded taking time out to deliver the baby and miss a few appointments. I think she fell in love with the guy.''

Transference. Catherine wondered how she'd deal with it when she opened her own practice. "It's not uncommon for patients to develop strong feelings for their counselor.''

"If she liked him so goddamn much, why the hell couldn't he make her better?" It was a cry of anger. And pain.

"I'm sure he tried."

"Trying doesn't cut it if you strike out, doll."

Catherine felt a stir of uneasiness. "Dr. Whitmire wouldn't have been able to prescribe medication until after the baby was born. And sometimes counseling by itself isn't enough." A thought occurred to her. "Did the two of you ever see Dr. Whitmire for joint counseling?"

Joe scowled and looked away. "So now it's my fault?"

"What's your fault? Her depression?"

"I was getting a lot of good press that year, okay? When you're playing hot and signed with a farm team, you can't miss practice and games, or you might miss the one time that scout is sitting out in the stands. I couldn't lie on a couch and blow my shot at making The Show."

"Of course you couldn't—"

"I took a whole week off when Allie was born until Vicky got back on her feet. She loved the baby— you can ask my mother. Mom was with her for three weeks after I got back in the game schedule. When she left I thought Vicky could take care of the baby by herself no problem." He shifted to the edge of his chair, positioned to spring up. "I mean, other women go back to office jobs after four weeks, don't they?"

"Joe—"

"It's not like Vicky had an eight-to-five job. All she had to do was take care of one little baby—"

"Joe, *stop*." Catherine's stomach clenched in queasy anticipation. "Allie told me her mother died of complications after she was born. Exactly how did Vicky die?''

The defensive gleam in his eyes vanished, replaced by staggering anguish and guilt. "She slit her wrists an hour after Mom left. I came home that night and found Allie squalling in her crib. Vicky was in the bathtub..." His large frame shuddered.

Even though some part of her had guessed, Catherine's breath whooshed out.

"You once wanted to talk about my 'aversion to marriage.' Well, now you know the truth. I can't handle being responsible for someone else's happiness. When the pressure's on, I don't even step up to the plate, much less take a swing at the pitch. I killed my wife as sure as if I'd held the razor blade.''

Catherine's lungs inflated so fast she got dizzy. "That's melodramatic nonsense! Did Dr. Whitmire warn you Vicky might have suicidal tendencies? Prepare you for handling postpartum depression? Call you when she didn't schedule an appointment after the baby was born?''

He shook his head warily.

No wonder he had no respect for her profession. "A thorough evaluation and a conscientious counselor could have advised you to take preventive steps. But even then there's no guarantee Vicky wouldn't have taken her life.''

"I wasn't there for her," he insisted.

"Listen to me, Joe. If she'd waited to use that razor blade until right before you were due home, her attempt might have been the proverbial cry for help. But she didn't wait. In fact, it sounds like she made damn sure she'd succeed.''

He looked a bit stunned.

She leaned forward and took his hands into her own. "Maybe you weren't the most supportive husband. Maybe you could have been more sensitive, I don't know. But I *do* know that each and every one of us is responsible for our own happiness—no one else can make us happy. If Vicky really wanted to kill herself, nothing short of twenty-four-hour observation or physical restraint would have kept her safe." Her thumbs massaged his knuckles. "It's not your fault, Joe. Let it go."

For an instant his beautiful brown eyes were free of all pretense, his fear a precious gift of trust. "It won't change anything. I'll still be a screwup."

She squeezed his hands. "No, you'll be standing at the plate, swinging at every pitch. That's all anybody expects. When it gets right down to it, that's all any of us can do."

JOE GAZED at the deepening twilight and sipped his cabernet. Catherine had insisted on doing the dishes alone after their spontaneous meal of soup and sandwiches. The backyard patio provided needed distance and a chance to think.

He rehashed their conversation at length, one phrase replaying over and over in his mind. *It's not your fault, Joe. Let it go.* His rigid stance gradually relaxed. As if awakening from a dream, he grew aware of the beauty surrounding him.

Crickets sawed a high-pitched tune. A warm breeze rustled the leaves in a towering pecan tree. Roses swayed seductively against the tall wooden fence. Within this patch of paradise, a measure of peace settled into his heart. Maybe in time he actually *could* let it go.

He wandered toward the fence and breathed in the spicy-sweet fragrance of at least a hundred blooms. One perfect white blossom caught his attention. Reaching out, he touched the velvety petals and thought of Catherine's skin.

A swirl of emotions hit him harder than Carl's punches. Lust, possessiveness, respect, wonder—a longing of the soul he'd scoffed at when playing the lead in *Romeo and Juliet* all those years ago. But the bard had known his stuff. Forbidden love tempted like the apple lured Eve.

The back door opened and closed, drawing his gaze. Catherine walked toward him carrying the bottle of cabernet and a filled wineglass. The dark liquid remained level even when she stepped from flagstone onto grass. He never tired of watching her move.

She reached him and topped off his half-empty glass without asking for permission. "We might as well finish the bottle. You don't have far to drive." Her mischievous glance slanted up to the garage apartment.

Smiling, he nodded at a wrought-iron bench sheltered under the spreading tree branches. "Want to sit for a while?"

She hesitated, then shrugged. "Sure. I forget how nice it is out here once the sun goes down."

As if on cue, an ornate gas lantern installed behind the bench flared into life. They settled onto opposite ends and sipped their wine.

Lamplight flickered over her arresting face and highlighted details: the almost straight dark brows adding to an impression of serious intensity; the elegant thin nose that made him think of royalty; the prim little mouth that could prune up in displeasure or spread in a smile so dazzling he forgot his own name. Robert had cut her black hair into a youthful tousled cap. Mesmerized, he watched a blush rise up her graceful neck.

"You're staring," she murmured.

"I was wondering whether you look like your father," he lied smoothly. "Will I recognize him at the party, or will he be the one holding a rose in his teeth?" Her floating laugh buoyed his spirits.

"I'll introduce Father to you. I don't resemble him except for my nose. That's the only Hamilton feature I inherited."

"Then your mother must've been very beautiful."

This time her blush reached her roots.

He suddenly wanted to know everything about this confident, bashful woman. "You know, I've heard more than enough about the pretentious Hamiltons. What about your mother's side of the family? Tell me about her."

Every line in her body grew taut. She took a small sip of wine.

He frowned. "I didn't mean to bring up painful memories. You said she died when you were young, so I thought... Oh hell, I guess I didn't think, period."

"It's okay. I'm not used to talking about her, that's all. Father never did, and he never answered my questions about her, so eventually I stopped asking."

Joe cocked his head. His own mother still talked about his father as if Big Joe might walk in any minute and pop open a beer. "You really don't know anything about your mother?"

Two spots of red stained her cheeks. "I didn't say that."

"But you said your father wouldn't answer your questions. Does that mean you talked to one of your mother's relatives?"

She shook her head.

"A friend, then, or someone she went to school with?"

"No."

"C'mon, Catherine, what's the big mystery? Did you find her secret diary in the attic? Get an anonymous letter? Dig up her bones planting flowers in the yard—"

"No, no, *no*. Would you please just drop the subject?" She was breathing hard and avoiding his eyes, her turmoil as genuine as it was baffling.

A thought clenched his fists. "Has your father warned you not to talk about this, Catherine?"

She choked on a laugh and groaned, "No-o-o."

He narrowed his eyes. "I can tickle it out of you. Two minutes with these babies—" he wiggled his fingers "—and you'll sing like a canary."

Raising her wineglass, she drained the last sip and faced him with an expression of pained resignation. "Three years ago I hired a private investigator to track down my mother."

"Track her down? You mean her family?"

"No, I mean her. She isn't dead, Joe. That's something my father made up to save face with his friends. I follow along because it's...simpler."

It was his turn to drain his wine. Finished, he set both their glasses on the ground, slid across the bench and took her hands in his. Something told him she'd need his support now just as much as he'd needed hers earlier.

"Okay, doll, give it to me from the top."

"It's a boring story."

"Does it have anything to do with caviar, grammar, art, French cuffs or fruity bouquets?"

She managed a small smile. "No."

"Then I won't be bored. Go ahead. Shoot."

Her story didn't bore him—it broke his heart. He tried to keep a neutral expression while she described a childhood devoid of love but filled with rules and codes of behavior. Every wrong utensil picked up from beside her plate, every musical note fumbled on the piano, every *B*, instead of an *A*, on her report card brought stern reprimands and comparisons to her mother's inferior intelligence and breeding.

Joe looked down at the delicate hands he held and felt a fierce urge to shield her from further pain. "So you knew your mother was alive?"

"Not until I was sixteen. Before then, my mother was this secret part of Father's past we didn't talk about in public. I could tell some people felt sorry for me that my mother had died, but I was glad she was dead. I *hated* her for making Father ashamed of me."

"What happened when you were sixteen?"

Her mouth thinned. "For years I'd buried myself in libraries during summer vacation to help Father with his research papers. Getting published in reputable journals was essential to his career. Anyway, it was pretty tedious work to track down the obscure information he wanted."

Remembering his own summer days of hot sunshine, sweaty baseball games and cold plunges into swimming pools, Joe asked, "How'd you stand being cooped up?"

"I was still trying to please Father at that point. But the summer I was sixteen my two best friends applied for a job working the concession at a movie theater. Scooping popcorn and filling cups with ice sounded like heaven to me. I took home an application for Father to sign and he went ballistic. Same song and dance, only worse than ever. I finally started screaming back, asking him why he'd married my mother in the first place if she was so trashy." Her brows drew together.

"And?" he prodded.

"And then he told me the whole sordid truth." She searched his eyes anxiously. "You sure I'm not boring you?"

"I live for sordid truths. What did the pretentious bastard tell you?"

The tension in her face relaxed. She seemed pitifully grateful for his outrage on her behalf. "Before Father met my mother, he was teaching psychology at a small college in Connecticut and living with his elderly mother. He was the last male in the Hamilton family—his own father had been dead for years—and he hadn't produced a son *or* made his mark in the academic world. One Friday he got restless and drove to New York to get away from it all.

"He met mother in a coffee shop on Fifty-seventh. She was an aspiring actress of course, waiting tables until her big break. Father blames the attraction on temporary insanity, and it must have been contagious, because by Sunday afternoon they were driving back to Connecticut as husband and wife. I was born exactly nine months later."

Joe watched the tension creep back into her face and braced himself for the sordid part.

"He said he tried to make it work, but she was uneducated, unsophisticated...uncontrollable. She embarrassed him in front of his friends and colleagues and even made passes at the younger ones. When I was three, she took off with an actor performing at the local dinner theater and never looked back."

Pretty sorry tale, but he'd heard worse. "Your father never divorced her?"

"About six months after she left, he traced her to New Orleans. She was alone by then and waiting tables. He offered her five hundred dollars to sign divorce papers giving him uncontested custody of me. She held out for a thousand."

Now the story was sordid. "And he told people she'd died?"

Catherine pulled her hands abruptly from his grasp and hugged her stomach. "Terrible, isn't it? But he moved from Connecticut heading south through a series of college professorships. It wasn't likely he'd meet anyone who'd known my mother. Widowerhood was so much more...dignified than divorce. I think Father actually believed the story himself after a while."

Catherine rose gracefully, walked a few steps, then stopped, her focus on something only she could see.

"What did you find out about your mother, Catherine?" She was quiet for so long, at first he thought she wouldn't answer.

"She never remarried, so I don't have stepbrothers or sisters. I used to wonder about that a lot. She manages a truck stop in Columbus. She was working there long before Father and I moved here from Alabama. Columbus is just fifty miles away, Joe, can you believe it?''

Drawn by the longing in her voice, he stood up and moved to her side. ''Maybe it's fate.''

Her startled gaze rejected the obvious.

''Maybe you should go see your mother, talk to her, hear her side of the story.''

She shook her head violently. ''No! If she'd wanted to see me, she could have contacted me just once...'' Her voice broke on the last word and her shoulders bowed.

With a soft curse he pulled her into his arms and gathered her close, aching for the lonely girl who'd been abandoned to a cold son of a bitch for a thousand bucks. How had she turned into such a compassionate and loving woman? He struggled to keep the anger he felt for her parents out of his tone.

''You don't know the circumstances, honey. Maybe she thought you wouldn't want to see her. Maybe she was embarrassed. Hell, there's probably a real good reason she didn't contact you. But even if there's not, I think you should find that out, too.''

Catherine burrowed her face deeper into his shoulder. ''You think I should go see her?''

He suppressed a smile at her muffled voice. ''That's what I think. Not knowing is eating you up inside, like Vicky's suicide was doing to me. And a friend once told me that running away isn't the solution. You've got to confront your fear in order to let it go.''

She stood quietly in his arms.

He rubbed her back in lazy circles, letting her think about what he'd said. He wasn't in any hurry. Her head was the perfect height on which to rest his chin, her body the perfect cushion for his harder angles and planes. Better than a brand-new mattress any day.

She stirred against his chest and raised her face. "Your friend sounds exceptionally astute." The sass was back in her eyes.

He slid a playful finger down the slope of her nose. "Yeah. And she's smart, too."

As they grinned at each other like fools, like *friends,* a strange warming pleasure unfurled in his chest. It took a full minute for him to identify the feeling as happiness.

Her expression grew solemn, her bewitching green eyes huge. "Thank you for being my friend, Joe."

His senses leapt to attention. The smell of her citrus shampoo, the feel of her breasts sliding up his chest as she rose on tiptoe, the sight of her raised mouth—he experienced them all as exquisite torture. Then her lips brushed his in a petal-soft caress.

Desire flooded hot and insistent and harder than a baseball bat. He closed his eyes and made himself picture Catherine at the altar in a wedding dress.

She sank back down to flat feet. "I shouldn't have done that, huh?"

"No, no. It's fine." Like hell. The groom standing at the altar in the penguin suit wasn't Carl, but Joe.

She squirmed to get free and his eyes popped open. She looked delightfully flustered.

"Please let me go."

He stared down at his hands clamped on her hips and willed them to move. A long minute later he met her embarrassed gaze. "I don't seem able to do that."

Her brows slashed down. "What do you mean, you don't seem able? Just lift your hands and let me go!"

He shook his head and walked slowly forward, his hands steadying her hesitant steps backward. "I can't let you go until I do something first."

"What in the world are you talking about?" She stumbled and he discovered what a sweet little tush she had. "What do you have to do?"

Her back hit the wide tree trunk. He braced a palm on each side of her head and met her shocked eyes.

"This," he muttered hoarsely, then lowered his head.

CHAPTER THIRTEEN

CATHERINE'S HEART went into fibrillation as she realized Joe's intent. She flattened her palms against his chest and pushed, but she might as well have tried moving her brick house for all the good it did her. His face came closer, his devil-dark eyes glittering, his hard mouth softening.

She'd wondered for so long what it would be like to kiss him. Now she would finally know.

Tilting up her face, she closed her eyes and gasped as his lips brushed the skin beneath her ear. Warmth radiated from his busy mouth in shimmering circles. Whatever he was doing felt wonderful, an erotic combination of gentle suction and soothing tongue. Her head lolled back against the tree and she realized he was not so much kissing her as branding her.

She might have protested if her vocal cords hadn't gone limp—along with every other part of her body.

He made a low velvety noise in his throat and lifted his head. "I've wanted to do that since you swigged a beer in The Pig's Gut."

Her eyelids wouldn't open all the way. She followed the line of his hard jaw and the satisfied curve of his mouth with her slumberous gaze.

"When you look at me like that..." His head dipped under her chin and he nuzzled the base of her throat. "God, Catherine." It was a groan. "Do you feel what you do to me?"

She felt the rough bark against her shoulder blades and the steel curve of his thighs against her own. She felt the rasp of his whiskers on her throat and the pounding of his heart beneath her palms. She felt the rigid evidence of what she did to him pulse against her belly, and the answering surge of heat between her legs.

She felt womanly and powerful and sexy, because this man thought she was. And that freed her inhibitions as nothing else could.

"I feel a lot of things, Joe. But I want to feel more."

Sliding her palms down his T-shirt, she tugged the hem from his jeans, ducked her fingers underneath and found the naked skin of his back. They both drew in a sharp breath. She released hers in a wondering sigh.

She'd seen him bare-chested, known he was lean and perfectly proportioned. But, oh-h-h, to *touch* him. He was like sun-baked marble, hot and smooth and rippling with muscles, and so tall she had to stretch in order to reach his shoulders. The action flattened her breasts against his chest. He tensed, then pressed a string of feverish kisses over her neck, her jaw, her cheeks—everywhere but the lips that ached for his possession.

In retaliation, she withdrew her palms from his back and skated them up his stomach, intrigued by the silky prickle of hair that thickened the higher she went. She spread her fingers in delight and brushed two flat nipples in passing. His in-drawn hiss brought her hands wandering back to investigate.

She'd never indulged her curiosity during past romantic encounters. Shyness or awkwardness or indifference had always kept her from exploring. But with Joe she felt like a child given a fascinating new toy. She wanted to take him out of the box and examine all the pieces and play to her heart's content. He bore her skimming hands with a control she didn't question. This was Joe. He wouldn't hurt her.

"Are you having fun?" he asked finally, his voice strange and thick.

She circled a pebbled disk with her fingernail and peeked up through her lashes. "Yes, I am, thank you. And you?"

The cords of his neck looked ready to snap. He made a gravelly sound in his chest and closed his eyes, his expression close to agony.

The she-devil within her wanted to test his limit, to push him over the edge. She inched her hand down his ridged abdomen and felt his muscles contract. Her boldness astonished and excited her. He seemed to be holding his breath, which excited her even more. The heel of her hand bumped over his belt buckle and reached its destination.

"Oh, my," she murmured softly, his hard shape scorching her palm. She curled her fingers a teensy bit—

"Witch!"

His thighs crowded forward, his head swooped down. He slid his fingers into her hair and captured her lips, holding her hard against his mouth. The warm invasion of his tongue sent an electric sizzle streaking to her toes. She yielded to his domination with a sense of feminine awe.

It was a deep kiss, a man's kiss, as branding in its own way as the mark he'd probably left on her neck. Weakness spread through her limbs. She clung to his shoulders and would have fallen if not for the tree bracing her spine.

He lowered his hands without breaking the kiss and worked open the buttons of her blouse. Parting the silk, he peeled back a lacy cup with one blunt fingertip, bent his head and washed her in wet heat.

Catherine moaned. Never in her life had she felt like this, drugged with passion, oblivious to everything but the mindless needs of her body. Arching her back, she gave herself up to the building storm of sensations and trusted Joe to keep her safe. To anchor her to the ground.

Suddenly the whirlwind stopped.

Dazed, she watched him tilt his head and grow still. A sweep of air chilled her breast and she struggled to remember where she was.

"Damn!" Grasping her waist, he swung her around to the opposite side of the tree as if she weighed no more than a child. "Allie's home," he explained, easing her down onto her feet. He tucked in his T-shirt with savage thrusts. "Button your shirt and I'll head her off at the pass."

With dawning horror, she heard the slam of a car door and an exuberant, "Thanks, Mrs. Bass!"

She looked up only to be driven back against the tree by Joe's hard swift kiss.

He raised his head and stared urgently into her eyes. "Don't analyze this to death, Catherine."

Before she could answer, he was gone.

She shivered as if a blanket had been ripped from her cozy bed in wintertime. Awareness returned. She

blinked down at her right breast, shocking and pale
except for a few spots of redness. Whisker burns, she
realized, jerking at the sound of Joe greeting his
daughter in the driveway. She slipped up her bra cup
and fumbled with her buttons.

If she and Joe hadn't been interrupted . . . Her face
grew hot with embarrassment at the realization she'd
almost fulfilled her father's predictions. Making love
against a tree was in keeping with her mother's leg-
acy.

Allie chattered all the way up the garage-apartment
stairs. She was preoccupied with her skating adven-
ture, thank heavens, or she might have noticed the
Jezebel huddled guiltily behind the tree.

Holding her breath until she heard the apartment
door open and close, Catherine slunk to the bench,
snatched up the empty glasses and wine bottle and
managed to reach her kitchen door without anyone
screaming, "Slut!"

Once inside, she collapsed in a chair and set her
burden down. The four wine bottles sneered at her
from the tabletop.

She glared back. "Okay already. So I won't swallow my tastes from now on."

An easy promise to keep. Much easier than the one
she needed to make—which was never to repeat what
had happened out there under the tree. Because no
matter how wonderful Joe had made her feel, he'd
also made his position clear. No commitments beyond his daughter. Certainly no wife. And Catherine
wanted to be a wife and mother more than she wanted
mind-blowing sex. She did, dammit.

Reaching for the *fumé blanc,* she swigged a swallow straight from the bottle. Despite her best inten-

tions she relived the glorious feeling of kissing Joe Tucker. She'd wondered for so long what it would be like, and now she knew.

But, dear God, she wished she didn't.

TWO DAYS LATER, Catherine glared at the fabulous kisser blocking her exit from his small kitchen and wanted to kick him into Oklahoma.

"Look, you stubborn man. I brought the overnight bag Allie needs. I drank the Coke you served me. Now move and let me go home."

Joe gave her old shorts and T-shirt a once-over. "You probably *should* change into something nicer. I'd hate to see you make a bad impression on your mother."

"Well, *excuse me* for offending your delicate sensibilities, but I was cleaning the bathroom when you called. As for my seeing my mother—" she stepped forward and tilted back her head "—if you don't stop badgering me about her, I'll have to put a curse on you. I can do it. I'm a witch, you know."

"I know."

His gaze sharpened and she caught her breath, shaken by the realization he wasn't nearly as indifferent to her as he'd pretended since their kiss. She retrieved the threads of her anger and stitched on.

"My mother and I have gotten along just fine for thirty years without seeing each other. You are *not* driving me to Columbus today. No way, forget it, nothing doing. Capital *N* capital *O*. NO!" She set her hands at her waist. "Now, is that plain enough, or should I continue?"

Joe shouldered past her and opened the refrigerator door. The instant he pulled out a plastic container, Romeo and Juliet came running.

Catherine ignored her chance to escape. "Well?" she said loudly over the discordant meows.

Popping open the lid, Joe tilted the container in front of Catherine's nose. "Fish stick for the road? Riding on an empty stomach can make you carsick, you know."

She bit her lip, looked at his boots and shook her head. "Unbelievable."

"No, it's true. I blew beets all over the back seat when Dad wouldn't stop for a burger on the way to—"

"Can I give you a little advice, Joe? Next time you clean your ears with a Q-Tip—" she reached out and patted his arm "—stop pushing when you meet resistance."

The milling cats blocked her grand exit, or she might not have heard Joe's low chuckle. Some of her irritation faded.

Romeo leapt onto the counter and swiped an impatient paw as far as he could reach.

Juliet plopped down and rolled to her back.

Catherine watched Joe look from the dainty black feline sprawled in adoring supplication on his boots to the huge belligerent tabby demanding a fish stick *now*.

"No contest," Joe told the tomcat, then bent to feed Juliet her treat first.

"Can I have one?" Allie yelled from the sofa.

Catherine moved into the main room. Softball camp had a two-day break between sessions, and the excited girl sat packed and ready for her trip to the beach.

"Didn't you have breakfast?" Catherine asked. "It's an hour's drive to Galveston, and the Basses may not stop for lunch right when you get there."

"I ate."

"Good. So what'd you have?"

Allie shrugged. "Oreos and a Coke."

Catherine turned around and arched a brow at the girl's eavesdropping father.

Joe ducked back into the kitchen.

Chicken. Stifling a smile, Catherine walked to the sofa and sat knee to knee with Allie for a private conversation.

"You know, grabbing whatever's handy to eat is okay every once in a while, but those four basic food groups your teachers talked about in grade school really *are* important."

Allie rolled her eyes.

"No, I mean it. Growing bodies need plenty of milk, fruits and vegetables. They didn't make you learn that stuff to bore you—that's what memorizing the state capitals was for."

A grudging smile pulled at the girl's lips.

"I know it's hard, honey, especially when you don't have your Gram to grocery shop and cook for you and Joe anymore. But hey, if you're this pretty, this smart and this good an athlete right now, just think what a balanced diet will do for you. Tommy will have to beat the other guys off with your softball bat."

Allie perked up. She'd confided in Catherine the day before about events leading up to Tommy's undivided attention.

"Do you really think he'll call me?"

"Honey, I think he'll be camped out waiting on your doorstep when you get home."

"Cool."

Allie's engaging grin produced a curious mixture of happiness and pain in Catherine. With her father flying from England in four days, her tenants would be returning soon to their own apartment. She studied the girl's heart-shaped face and realized how much she would miss seeing it daily.

"Your hair has really grown since you've been here," Catherine observed, brushing the girl's bangs aside and holding them in place. "Time for a trim. It's a pity to hide these beautiful eyes."

The eyes under discussion filled with heart-wrenching neediness, an emotion Catherine understood all too well.

Releasing the silky strands, she rubbed the backs of her fingers against the girl's cheek before lowering her hand. "I don't mean to sound preachy, but it's just that…well, I love you, Allie. If I had a daughter, I'd want her to be exactly like you. You've done a fine job of taking care of your father. But you need to take good care of yourself, too. Will you promise to do that?"

With every word Allie's eyes had grown brighter. Now they welled with tears. "You'll come see me after I leave, won't you?"

Catherine silently vowed to give this remarkable girl her love and support for as long as needed. "Nothing could keep me away." She dabbed her own eyes with the corner of her T-shirt, laughed self-consciously and patted Allie's knee. "You'll have fun in Galveston. Got your bathing suit?"

"Yep."

"Sunscreen?"

"Holly's mom said they have plenty."

"Don't forget to *use* it. Got your pajamas and two changes of clothes?"

"Yep."

"Toothbrush?"

Allie opened and closed her mouth. "Be right back," she said, jumping up and running toward the bathroom.

No longer able to ignore the prickling sense of being watched, Catherine turned.

Joe stood just outside the kitchen, his muscular arms folded, his long legs braced apart—his virility a beacon both drawing her to and warning her away from dangerous waters.

She met his dark possessive eyes and for one breathless instant was pressed against a tree, her mouth being taken as thoroughly as her body ached to be filled.

Allie jogged back to the sofa, snapping the sexual tension between the adults. "Good thing I went in there. I forgot my hairbrush, too." She knelt on the floor and zipped the items safely into her borrowed luggage. Her ingenuous gaze moved from Catherine to her father and back.

"So are you gonna let Joe take you to Columbus?"

Romeo leapt up beside beside Catherine and butted his nose under her hand. "If you heard us talking, you must have heard me say no."

"I think you should go see your mom. You know, talk a little or something."

Romeo gave a distressed growl. Catherine un-clenched her hand from his fur and shot Joe a black look. His guilty shrug didn't excuse him for provok-ing her into airing her dirty laundry earlier.

"So you'll go?" Allie persisted.

"You don't understand, honey. It's not that sim-ple."

"I understand that grown-ups make things too complicated."

"Allie..." Joe warned.

The girl cast him a "what'd I do?" look, then turned back to Catherine. "Aren't you curious about her? Don't you have a million questions you wanna ask?" She buried her nose in Romeo's fur, then looked up with a perplexed expression. "I'd give *anything* to have a mother, but you don't want the one you have. It's not like she abused you, or any-thing, 'cause you haven't even *seen* her in thirty years. So how come you don't want your mother, Cather-ine?"

Catherine's stomach churned. For one of the few times in her memory, she didn't know what to say.

BEHIND THE COUNTER at Columbus Truck Stop, Mary Lou set a bowl in front of Nate and smiled. "If I didn't know any better, I'd think you've been look-ing forward to this for a while. How many weeks have you been dieting?"

Her friend held up a palm and spooned in a mouthful of peach cobbler. Eyelids drifting shut, he moaned deep in his throat and shuddered before opening his eyes and fixing a dreamy gaze on his fa-vorite dessert.

"Good grief, Nate, this is a G-rated restaurant. Show a little restraint, or I'll have to take that away from you."

He curled protective forearms around the bowl. "Touch this and you're a dead woman."

She laughed, something she seemed to do a lot these days. "Quit growling and enjoy. You deserve it after getting into those tuxedo pants."

Checking the other customers to make sure Irene had things under control, Mary Lou propped companionable elbows on the counter as he continued eating. "You looked pretty spiffy walking down the aisle with Cindy on your arm. And she looked beautiful."

Pride softened Nate's bulldog features. "She did, didn't she? Hey, that reminds me. The photographer got some great shots of you and John at the reception. Think you might want some copies made?"

Heat bloomed in her cheeks. "Maybe. Could I look at the proofs first?"

"Sure thing, honey." His hazel eyes twinkled affectionately. "I'm real glad to see you so happy. It's about damn time you let a man into your life again. Now if you'll just let him into your bed, I'll quit worryin' about you altogether."

Had any other man told her that, she would have frozen him with an icy glare. But Nate had watched her perfect that glare as a young waitress recovering from heartbreak. He truly cared about her welfare.

"How do you know I haven't pulled back the covers already, Nate Dawson?"

Pushing up from the counter, she headed for the coffeepot, her ears trained behind her for his response. Silence, then a booming laugh. She grinned in satisfaction. Although she hadn't taken that crucial step with John yet, it was fun to go one up on an incorrigible tease like Nate.

She bustled back to work, her thoughts filled with John. Her first public appearance as his date last week had been blissful. His unpretentious manner and enthusiastic polka at the reception had charmed the working-class wedding guests. She could almost believe their relationship had a chance. Of course, the real test would be attending, as a couple, one of *his* social events.

As if her thoughts had conjured him up, the front door jangled open and John walked in. Happiness hummed through her body. He saw her immediately, his handsome face alive with pleasure as he strode to the counter and slid onto a stool.

Without having to ask, she shoveled ice into a glass—halfway to the rim and no more—then drew a Diet Coke from the dispenser. He reached for it, grinning that damned grin, the one that said he knew her carefully controlled expression was a lie and he could prove it anytime he wanted.

The front door opened again. A man and woman entered with the look of people searching for the washrooms. She gave Samuel, the cashier, a nod to steer them the right way.

"So Grace must still be running a fever," John said, recapturing her attention.

"If she is, I'm not sure it's from a virus. I think her new boyfriend has a few days off. She used up all her vacation time last month."

"I wish *you* would take a vacation. Your boss wouldn't begrudge you a little R and R. In fact, he could use some himself." His dark brown gaze intensified.

Flustered by the underlying sexual current, she nodded toward a trucker who'd finished his meal. "Let me take care of Larry and I'll be right back."

She was giving the burly trucker his tab when she noticed the strangers a second time. They hadn't wanted the washrooms after all, but were standing at the Please Wait to be Seated sign.

She turned to Irene and called, "Customers in front."

The waitress glanced toward the sign and nodded at her boss.

Mary Lou thanked Larry for his business and watched him lumber past the striking pair. She studied them from under her lashes while clearing dishes.

The man was tall and dark, not handsome exactly, but so one-hundred percent male her gaze would have lingered if the woman hadn't exerted such a strong pull. She was tall, also, with black hair, skin as pale as Mary Lou's and a graceful slimness emphasized by a belted white sundress.

Irene approached the couple, and Mary Lou focused on wiping the counter with a sponge. But something about the woman tugged at her. She lifted the stack of dishes and stole another peek, startled to see Irene pointing a finger straight at her.

The woman turned. Her black-fringed pale green eyes collided with Mary Lou's, and time was suspended.

It was like looking at her own eyes in the mirror.

The blood left her head. She swayed and her fingers slackened. The dishes hit the floor with an exploding shatter, and her panicked gaze jerked away.

For a big man, John made it around the counter in record time. His arm wrapped around her waist seconds before her legs would have collapsed.

"Take a deep breath, Mary Lou. I've got you. Can you walk?"

She nodded woozily. "I'm okay."

"Come on over here and sit." He led her to a back corner booth of the diner and helped her ease down. Irene rushed over and hovered anxiously.

Mary Lou made herself look up and smile. "I just got a little dizzy. I'm fine now, really. But could I have a glass of water?"

"I'll get it." Irene exchanged a concerned glance with John before dashing off.

Mary Lou refused to look beyond her clasped hands, afraid of what she might see, even more afraid of what she wouldn't. For too many disappointing years she'd studied every female coming in that door who fit the right general age and description. Maybe the Lord had felt her relaxing on the job and had created a false alarm to keep her on her toes.

"Here's your water."

"Thanks, Irene," John said. "Why don't you see what you can do about that mess behind the counter? She'll be fine. I'll stay with her."

Mary Lou sipped the water and took strength from his competent presence. Especially when, over the rim of her glass, she saw the tall couple approaching her booth. She set her water down with a sense of unreality.

They stopped nearby, the man supporting the woman's waist as John had supported hers earlier.

"Can I help you?" John asked, stepping protectively in front of Mary Lou.

At that instant she made a decision. If John still wanted her after today, she would hand him her heart on a platter.

"Joe Tucker," the man said, extending his hand for a brief shake. "My friend here would like to speak with Ms. Denton."

She saw the exact moment John noticed the uncanny resemblance between her and the younger woman. His eyes widened and he looked to her for guidance.

Despite her sweating palms, she spoke firmly. "It's all right, John. Thanks for your help, but I think I'd like to be alone with Mr. Tucker's friend if you don't mind."

John held her gaze a probing few seconds, apparently reading something in her expression that told him not to argue. "If that's what you want, Mary Lou. But call out if you need me. I'll be at the counter."

A big silver platter, she vowed to herself, holding her smile until he walked away.

The man named Joe Tucker guided his friend to the booth and helped her slide onto the opposite bench. His mink brown eyes were tender in so rugged a face. "Are you sure you don't want me to stay with you?"

The woman shook her head but reached for his hand. He took it instantly, their clasped fingers an eloquent exchange of strength and trust.

He turned to Mary Lou and his eyes hardened. "We should've prepared you first, Ms. Denton. I see that now, and I apologize. But I won't let you upset her." It was an unmistakable warning.

Mary Lou nodded her understanding, her throat thickening as one of her most important questions was answered.

Her daughter loved—and was loved by—a good man.

He released the hand in his with obvious reluctance. "I'll be at the counter watching if you need me, Catherine."

The name arrowed through Mary Lou's heart. Memories bled free: a tiny rosebud mouth fastening to her breast; a small slim nose lifting royally at the word no; happy little giggles erasing Mary Lou's despair when Lawrence had been particularly hurtful.

She studied the face in front of her eagerly. Catherine the child had matured into a stunning woman, her face possessing a character and humanity that outshone conventional beauty. The love Mary Lou had kept alive with old memories grew stronger with the new data. Her questions clamored to be answered.

One rose above the others and escaped in a whisper. "Why now, Catherine? After all these years, why come see me now?"

Resentment chased coolness across green eyes so like her own. That slim nose, not so small anymore and as imperious as her father's, lifted a royal notch. "I suppose I wanted to know why *you* didn't come see *me*."

The aftershock was more devastating than the original quake. This was too much to absorb. "But your letter..." Mary Lou shook her head to clear the dazed confusion from her brain. "You told me not to contact you. That you needed to concentrate on getting your degree. That your father was the only parent you wanted, or needed." The pain of reading those words came flooding back, no duller for having been stored almost fifteen years.

"What letter? I never sent you a letter."

"Of course you did. After your eighteenth birthday."

Confusion winkled Catherine's smooth brow.

Mary Lou forged ahead. "Except for sending you a birthday card every year, I stayed away just like the court ordered until you reached your majority. Then I was so nervous about seeing you, so afraid you would hate me after what Lawrence must have told you..."

Her daughter's tightening mouth confirmed Mary Lou's fears. "So I sent you a birthday present that one time. A carousel music box because you used to love riding merry-go-rounds. And a huge card. With roses on the outside and a long personal note inside..." Her voice broke. She lifted a trembling hand and covered her eyes.

She'd labored for days composing her request to enter her eighteen-year-old daughter's life again. Catherine's rejection had almost destroyed her.

"Father told me the music box was from him."

The horror in that strained voice brought Mary Lou's hand down.

"I never got your card. I never got *any* of your cards, Mother."

Mother. Mary Lou swiped impatiently at a tear.

Every smidgen of color vanished from Catherine's face. "If you got a letter from me, then someone else wrote it. Someone who wanted to keep us apart." Her implication was clear, along with the bitter pain it caused her.

"But...the letter was handwritten. I know your father's handwriting. It wasn't his. Lawrence couldn't have been that cruel." But of course that wasn't true. How could she have been so naive a second time? Mary Lou dashed away more tears.

"What did you say about a court order?"

"What? Oh, the custody judgment." She'd never tried to contact her daughter after that first attempt, deciding that learning the truth about her beloved father would hurt Catherine more than it would give Mary Lou satisfaction. But now... "Those people *lied,* Catherine! I was totally unprepared at the trial—"

"Custody judgment?" Catherine interrupted, her expression stark with shock. "You fought Father for custody of me?"

Mary Lou blinked. "Of course. You were my baby. I would have died for you. I nearly *did,* when they took you away from me. You...didn't know about the trial?" She looked into her mirror-image eyes and saw fragile wonder and unshed tears.

Catherine shook her head. "Father said you were glad to sign over custody. He told me you'd said I would only hold you down."

Mary Lou grew still, the enormity of Lawrence's deception and her own tucked-tail defeatism squeezing the air from her lungs. If she dwelled on what she'd lost, she would lose her mind. But by the grace of her daughter's courage, she had a chance to salvage their future relationship.

Stretching both hands across the table, she turned her palms up and waited. Seconds passed as her heartbeat thundered in her ears.

Then Catherine's hands crept from her lap, inching forward to clasp her mother's fingers for the first time in thirty years. Neither woman broke the connection to wipe the tears rolling down her face.

"I *never* stopped loving you," Mary Lou said, her voice fierce with truth. "Not once since the day he took you away from me. Your father lied to you, Catherine. And it's time you learned what really happened."

CHAPTER FOURTEEN

CATHERINE STARED blindly out the Bronco's passenger window, grateful for Joe's silence and the setting sun. Her emotions needed a quiet dark place to whimper and lick their wounds.

Her father's betrayal was beyond forgiving.

The woman Catherine had left behind in the truck stop was nothing like the wife Lawrence Hamilton had described. Several hours in Mary Lou Denton's company had proved her to be articulate, demure and smart. John Chandler had called her one of the most responsible and savvy business managers he'd ever employed. Despite his obvious personal interest, Catherine didn't doubt his word.

She'd finally remembered where she'd seen his name—on her engagement-party guest list. Carl had expressed hope that the prominent businessman would attend their little affair.

Even if her mother's character hadn't been endorsed, Catherine would have still believed Mary Lou's story. It was too sickeningly plausible. And the pure unconditional love shining in the gaze she'd turned on Catherine couldn't be faked.

That single fact overrode an entire lifetime of her father's disapproving guardianship. She heard a tiny moan, and realized it had come from her.

"You okay over there?" Joe asked, casting her a sharp-eyed glance.

She tried to smile, but her facial muscles wouldn't cooperate. "I've been better."

"We're almost home, doll. Hold on a little longer."

She laid her head back against the seat, thinking that Joe had shown her more kindness in the past few weeks than her father had in all the years they'd lived and worked together. Control was Lawrence Hamilton's substitute for love. He'd been so obsessed with molding his daughter in his own image that he'd used despicably low means to justify the end.

Like hiring a high-powered divorce lawyer, who later ran for governor of Connecticut with the Hamilton family's endorsement. Like obtaining affidavits from a series of Mary Lou's alleged past lovers. Like bribing sworn testimony from a dinner theater cleaning lady who'd walked in on the theater's male director, Mary Lou and her child during an "assignation."

Only according to the cleaning lady, the director had been fondling the child, not the woman.

"Catherine?"

She jerked out of her unpleasant thoughts and blinked at her surroundings. The Bronco sat parked in her driveway. It obviously wasn't the first time Joe had called her name.

"I'm sorry, Joe, I...can't seem to get a grip."

His eyes gentled. "Let's get you inside."

She found herself hustled into the house, guided up the stairs and propped against her bathroom door while Joe started a tub of water. The sight of his brawny forearm testing the temperature brought a faint smile to her mouth. He adjusted the taps, then rose to his full height.

"You want to get a robe or something from your room?"

She shook her head, the effort depleting the last of her energy.

Frowning, he brushed past her and clomped down the hardwood floor hallway. Her eyelids drifted shut. She heard drawers sliding open and closed, then the squeaky hinge of her closet door. More distant clomping. And suddenly he brushed by her again trailing that yummy Joe smell—a mixture of sun and wind and big male animal. She lifted drowsy lids and saw him toss her long terry cloth robe on the closed commode.

He cut off the tub faucet and turned, avoiding her eyes. "That's about all I can do here. You need anything else?"

"Give me a hand with my zipper?" She faced the door, leaned her forehead against the wood and waited. After a long moment he stepped behind her and did as she requested with one quick *zing!*

He was in the hallway before she lifted her head.

"Joe?" she called, halting his retreat. He didn't quite turn all the way around. "You're not leaving, are you? I mean, you'll wait downstairs?"

He released a drawn-out breath. "Yeah, I'll wait."

"Thank you," she said softly, closing the door on the sight of his broad back heading toward the stairs.

She stripped off her sundress, undergarments and sandals and sank into the tub. Heavenly. Joe's vow to remain single was depriving some lucky woman of a wonderful husband.

Dangerous subject, that. Her mind searched for a diversion and offered up her mother's horrifying description of the divorce trial.

There had been just enough truth in the cleaning lady's testimony to nail the lid on her mother's coffin. Mary Lou *had* landed a role in the dinner theater's latest production. Mary Lou had taken her daughter to a late rehearsal and accepted the director's offer of a cup of coffee in his office. He'd given her little girl paper and crayons and then sat cross-legged on the floor beside Catherine to watch her scribble. Mary Lou'd had no idea the kindly director had been arrested three times—for child molestation.

She'd been helpless against her husband's unexpected and heinous charge. Rallying as best she could in her own defense, she'd failed to prevent the judge's harsh ruling. Her later court appeal had been denied. Only her knowledge that Lawrence loved Catherine, however misguided and warped that love was, had kept her from attempting to kidnap her daughter and run.

As Catherine lathered herself with rose-scented soap, she thought that maybe Joe was right. Maybe they were all just pawns in the end. If so, then she'd wasted precious time trying to create a future she had no control over. What she *should* be doing is wringing the gusto from each and every minute, before her position on that giant celestial chessboard moved again.

She slid underneath the water, blew bubbles and came up dripping but invigorated. It was all so clear now. She would sever ties with her father. That much was a piece of cake. But the other—breaking her engagement to Carl—that would be tough.

She would do it, though, because they both deserved better than a loveless marriage. She had her parents' example to thank for her new attitude. And, of course, Joe. The screwup whose image of himself was slowly starting to match the gentleman he'd always been inside.

What would calling off her engagement before he had a chance to prove he could win the bet do to his self-esteem?

Frowning, she rose from the tub, lifted her robe and did a double-take. A shimmering cream satin nightgown lay draped across the commode like a forties' movie queen.

Why, out of a drawer full of chaste cotton garments, had Joe selected the one item she'd purchased for her wedding night? Shivers raced over her skin.

She had the distinct feeling that somewhere up there in the sky, her pawn had just been moved.

JOE RUMMAGED in the kitchen pantry and pulled out a can of chicken noodle soup. Catherine had to be hungry. Her mother had ordered burgers all around, but while he and John had polished off theirs, the two women hadn't touched a bite.

The truth was he'd had to swallow past a huge lump in his throat himself. Come to think of it, John had looked a little misty, too. The reunion between mother and daughter had played out like a scene from a two-hanky chick's movie.

Dumping the soup into a pan, Joe set it on a glowing burner and propped his hip against the stove. He was happy he'd had a part in Catherine's gaining a mother, but sorry as hell she was hurting so much over her father.

Talk about manipulation! Lawrence Hamilton's shenanigans made Big Joe's prodding seem amateurish by comparison. Keeping his fist out of Hamilton's face was going to be Joe's biggest challenge at the party.

He glanced toward the doorway, wondering what was taking her so long. He'd gotten the impression that she would come downstairs after her bath, that she needed a friend to be with her for a while.

Is that why you picked out the sexiest nightgown in her drawer, old friend?

A rush of heat flooded his face, then his loins. The sight of the plastic Snow White doll standing amid the crystal ornaments on her dresser had made him pause. He'd felt uncomfortable invading her privacy, going through her stuff; so, intending to get out quickly, he'd plunged his hand through cotton. And then he'd touched satin.

He loved satin. A lot. His fingers had gathered a pinch and pulled. Next thing he'd known the slinky gown was hanging over his arm beneath a terry-cloth robe like the one his mother wore. He wondered what Catherine would think when she saw what he'd brought her.

Again he glanced at the doorway. She'd acted strange in the bathroom, sort of detached and dreamy. A stir of uneasiness came and went. She was probably enjoying an extra-long soak, that was all. Might even have fallen asleep in the tub. He straightened swiftly.

Turning off the burner, he strode out of the kitchen, through the living room and into the foyer. "Catherine?" he called up the staircase.

Silence.

Climbing a step, he paused. "Yo, Catherine, are you all right?"

Nothing.

He took the stairs two at a time, hit the hallway at a lope and skidded to a stop in front of the open bathroom door. Moist, rose-scented air curled a seductive finger under his nose. He stepped inside and noted the empty bathtub, the puddle of water on the floor, the terry-cloth robe folded neatly on the tiled counter. His gaze snapped to the closed toilet seat.

No satin nightgown.

Don't be stupid, Tucker. He backed out of the bathroom and into the hall. *She's vulnerable right now and you have to be strong.* He turned and headed for the staircase. *She doesn't belong to you, and you're not good enough for her, anyway.* He passed by the stairs as if in a trance, his steps pulled by a force stronger than caution, more insistent than honor.

Drawing close to another open door, he slowed and stopped on the threshold, his muttered oath part curse, part prayer.

The room was lit by two squat candles flickering on the nightstand. Catherine sat in the middle of the bed, her legs tucked primly to the side. Candlelight caressed white skin and ivory satin with a shadowy, lapping motion. Her cat-in-the-dark eyes were mysterious and watchful.

"Why didn't you answer when I called?" he finally managed.

"I wanted you to come to me."

Lord have mercy. She couldn't mean it like it sounded. He looked at the nightstand, the dresser— anywhere but at her. "Is there something you need?"

"Yes, please."

Her throaty whisper lingered in the quiet, waiting...pulling...dragging his gaze back to her heavy-lidded eyes.

"I need *you,* Joe."

His heart stopped, then lurched to rib-cracking life. "You're tired. Your emotions are strung out from here to Columbus. Tomorrow you'll feel different. Go to sleep."

"Come here."

Oh, God, he thought, *don't do this. Not when I'm trying to be responsible for once in my life!*

"What about Carl?" he said desperately.

Something flickered in her eyes and she started to speak, then looked down and smoothed the bedspread. "We'll have a marriage of convenience, Joe. Our hearts aren't involved."

Savage triumph swelled and died. He'd seen the way Pretty Boy looked at her these days. "What about your private practice? Because I guarantee he won't foot the bill if he thinks there's anything between us. Are you willing to risk everything, Catherine? Stop for a minute and *think.*"

She flung up her chin. "I don't want to think. I'm tired of thinking! Thinking is for dried-up academics who plan every trip to the john."

He winced at the phrase he'd once thrown at her so cruelly.

"Tonight I want to *feel,* not think, like I did when you kissed me under the tree. Please help me feel something besides pain." She lifted her slender arms and opened them in invitation.

He closed his eyes against the sight, knowing he should walk away, rooted in hellish limbo on the threshold. "You'd hate me later," he predicted.

"But if you leave, I'll hate you more."

The soft conviction in her voice raised the hairs along Joe's arms. A rustle on the bed flared his nostrils. He opened his eyes and stiffened.

She stood and walked toward him, a fantasy vision in the floor-length satin gown. Its thigh-high slit flashed a long shapely leg with every second step. He smelled her as she drew near, the blend of roses and natural female so imprinted on his brain he could have picked her out blindfolded in a room full of women. Sweat beaded on his forehead.

When her bare toes touched his boots, she stopped and lifted her hands. "One minute with these babies—" she wiggled her fingers "—and you'll do anything I want."

"Catherine—"

"Shh." She pressed two fingertips against his lips, then trailed them over his cheek, his nose, his increasingly damp brow. "Are you hot, Joe?"

The passion he'd felt under the tree was nothing— a boy's hunger—next to the ravenous heat in his blood now. Then, he'd caught her by surprise. Tonight, she'd come to him.

She twined both arms around his neck and looked up through her lashes. "I'm hot. In fact, I'm burning."

Staring into the green flames of her eyes, he felt poised on the rim of a volcano. "You know this is wrong, Catherine," he said, trying one last useless time.

"Then why does it feel so right?"

Reason fled. He jumped in with both feet. His open mouth lowered to her warm waiting one, and the earth's molten core closed over his head. Searing, bubbling, roaring in his ears.

Her hands delved into his hair and his did the same to hers, threading the sleek wet strands and cupping the back of her head. He slanted his mouth for deeper access and silently invited her to join the thrusting dance. She did, startling him by leading as often as she was led.

The tongue that could flay him with words stroked his mouth like an experienced courtesan's, making him wonder what else it could do. She broke the kiss and tilted his head, swirling her tongue in his ear and providing at least one erotic answer.

She seemed as hungry as he was, her mouth eating him up in small nibbles, taking a piece of his earlobe, his jaw, his Adam's apple. Latching onto the vulnerable spot on his neck he'd claimed for his own on *hers* when he'd backed her against a tree.

He slid his hands down bare skin to her satin derriere and cupped the slippery curves. The liquid fire rose, pulsed, threatened to erupt. He squeezed the flesh-warmed satin filling his hands, then slipped an arm beneath her knees and swept her up against his chest. If he didn't slow things down he'd be done for, and he'd waited too long, wanted to please Catherine too much, for him to let that happen.

He carried her to the edge of the bed and sat, positioning her as he wanted in his lap. "Let's just sit for a minute, okay?"

She searched his eyes, her hesitancy changing to cat-that-ate-the-fish-stick satisfaction. "Your thighs are so hard they don't feel human," she murmured, testing the muscles with a probing touch. "All those deep knee bends behind the plate must be better than a StairMaster."

He made a noncommittal sound, his attention focused on her shifting bottom. Grinding his teeth, he cursed himself for not putting more space between them.

Her fingers fluttered over the biceps of his left arm and settled like a white dove. "You're very strong and you have a beautiful body. But you want to know what's really sexy?"

Did a pitcher chew tobacco? "What?"

"Your brain."

He peered suspiciously down at her upturned face. "My what?"

"Your brain. Watching you these past weeks, seeing you stop hiding your intelligence behind all that brawn..." Her eyes darkened with unmistakable desire. "There's nothing you can't do now if you set your mind to it, Joe. That's incredibly sexy."

So much for slowing down. He gathered her close in his arms and rocked a joyful moment. "Ah, Catherine. Only you can compliment my brain and give me the hard-on of a lifetime."

"I can?" She pushed away from his chest and studied him hopefully.

Half-laughing, half-groaning, he scooted her to one thigh, captured her hand and curled her fingers over the proof.

"I did," she stated, her voice wondrous, her expression awed.

Suddenly he couldn't breathe for the emotion filling his chest. She'd had so little love in her life, this warm and giving woman. She deserved to wallow in it, to drown in it, for the rest of her days on earth.

And worthy or not, he wanted to be the one to give it to her—not some goddamn Pretty Boy.

"Joe?" The hesitancy was back in her eyes.

His face must look as fierce as he felt.

"We've sat long enough," he said, cinching his arms around her waist and falling back, back onto the soft springy mattress.

She sprawled across his chest, but he rolled with her until she lay beneath him, wide-eyed and expectant, her kiss-swollen lips parted along with her legs. He rose up on his elbows and she thrust beneath him once as if unable to help herself.

It was all he could do not to get free of his jeans and bury himself deep and hard and *now*.

"Easy," he whispered, dipping his head to kiss a creamy shoulder, a delicate collarbone, the V of her gown's plunging neckline.

He slipped the thin straps off her shoulders and peeled the sensuous material down, exposing translucent white flesh softer than her fine satin gown. As he paid homage to her small perfect breasts, her breathing changed to soft aroused pants. He lavished attention on her narrow rib cage and the sweet valley between her hipbones, thrilling to the restless moan he wrenched from her throat.

When he moved lower she stopped breathing altogether. He lifted his head. Her passion-drugged eyes flickered with embarrassment, and he knew she'd never experienced this before.

"Let me, Catherine," he pleaded hoarsely, waiting in ardent agony for some sign of permission, receiving it with the simple drifting shut of her eyelids.

Growling a rumble of satisfaction, he lowered his head and loved her good and well, her mounting pleasure causing his own excitement to build until he thought he would burst when she found her release.

During her float back down to earth, he shucked his boots, jeans and shirt and lunged up to cover her naked flesh with his. In one swift thrust, he buried himself where he'd wanted to be for more weeks than he'd like to admit. "Ah, yeah, this feels good. This feels right." He sighed. "Now, if I could only say something brainy..."

Catherine opened dazed eyes and smiled. "Put a little muscle into it, Tucker."

God, he loved this woman! Raising up on his elbows, he gave her a slow, crooked grin. "Whatever you say, Teach."

CATHERINE WAS ROUSED from the depths of her coma by a tickling sensation on her shoulder. She burrowed her face deeper in her pillow and started to sink back into oblivion. The tickle persisted, trailing like insect legs down her outflung arm.

Her eyes popped open. She scrambled upright and slapped wildly at her arm, searching the rumpled sheets for the vile intruder in her bed and seeing long masculine fingers, instead. Her gaze traveled past wrist, hair-dusted forearm and sculpted marble shoulder to an irresistible grin and teasing dark eyes.

"Mornin', doll."

When had the word ceased to be offensive and become a treasured endearment? "Good morning."

Joe clasped his hands behind his head on the pillow, his grin fading as his gaze lowered. "A damn good one."

She reached for the sheet and pulled it to her chin, struck by belated shyness. Ridiculous, considering the intimacies they'd shared throughout the night. Oh, what had she *done?*

"You're analyzing, Catherine. That's never a good idea the morning after. Things seem too different. You need time to adjust. We'll sort this out later when you know exactly how you feel."

His sensitivity didn't surprise her, not now that she knew him so well. Knew exactly how much she loved him. The rest was a confused tangle, but that much was clear.

She studied the picture he made against her flower-sprigged pillowcase, recording it in her memory to bring out in the lonely days ahead. His dark tousled hair, his beard-shadowed chin and jaw, the swelled biceps framing his face, the sheer manliness that made other men seem less masculine, however unfair that was.

"Come here," he said, his voice low and gruff, his eyes telling her she was desirable and wanted, if only for the moment.

But the moment would pass.

Despite her brave intentions, her smile trembled just a bit. "What happened to letting me sort out how I feel?"

"Maybe I want to refresh your memory."

They exchanged a long intense look filled with re-membered passion, and heaven help her, the sweet melting process began again.

"Come here," he crooned.

She leaned forward, drawn by the mesmerizing tether of her lover's eyes.

A sudden noise broke the connection. A noise sus-piciously like the front door opening downstairs. She saw her startled shock reflected in Joe's eyes, then he was whipping back the covers and pulling on his jeans.

"I didn't check the lock last night. Anyone have a key to your house?"

"Father. But he isn't due for three days."

Joe zipped up, nodded grimly and said, "Stay here."

Adrenaline shot through her as he moved into the hallway. She thrashed her way out of bed, slipped on her discarded nightgown and searched the room for a weapon. Idiot manly man, did he want to get himself shot? She grabbed the portable phone with the vague intention of calling for help and crept into the hall.

Joe stood frozen at the top of the stairs, his gaze riveted on something—or someone—below. Oh, God. She started to punch in 911.

"Enjoy your lesson, Tucker, or were you the teacher in this case? Lord knows she could use some tutoring in that area."

Carl. Horror paralyzed her poised finger.

Menace emanated from Joe in waves. "I'm gonna let that slide, considering the situation. But watch yourself, buddy. You won't get a second chance."

"Just who gave whom a bloody nose, you filthy bastard? Where is she? I want to talk to her."

"You'll have to talk later."

"The hell I will. *Catherine?*"

"Don't do it, Wilson. Turn around and walk back down those steps. You're not thinking straight right now." Although his voice sounded calm, Joe's fists were clenched, his legs braced for a fight.

Trapped in a living nightmare of her own making, Catherine walked slowly forward. "I'm here, Carl," she called. "Don't do anything foolish."

She ignored Joe's warning glance and moved up beside him. It took every ounce of Catherine's courage to meet Carl's eyes.

They were as cold as liquid nitrogen.

"So tell me, Catherine, was he compatible?"

Shame swept through her from head to toe. No man deserved this from his fiancée, no matter how loveless the bond. She'd agreed to marry him knowing full well his reasons for asking. She'd owed him her respect at the very least.

He set a large bag on the step above him, his smile caustic. "My little romantic surprise backfired, I see. Since I'm too late to help you work up an appetite, darling, I'll just leave this here. You must be starving."

She read the name of an exclusive bakery on the bag just as the scent of warm Danish reached her nose. To her utter humiliation, her stomach growled loudly.

He held up a key and placed it beside the bag. "Please return this to your father. I'm afraid I can't be the protector he wanted any longer. You'll have to find another fiancé for the job—*if* you can." His sweeping look made it insultingly clear what he thought of her chances.

Standing there in her crumpled satin nightgown, knowing her wild hair and abraded skin branded her like a scarlet letter, she made a small sound of distress. Suddenly Joe's arm curled around her waist and hugged her to his side.

"She's already found one, buddy—*if* she'll have me," Joe said in a hard tight voice.

Her heart soared. She flung her head back and searched his beloved face. His gaze moved from Carl's to hers, the competitive glitter in his eyes changing to inscrutable watchfulness.

He doesn't want this, she thought, wondering how a shattered heart could continue beating.

His awakened sense of responsibility, his gentlemanly instincts—those were what had prompted his offer. He'd told her often enough that he didn't want or need a wife. To love him as she did without receiving his love in return would be a thousand times worse than a marriage of convenience.

"I hate to interrupt this touching scene," Carl said acidly, "but, Catherine, there's a little matter of my parents and two hundred guests we need to discuss. Shall I come back in, say, an hour?"

Removing Joe's arm from her waist was the hardest thing Catherine had ever done. "That's fine, Carl, it will give you time to adjust. When you come back, we'll sort this out and see how you feel then. Maybe we can salvage something from the mess I've made of things."

CHAPTER FIFTEEN

JOE ZIPPED UP his last bag and hoped he hadn't forgotten anything. Two mornings ago Catherine had made it clear he had no place in her future. No way was he coming back.

He scanned the apartment one last time, his eyes straining with the effort to memorize details. The bright colors and wall art he'd found so irritating that first day seemed interesting and provocative now. Over the past month his attitude about a lot of things had changed—especially about himself.

He would never be perfect, not by a long shot. But if there was any chance he could influence his future, he was willing to give it a try. He'd much rather make his own decisions and accept the consequences than drift along at the mercy of someone else's agenda.

According to Norman, Joe's new confidence and polish really showed on his latest demo tape. Copies of the tape had hit the post office yesterday and, with any luck, would generate some promising interviews. His participation in Catherine's crazy bet would've been time well spent.

If only he hadn't fallen in love with her.

Juliet slunk out from under the sofa and rubbed against his leg. Joe crouched down into a catcher's squat and stroked her arching back. The steady ache in his chest intensified.

"So what's Romeo's secret, girl? I seem to've lost my touch."

When Catherine had pulled away from him on the stairs and scrambled to get back into Pretty Boy's good graces, everything in Joe had grown cold. The worst part was knowing she'd been right to do it. As much as he'd wanted to play Prince Charming come to the rescue, the castle and all its riches belonged to Carl. He doubted anything else could've kept him from fighting like hell to change her mind.

Snow White deserved her happily-ever-after.

Looked like she'd get it, too, because she'd told him yesterday the engagement was still on—party, bet and all. He could imagine what she must've told Carl in private to pull that off. Probably something about sowing her last wild oats, along with assurances that Joe was out of her system now.

Thank God he hadn't blurted out his feelings during their incredible night together. Catherine was just starved enough for affection to choose his love over Carl's offer of certain security. He probably would've let her, too, if not for the lessons in responsibility he'd learned at her hands. The irony was laughable.

Sighing, he gave Juliet a final affectionate scratch, saluted Romeo perched on the green patio table and grabbed a suitcase in each hand. He heard Allie pound up the stairs just as he reached the door.

It burst open and she looked beyond Joe to the two cats.

"No," he said before she could open her mouth. "And you better not've asked Catherine if you could take them home with you. You didn't, did you?"

"I said I wouldn't, and I didn't. But Jo-oe, *look* at them."

He cast a reluctant glance over his shoulder at the two felines staring at him as if their last fish stick on earth was walking out the door.

"They'll be all alone for at least a month until a fall-semester student rents the apartment. I don't want them for keeps, I just want to...borrow them." Allie's chin jutted forward, the obstinate angle hardening his resolve.

He stepped out into the morning sunlight. "Check to see that you haven't left anything behind, then shut the door good. I'll meet you at the Bronco."

Damn, he thought, descending the stairs with the image of Allie's mutinous expression for company. As if it wasn't hard enough leaving without her badgering him about the cats.

He opened the rear of the truck and slid the two suitcases into the spot he'd cleared for them. Amazing how much more stuff they were taking home than they'd originally brought.

The apartment door opened and closed. Allie's heavy stomps on the cedar stairs alerted him to the fact that her mood hadn't improved.

Well, neither had his.

He slammed the tailgate shut and turned to face his daughter. "Ready?"

"Why *can't* we take them, Joe? I'll clean the cat box, I promise, and you know they don't eat much. Just let me ask Catherine—"

"Listen to me, Allie. Those cats don't belong to you. And no matter how much you love them, Catherine loves them more. Do you think she's gonna let her babies get hungry or lonely? Not a chance. So quit nagging me and let's get this show on the road."

"But here she comes. It won't hurt to ask her."

He began to wonder if those straight *A*'s on her report cards had been forged. "Cats get upset when they're moved. Do you really want to tear them away from their home and take them to a strange place just so *you'll* be happy? Sounds pretty selfish to me."

"What's this I'm hearing?" Catherine asked from behind Joe, sending a bittersweet spike through his heart. "Allie, why didn't you tell me you wanted to take Romeo and Juliet home with you?" She moved forward and draped her arm around the girl's shoulders.

"Joe told me not to ask you. He says I'm nagging him."

Ignoring his daughter's fingernail-on-a-blackboard whine, Joe transferred his irritation to Catherine. If she'd said yes to his marriage proposal, this wouldn't be an issue. Allie would have the pets she'd always wanted and the mother he'd only recently learned she'd "give anything" to have. And what would he have?

"If your father didn't want you to ask me, he must have had a good reason," Catherine said firmly.

I'd have a lover who's also my best friend.

Allie made a face. "He's just in a bad mood. He's been grumpy ever since I got back from Galveston. Please, Catherine? Could I take them with me for a few weeks?"

Joe had been on the receiving end of those pleading spaniel eyes enough times to know how tough they were to resist.

Catherine removed her arm from the girl and stepped back. "It's up to your father."

Quickly masking a spark of triumph, Allie dragged her soulful gaze to Joe. "C'mon, Joe, it'll be fun."

The magic phrase, the one he'd used for years to wheedle cooperation from her. His temper snapped. "I've had about all the manipulation I'm going to take from you, Allie. When I tell you no, it doesn't mean maybe, or ask me twenty more times, it means respect my judgment and keep your complaints to yourself. Is that understood, young lady?"

Her eyes grew huge. "But Joe—"

"Is that understood?"

As father and daughter stared at each other a long measuring moment, there was a subtle shift in the balance of power between them.

"Yes, Dad."

"Good. Now tell Catherine goodbye again and hop in the Bronco."

Allie moved into Catherine's open arms and hugged her fiercely. "You'll help me shop for school clothes like you promised? You won't forget?"

Catherine's lids squeezed shut briefly. "Of course I won't forget. We're talking shopping here."

Allie pulled back and grinned. "Thanks, Catherine. Guess I'll see ya soon, then." She jogged to the passenger side, climbed in and slammed the door.

Fumbling for his jeans pockets, Joe shoved his hands deep to keep them from doing something stupid. The goodbyes in his life had always been filled with guilt. This vise squeezing his ribs, this knowledge that walking away would rip out his heart and leave him hollow and bleeding . . . well, if this is what Vicky and Allie had endured, he was surprised they hadn't hated him.

He looked down and toed a crack in the driveway. "So I'll show up Saturday night at about eight-thirty, right? I've gotta admit I'm kind of nervous." Kind of? Ha!

"You'll do great. I'm very proud of you."

His head came up. Moisture glinted in her eyes like dew on spring grass. He waited until he could trust himself to speak.

"Don't jump the gun. I haven't convinced your father yet."

"I'm not talking about your party manners, for heaven's sake. Don't you realize what happened a minute ago?"

He stared at her blankly.

"Allie called you Dad. How long has it been since she last called you that?"

Lord have mercy. "Not since she was about six."

"Welcome to fatherhood, Joe. It might not be as much fun as never-never land, but with Allie for a daughter, the magic will never end."

CATHERINE SLIPPED into the Wilsons' downstairs guest bathroom, locked the door and set her beaded bag by the Italian marble basin. She'd orchestrated the evening with unnatural calm, but now that it was time to conduct, she was a bundle of nerves. So much could go wrong.

Turning the cut-crystal faucet, she held her wrists beneath a stream of cold water and prayed for courage. She'd agreed to masquerade as Carl's adoring bride-to-be, thus saving his parents the social embarrassment of their lifetime, on two conditions.

First, he must not under any circumstances reveal that either the bet or their engagement was off. Second, he must facilitate the surprise she had planned for her father.

She'd confessed everything regarding her flawed pedigree, including the vaulted Dr. Hamilton's lowly character. Shocked and subdued, Carl had readily consented to her terms. Especially after she'd threatened to stage her surprise in front of their guests should he not cooperate.

She switched off the water, patted her hands dry and vowed to give Joe his chance to mingle as Sebastian Doherty, intellectual and social equal to society's darlings. Maybe after tonight her student could be comfortable with the real Joe Tucker—the man somewhere between dumb jock and aristocratic snob. The man she loved.

Catherine met her own stricken eyes in the mirror and shook her head.

No, she wouldn't think about that now. Not when she needed to be strong for the upcoming confrontation with her father. Her stony aloofness since she'd picked him up from the airport yesterday had prompted more attention than he'd shown her in years. But she'd purposely kept up the silent treatment. If all went according to plan, he wouldn't dare interfere in her life again after tonight.

Fumbling in her bag, she withdrew a gold tube and freshened her lipstick, drawing confidence from knowing she looked damn good. The bright red cocktail dress she'd seen on her shopping trip with Joe actually looked better on her than it had on the store-window mannequin.

High-necked, cap-sleeved and form-fitting to three inches above the knee, it whispered expensive and classy—from the front. She turned slightly and eyed the expanse of white skin narrowing to a point below her waistline. A rhinestone bow perched on the dip just before her buttocks swelled.

From the back this dress said, "Follow me, big boy," and earned every penny of its outrageous price tag.

Okay, Catherine, you've stalled long enough. Time to put up or shut up.

Squaring her shoulders, she left the sanctuary of the bathroom and headed for the formal living room, amazed at the number of guests who'd arrived during her short absence. Lilting music from a string quartet softened the geeselike chatter of humans. She immediately spotted her father among the flock.

Tall and white-haired, with sharp angular features and the bearing of an eagle among lesser fowl, Lawrence Hamilton stood next to Carl, pontificating about something or other. Two distinguished-looking couples in their fifties completed her father's enthralled audience. Catherine accepted a glass of chardonnay from a passing waiter and headed for the performance.

"Consider a recent study conducted at Stanford Business School to determine the best predictors of success in business," her father was saying. "The scholastic records of graduates were compared with their positions in the business world ten years later. The only consistent variable that could predict success was verbal fluency."

As Carl made room for her in the semicircle, the others smiled a quick greeting.

"So you're saying that most successful men are good communicators?" Dusty Black asked, throwing his wife, Dawn, a smug look.

"That's right. They're able to sell themselves, their services and their companies—all critical skills for running a corporation. The designers, researchers and programmers of the world will never get paid as much as the Lee Iacoccas..."

Catherine tuned out her father's voice, refusing to listen to such a narrow-minded view of success. How many CEOs were happy with themselves and their lives? How many of them had a positive impact on the people around them?

She sipped her wine and glanced toward the foyer for the third time in as many minutes. Charlotte and Jeffrey Wilson opened the door to more arriving guests, none of them familiar to her. She and Carl had been excused from front-door duty in honor of her father's brief visit. He was heading for an airport hotel after the party and would fly back to England tomorrow.

Lowering her glass, she winced as her fingers slipped on the condensation. Wine sloshed over the rim and hit her father's polished dress shoes.

He stopped in the middle of a sentence and looked down his long Hamilton nose at the offending liquid. "And then there's the *nonverbal* form of communication." His gaze slowly lifted. "If I'm boring you, Catherine, surely you could find a less dramatic way to tell me?"

His charming smile swept his audience and prompted chuckles, but not before Catherine had seen the unguarded flash of displeasure in his hazel eyes. A month ago it would have devastated her.

She patted his arm and offered the group her own falsely bright smile. "Father *loves* high drama. He's too modest to admit it, but he was an excellent actor in his younger days.''

"Really, Lawrence?'' Dawn's dark eyes lit with speculative interest. "You know our Hospice House fund-raising ball is staging a melodrama prior to the dancing. We could certainly use a volunteer with experience.''

"I'm afraid my daughter is mistaken.'' He glanced warily at Catherine. "I don't know where she got the idea I was in the theater.''

"Who said anything about the theater? I said you could act.'' Catherine turned to the attractive older woman and forced a teasing note into her voice. "According to an old friend of the family, Father wasn't *always* the proper professor. It seems he could talk a courtroom judge into believing anything.''

Smiling nearly cracked her face, but it cued her audience to laugh along with her "little joke.'' She risked a glance at her father and met his shocked stare.

He suddenly looked every one of his sixty-seven years, and her reflexive desire to make him happy, to please him at any expense to her own pride, both shamed and angered her.

"Carl, dear?'' Dawn said, the odd edge in her voice capturing Catherine's attention. "Who is that arriving just now?''

As one, they all turned and looked toward the front door. Despite the fact that there were three men and two women crowding the foyer, there was no doubt in anyone's mind who Dawn meant.

He stood alone and apart, a sophisticated pirate preparing to conquer and claim.

His charcoal gray Valentino suit would have made an ordinary body seem athletic. On Joe's powerful physique, the double-breasted jacket and full legged trousers made him a feast for feminine eyes, an irritation to those of his own sex. A snowy white shirt and peach silk tie were the perfect foil for his bold dark eyes and hard-planed face.

She wanted to rush over and let every woman know he was *her* sophisticated pirate. He *could* have been hers if only she hadn't been so damn noble. And, oh, it hurt. It hurt so much!

Catherine dragged her gaze away and noted Carl's bristling hostility. Definitely not a part of their deal. She pulled herself together and smiled.

"Isn't that Sebastian Doherty?" she asked Carl pointedly. "You introduced me at the country club last week. He's visiting Houston on business, and you invited him to our party. *Remember,* darling?" She grasped his arm and sneaked a hard pinch.

"Ah! So it is, Catherine."

"Any relation to the Philadelphia Dohertys?" her father asked.

Carl continued staring at the foyer as if ready to unsheath his sword. Her elbow found his ribs.

"Um! I believe he is, Dr. Hamilton. Rumor has it he's looked at several large pieces of commercial real estate. Very hush-hush about his intentions of course, but relocating Doherty Enterprises does seem a logical assumption."

If he'd been a dog, her father's ears would have been standing straight up. From the others' expressions, Joe's fictional prestige would spread faster than the common cold among the gossiping crowd.

"Excuse us, please, while we make Mr. Doherty feel welcome," Catherine said, drawing Carl with her to the entryway.

Charlotte looked up with a relieved expression as they drew near. Her Grace Kelly poise and blond beauty held a hint of censure. "Ah, here they are now, Mr. Doherty. Carl, shame on you for not letting me know you'd invited a special guest."

Catherine added warningly, "Yes, shame on you for forgetting something so important. Sebastian must have felt extremely awkward." She turned and extended her hand to Joe. "We're so glad you could squeeze us into your busy calendar, Sebastian. Thank you for coming."

His ebony gaze swept over her and glittered with appreciation. "I wouldn't have missed it for anything."

Their hands met, and everything female in her merged with his heat and strength. The connection pulsed with life. She looked into his eyes and almost hated him for making her heart hammer, her mind sharpen, her senses vibrate as no other man ever had or, she suspected sickly, ever would again.

She jerked back her hand. "Do let us introduce you to our friends, won't you?" Had he noticed her slight breathiness?

The satisfied curve of his mouth said he had. "I'd be delighted."

Delighted, she thought, marveling that a word so foreign to Joe could sound so natural from "Sebastian." With the two men in tow, she set out to introduce her prize student to the Wilsons' friends and protect his true identity from discovery.

Tight clusters of guests flowered open at their approach, offering obligatory congratulations to Carl and Catherine before focusing swiftly on Joe. His role gave him free rein to use his extensive vocabulary, to practice his dry wit on an audience that appreciated rather than ridiculed such things. He collected admiration like pollen, moving on to each new group a bit more dusted with confidence.

In a circle including the Prewitts, talk of a successful dove hunt animated the men. Joe steered the conversation to bird dogs, segued into show dogs and walked away with Laura's heart and an invitation from Brad to flush up some south Texas quail in the fall.

A protective unit consisting of the Andersons and their two bodyguards loosened up as Joe discussed physical-fitness regimens. Interested eavesdroppers drifted into the group and asked questions press-conference style. Years of training camps and injury rehabilitation lent credence to Joe's advice. Catherine had to cut the questions short and physically drag him away in order to move on into the dining room.

They joined a slow-moving line leading to the buffet table where Charlotte, true to form, stood ready to reprimand the caterer should trays not be replenished immediately.

The woman's perfectionism rivaled her father's, Catherine realized. She would have spent her entire marriage to Carl trying to measure up to Charlotte's standards—and failing. At least loving Joe had saved her from that.

Riding a crest of gratitude, she hugged Carl's arm. "Isn't Sebastian amazing? The way he fits into this crowd, you'd never know he was from Philadelphia, would you?''

As Joe would say, Carl looked as if he'd just sucked on a lemon. "Maybe not. But then, I'm not as perceptive as your father, and I don't believe Sebastian's had a chance to visit with him yet... have you, old chap?'' He turned to the taller man with feigned innocence.

Joe appeared distracted by someone at the buffet table. "Hmm? Oh, I haven't had the pleasure, no. Will you excuse me please?''

He left the line and approached a pinched-faced elderly woman who was walking with a distinct hobble, trying with obvious difficulty to balance her plate. Speaking in her ear, Joe took the plate from her hands and began piling it with this and that, consulting with Charlotte and following his companion's gnarled pointing finger until there wasn't a smidgen of china showing.

Catherine and Carl weren't the only ones to gape. Martha Kendall's wealth was equaled only by her abrasive personality. Carl had once admitted she terrified even his mother.

Joe held out his arm, escorted Martha toward a row of occupied chairs lining one wall and stopped in front of a portly man stuffing shrimp into his mouth at a rate faster than he chewed. Whatever Joe said brought the man clambering up from his chair, his round face flushed. Joe proceeded to seat Martha as if she were the most important woman in his life.

She accepted the plate he'd filled, looked up with a coy smile and said something that made Joe throw back his head and laugh. The deep uninhibited whoops had people smiling throughout the room.

"You really love him, don't you?" Carl said for Catherine's ears alone.

Realizing he'd caught her staring unguarded at Joe, she didn't attempt to hedge. "Yes, I really do." She prodded him forward in the line, keenly aware of him studying her face.

"Good lord, you haven't told him. But why—"

"I have my reasons. If you care for me at all, you'll respect them and keep quiet." She held his puzzled gray gaze. "Will you do that?"

He reached up and stroked the pad of his thumb down her cheek. "He's a lucky man, Catherine."

Just then Joe walked back to join them in line near the buffet table, cutting off her chance to respond. Charlotte moved forward and patted Joe's arm.

"How fortunate for us, Mr. Doherty, that you decided to accept Carl's invitation. Martha can be...difficult to please sometimes. I don't believe I've ever seen her look quite so happy at one of my parties, and it's all thanks to you."

"Don't mention it. I'd do the same for you if your bunion were acting up," Joe assured her. Then he grinned. Not Sebastian's suave showing of white teeth, but Joe's patented, slow, sex-on-the-hoof grin.

Charlotte stared and seemed to have trouble breathing. Her beringed fingers fluttered to her diamond choker.

"Mother!" Carl exclaimed.

She jerked and blushed profusely. "I'll just see what's holding up that tray of shrimp," she murmured, bustling off toward the kitchen.

Watching, Catherine suffered a pang of sympathy for the older woman and an aching loss for herself. Never again to see that grin on a daily basis, never again to know firsthand the ecstasy it promised. How would she bear the emptiness?

"Oh, Carl, Catherine, *here* you are."

Catherine's gaze snapped to the dining-room entrance.

Jeffrey Wilson stood there eyeing his son urgently. "John Chandler and his date arrived a few minutes ago, and they're asking to see you both."

JOE GLANCED at the dining-room entrance, patted the feminine hand curled around his forearm and gently pulled away. The red-taloned fingers held tight. Damn! Catherine needed him, but he had to remember that Sebastian Doherty was never rude to a woman.

"I'm sorry, Mariel—"

"Marian," the blond-haired divorcee corrected. She'd stated her marital status right after the name he hadn't heard.

"Marian. I'm sorry, but you'll have to sample the caviar without me. I need to make an important phone call."

Without loosening her grip on his arm, she slipped her opposite hand into a long narrow shoulder bag and pulled out a portable phone. "No need to run off. I keep this handy for safety's sake. A single woman can't be too careful, you know."

Yeah, right. She'd probably have a mugger on his back in seconds flat—and follow him down.

He tried for a sheepish smile. "Okay, you caught me. I wanted to save us both the embarrassment, but the truth is I need to visit the men's room." He tugged, she gripped. "It's something I prefer to do alone if you don't mind."

Her smile was brittle. "Of course, go right ahead."

The instant she released him he headed for the door, catching Martha Kendall's gaze as he passed by. The old girl rolled her eyes in sympathy and he winked.

"I'll make you a plate," Marian called to his back.

He entered the living room and scanned the elbow-to-elbow crowd looking for a knockout lady in red. The party was in full swing now. Inebriated voices overpowered the la-di-da music he'd noticed when he'd first arrived. Hell, add a little smoke, change the wineglasses to long-neck beers, take away enough jewelry to buy a baseball franchise—and it wasn't much different from a blowout at The Pig's Gut. Hadn't Catherine said as much during each of his lessons?

She wasn't in the living room. A flash of red caught his eye...there! In the foyer. Huddled in fourth-down-inches-to-go intensity with her mother, John Chandler and Carl. Joe didn't know what they were up to, but he figured it had something to do with Catherine's father. And he intended to be there when she confronted him.

Returning his gaze to the crowd, he located Lawrence's dramatic white hair. The imposing man stood at the pass-through bar window. Reaching for a glass of wine, he made a production out of the swirl, sniff and sip routine.

Joe shouldered his way to the bar and heard the pretentious ass pronounce the wine fit to drink. "Mind if I join you, Dr. Hamilton?" he asked.

Lawrence turned and smiled with a semblance of real warmth. "Not at all. But how do you know my name?"

"Oh, I know quite a lot about you actually." Joe noted that the older man seemed to know who *he* was. Catherine's groundwork had paid off.

Lawrence tapped a manicured fingernail against his wineglass. "You probably saw me on Leno a few month's ago."

"No."

"Letterman?"

Jeez. "My days start before dawn. I'm usually asleep by ten."

"It must have been Oprah, then. She devoted a whole show to my book, *The Five-Minute Intelligence Test*. Her score caused quite a sensation in the media, you know, although I still say she studied the answers before going on air..."

As he droned on and on, Joe stifled a yawn. Lawrence Hamilton's ego could fill the Astrodome. There was no room left in his swelled head for anyone else, much less a needy daughter. Why he'd bothered fighting for custody of Catherine was beyond Joe.

"So how do you like Houston now that you've seen some of the city?"

Joe blinked and instant-replayed the question in his mind. "There's an energy in the business community I find invigorating. And the opera and ballet companies are world-class. I haven't visited the art museums yet, but I did go to a showing at Laurette Stimson's Gallery. Most impressive."

"Ah, I know the gallery owner well. Who was the artist?"

"Doreen Walden. Most of the paintings were from her 'motherhood' period."

Joe proceeded to describe several paintings and expound in elaborate mumbo jumbo, which he

watched Lawrence pretend to understand. When Joe
finally wound down, the older man gave him a companionable slap on the shoulder.

"Would you care to try a little of my favorite wine,
Sebastian?"

"I'd be honored, Lawrence."

Lawrence smiled expansively and turned to the
bartender as if he paid the guy's salary. "A glass of
the special-order cabernet sauvignon for my friend,
if you please. Ah, very good. Here you are. Tell me
what you think."

Joe took the outstretched glass and raised the rim
to his nose. "Mmm, nice blackberry bouquet with a
touch of...mint, is it? Yes, mint." He sipped and
closed his eyes. "Rich velvety flavors. Nutty young
oak. Blackberry, of course, and underlying vanilla.
All in all, a superbly balanced and finely resolved
vintage." He opened his eyes.

"Well-done!" Lawrence declared, looking appro-
priately impressed.

It was a beautiful moment, made more so by the
approach of Lawrence's "dead" ex-wife and her rich
and socially prominent boyfriend. Catherine and Carl
followed close on their heels.

"Drink up, Lawrence," Joe advised soberly. "I
think you're going to need it."

CHAPTER SIXTEEN

LAWRENCE SAW the entourage and grew pasty-faced.
The surface of his wine trembled. For an instant Joe
almost felt sorry for the jerk. He took the older man's
glass and handed it, along with his own, to the bartender.

"Why don't we all go into the library," Carl suggested tactfully, leading the way into a nearby hallway and through an open door.

Joe filed in last and took a coach position on the
sidelines, far enough away so as not to distract Catherine, yet close enough to see everyone's face and in-
tervene if she needed support.

The library lived up to its grandiose name: floor-to-
ceiling shelves jammed with books—not a paper-
back in sight; dark wood paneling, tufted leather
chairs and lots of brass doodads; thick Oriental rugs
on a parquet floor. Hell, they could've introduced
"Masterpiece Theater" in here.

And Mary Lou Denton, truck-stop manager,
looked right at home in an emerald green, off-the-
shoulder number that flattered her trim figure and
magnolia-blossom skin. In truth, she outshone their
hostess and rightful lady of the manor.

Backed up against the bookshelves like a cornered
animal, Lawrence couldn't seem to tear his gaze from
the wife he'd rejected and passed off as dead.

"Where . . . how . . . ?"

Catherine took one step forward and drew his gaze. "I hired a detective three years ago to find her, Father."

"Three years ago? Why didn't you say anything?"

"I only recently met Mother and learned what really happened when she left."

Lawrence darted a glance at Carl.

"He knows everything," Catherine said, studying her father's haunted eyes. Joe could see her attitude softening, along with her expression. "I think you realize that denying the truth is pointless."

"Whatever I did, Catherine, I did for you, for the Hamilton family name. I raised you to be a lady, and you are. At least . . ." His stunned gaze moved from daughter to mother and back. He lifted a shaking hand to his temple. "My God, when did you change so much? You look just like *her* now."

"Thank you, Father."

He lowered his hand, his green-gold eyes venomous. "It wasn't a compliment. Your mother attracted men like a bitch in heat."

John started forward.

"No!" Mary Lou said, stepping into his path and pressing her hand on his chest. She stared calmly into his murderous gaze. "He can't hurt me anymore. I'd still have to care about him for it to hurt."

"How very profound, my dear." Lawrence's voice was heavy with sarcasm. "And to think I bothered earning a Ph.D. when I had a veritable fount of wisdom at my disposal. Why, we might have world peace today if I hadn't been so blind to your abilities."

Joe's hands curled into fists. Carl murmured a protest. John tried to set Mary Lou aside. Only

Catherine paid no attention to her father. She exchanged a long loving look with her mother.

Mary Lou lifted her chin and slowly turned around. "Yes, you were blind. And bigoted and impossibly insecure. I never looked at another man, much less betrayed our marriage vows. I loved you, Lawrence, though God knows why. Back then I would have learned whatever you were willing to teach, become whatever you wanted me to be—if only you'd been man enough to trust me."

Lawrence drew himself up in chilly outrage. "Become whatever I wanted you to be? Really, Mary Lou, you forget I know your roots. Climbing the ladder to truck-stop manager is one thing, but passing yourself off as a woman of good breeding is quite another."

John growled low in his chest. "Look, you bastard—"

"Sebastian," Carl's voice rang out, swiveling every head in the room toward Joe. Lawrence's eyes widened in surprise. "You come from a family of distinction. What do you think of Dr. Hamilton's theory?"

Joe checked his watch in frustration. Thirty minutes to go in the damn bet, and he couldn't say a word. "I think it's too early in the conversation to give my opinion."

"On the contrary. As the intelligent sophisticate you've *proved* yourself to be, you owe it to Catherine's family to answer."

Lord have mercy, Joe thought, meeting the blond man's piercing stare. Pretty Boy was conceding the bet and giving him permission to reveal his identity.

Seeing his respect for Carl mirrored in the other man's gaze, Joe turned and focused on Catherine's father.

Lawrence looked embarrassed for the first time since they'd entered the library. "This is a private family matter. I must appeal to your gentleman's honor and ask you to leave."

Joe grinned in feral pleasure. "But I'm no gentleman. I'm not even Sebastian Doherty. I'm an ex-jock born and raised in Littleton, Texas. A month ago I didn't know a blackberry bouquet from a fistful of daisies."

"I . . . don't understand."

"Didn't score so hot on *The Five-Minute Intelligence Test,* huh, Lawrence? What I'm saying is, my background is more blue-collar than blue-blooded, but you believed I was a Doherty strictly on the basis of my hoity-toity B.S. What I'm saying is, you could've taught Mary Lou the same crap Catherine taught me, and high society would've accepted her just fine. What I'm saying is, these ladies have more true class in their pinky fingernails than you do in your whole pretentious ass." He walked forward to stand beside Catherine. "Now, just what part of that don't you understand?"

"This is outrageous!" Lawrence blustered. "Catherine, why would you do such a thing? Were you trying to humiliate me?"

"No, Father. You did that all by yourself."

"You planned it all? This impostor, your mother . . ." He shook his head as if trying to make sense of it all. "I can't believe you've been so manipulative."

"Why not? I learned from a master. But I won't be victimized by you any longer, Father. I'm hereby resigning as your research assistant. When you get back from England, I'll be living somewhere else. I don't want to talk to you or see you for a very long time—maybe never again.''

Lawrence looked stricken. Catherine looked almost as devastated.

''You can't resign,'' her father said.

She stiffened, then choked out a laugh. ''Thank you for putting things in perspective for me. It's nice to know your *work* will suffer in my absence. Because I *am* resigning, Father. And if you try to contact me or interfere in my life in any way, I'll tell the academic community what you did to Mother. So help me God, I will.''

''You'd do that? After everything I've taught you, everything I've done for you?''

''You taught me to doubt my self-worth, you deprived me of a mother who loved me, you advanced your career at the expense of mine. What you've done for me is despicable, Father. I need time and distance to think things through before I can consider forgiving you.''

His gaze searched each face in the room, found only hostility and returned to his daughter reptilian cold. He tugged his French cuffs and sniffed. ''Very well, Catherine, take all the time and distance you need. Because from this day forward, you're no daughter of mine. Do you understand me? *I no longer have a daughter.*''

Joe felt her tiny shudder as if it were his own. He nudged her palm with his knuckles, and she readily grasped his hand.

Then, tall and straight, beautiful and courageous, she lifted her regal nose. ''To be a daughter, one must have a father. And you, Dr. Hamilton, don't know the meaning of the word."

"WAKE UP, CATHERINE, you're home," Carl said, squeezing her shoulder gently.

Catherine opened her eyes and straightened up from the bucket seat's contoured hug. She hadn't been asleep so much as existing in an emotional vacuum. With blessed privacy only steps away, her numbness was fading fast.

She turned to the man who'd been surprisingly supportive after the nasty scene in his library. He'd calmed her father and stayed with him until a cab arrived, then had smoothed his abrupt departure with explanations of an early-morning flight.

"I don't know how to thank you, Carl. If you hadn't stood by me that last hour, I would have fallen apart."

"Somehow I doubt that. It's taken me too damn long, but I'm finally beginning to realize what a special woman you are." The garage spotlight filtered through the windshield and reflected in his thoughtful gray eyes. "You know, we don't have to call off the marriage, Catherine. We could have a good life together. I'd finance your counseling practice and we'd hire a nanny for the children—"

Catherine's swift kiss cut him off short. She pulled back and smiled gently. "Thank you again, Carl, but no. You're a good man. We'd have lovely children and an amiable relationship, but... I want more."

"You want Joe."

Yes, yes, *yes*, she thought. Spontaneous, outrageous, charismatic Joe. She bit her trembling lower lip and wished with all her heart she'd never set foot inside The Pig's Gut.

"Like I said before, he's a lucky man." Carl switched off the ignition and turned to get out.

"Wait," she managed. "Don't bother walking me to the door. I'm going to check on the cats. They're probably starving." She met his eyes and cursed herself for not reciprocating his unspoken feelings. "I'll be in touch. We'll decide how and when to announce our breakup, okay?"

"Yeah, sure. Good night, Catherine."

"Good night, Carl." She slipped quickly out of the car as the engine roared to life.

The powerful headlights beamed on her back while she walked up the driveway and climbed the garage-apartment steps. At the top landing, she unlocked the door, turned and waved.

Last chance, Catherine. It's not too late to stop him.

The car backed slowly out of her driveway—and out of her life.

The exclusive private practice he'd offered had lost its appeal a long time ago. She'd conceived the idea with her father and Carl's approval in mind. There were clinics begging for qualified counselors willing to work with the "unclean masses," as her father would have said. Digging in and getting her hands dirty would be a blessed distraction in the days ahead. And she could do so much good. Or at least she could try.

She pushed her way into the apartment, closing the door behind her with a quiet click of finality.

The cats came running and used her for a rubbing post, their purrs a soothing balm. She'd left the lamp

on for them, silly as that was. They could see fine
without it, and darkness didn't make them feel lonely.
They had each other.

She had only them.

"Hi, babies, did you miss me?" she crooned, a
confirmed spinster reduced to treating her pets like
children. She bent over and stroked what bits and
pieces of fur their constant weaving allowed. "Move
now so I can walk."

They didn't of course. She played soccer with their
bodies all the way to the kitchen, where purring es-
calated into meows at first sight of the dry cat food.
She filled each of their bowls, freshened their water
and wandered into the main room. The sudden pall
of silence grew heavy.

Everywhere she looked, Joe and Allie were there—
her impish grin brighter than the lamp, his big body
transforming the small apartment into a dollhouse.
Listless and dissatisfied, Catherine moved into the
bathroom and checked the medicine cabinet, the
bathtub ledge. She walked into the closet and eyed the
wire hangers, the empty shoe shelves. And finally,
wadded behind the roll-away bed in one corner, she
found a piece of evidence that they hadn't been a
dream.

She lifted the garment with two hands and spread
it wide...wider...envisioning Joe's broad shoulders filling the Astros jersey. Her fists drew together
and she buried her face in the crumpled material,
knowing she was torturing herself, inhaling his lingering scent just the same. Her eyes closed. A word-
less sound of longing escaped her throat. *Damn you,
Joe Tucker, for making me love you.*

Lifting her head, she threw the jersey toward the sofa, snatched up her evening bag and marched to the front door, intent on filling her lungs and mind with something besides *him*. Once on the landing, she locked the door and drew in deep gulps of air.

Ah, yes, roses. New-mown grass. And the faintest whiff of an earlier barbecue in the neighborhood. Crickets and frogs serenaded from the dark edges of the backyard. At this height, she was level with the branches of the huge pecan tree. Its canopy of leaves screened her view of the bench where she'd poured out her "sordid" story, the tree trunk where she'd first tasted real passion. A bleakness more complete than any she had known crept into her heart. Setting her purse on the cedar rail, she propped her elbows beside it, rested her chin in both palms . . . and sensed she wasn't alone.

" 'But soft! What light through yonder window breaks? It is the East and Juliet is the sun!' "

The voice came from somewhere below, its deep timbre producing a swell of wonder that took her breath away.

" 'Arise, fair sun, and kill the envious moon, who is already sick and pale with grief that thou her maid art far more fair than she.' "

Delivered in a velvet murmur, the words flowed naturally, melodically, stirring her modern heart as deeply as they'd affected women centuries ago.

" 'Be not her maid, since she is envious. Her vestal livery is but sick and green, and none but fools do wear it. Cast it off.' "

"Joe?" she whispered, knowing full well who it was. A shadowy shape moved directly into her line of vision.

" 'It is my lady. O, it is my love! O that she knew she were!' "

The garage spotlight kindled dark intense eyes raised in an unsmiling study of her face. It illuminated his broad forehead, his square jaw, the serious set of his mouth. He'd discarded his coat and tie and unbuttoned his shirt at the neck. Against the starched white collar, his throat arched strong and virile.

She drank in the details of his appearance because she didn't dare dwell on his last words. They'd been scripted, she reminded herself. And he was a talented actor.

"I'm impressed," she said thickly. "First Sebastian, now Romeo. Shakespeare is a difficult role."

"It depends on who's playing Juliet."

Somehow she dredged up flippancy. "Don't be modest—you're a natural. A lover not a fighter, remember?"

"There are times when a man should be both."

She straightened from the rail and hugged her stomach. "I'm too tired for riddles, Joe. Why are you here? What do you want?"

"You."

Her heartbeat stumbled, then broke into a wild gallop.

"Come here."

Her own words thrown back in her face.

He stood there, tall and strapping with the breeze ruffling his thick dark hair, so entirely what a man should be that it hurt to look at him. Her anger flared hot and righteous.

"Is this some kind of game to you? Because I'm not playing just to prove you can make me."

"Does he love you, Catherine? Does he take away your pain and make you *feel?* When you kissed him in the car, did he make you *burn?*"

"You were watching us?"

"Answer the question."

"You were watching us?"

"Yes, I was watching!" he roared. "I saw you staring into his eyes. I saw you lean over and kiss him. If you hadn't kept it quick I would've ripped his friggin' head off. Now answer the question, dammit. Did he make you burn?" His eyes glittered with a kind of savage anguish.

"No, he didn't make me burn!" she yelled back, close to tears. "He's never made me burn, or my heart pound, or my body ache—not like you have. Is that what you wanted to hear, Joe? Is your macho pride happy to know that I love you and not him?"

Her eyelashes fluttered. She sucked in a horrified breath. Grabbing her purse, she pulled out the key and whirled around to the door. Her hands shook so badly she fumbled inserting the grooved metal properly. The landing vibrated as feet pounded up the stairs.

"C'mon," she breathed. The key slipped in and she reached for the knob.

Large hands spanned her waist and pulled her against an iron body. Heat seared her bare back. A stubbled cheek pressed against her neck.

"You drop a bomb like that and expect to run away?" he rumbled in her ear. "I don't think so."

An agonizing, wonderful, miserable terror filled her heart. "Nothing's changed."

"Like hell," he muttered, turning her in his hands and pressing her spine against the door. His mouth came down hard and hungry on hers, and she was lost.

He kissed her deeply, possessively, as if he needed the taste of her more than he needed air. The hot succulent mating of tongues took her from embarrassed to burning in seconds flat. She threw her arms up and spread her fingers wide, thrilling to the hard strength beneath fine cotton, the thick hair cushioning his skull. His own hands seemed fascinated with her bare back, returning again and again to the point just above her rhinestone bow and teasing the edges of fabric. He suddenly pressed her tight to his loins and tore his lips from hers.

"Say it again," he demanded, his voice gruff with passion.

She lifted heavy eyelids and stared up with unfocused tenderness. "I love you, Joe."

He made an unintelligible sound low in his throat and captured her mouth again, his tongue delving deep and hard. His palms rose to bracket the sides of her breasts, his thumbs finding the sensitive centers with unerring accuracy. As always with him, and only him, she lost her inhibitions and matched his ardor, loving the wet heat of his mouth, the tumescence pressing into her stomach. Wanting more. So much more.

When at last he lifted his mouth, they were both breathing like bellows.

His dark turbulent gaze bore into hers. "You can't marry Pretty Boy, Catherine."

A perverse stab of irritation jerked up her chin. "Why not?"

"Because you're going to marry me."

She wilted like a pricked helium balloon while he watched her closely, his expression growing more grim with every passing second of her silence.

"I can see you're overwhelmed with joy."

Overwhelmed, yes. She couldn't speak for the confusion storming her senses.

"I know I don't have a job yet and I can't finance the fancy practice you've always wanted, but I'll work hard, Catherine. There'll always be food on the table and a roof over our heads. And Allie is crazy about you. She'd be thrilled to have you for a mother."

"And you? Would you be thrilled to have the burden of a wife?" Hating the threat of tears in her voice, she twisted her head and swallowed.

A strong hand spanned her chin and turned her face to his. The tender light in his eyes captivated her. She couldn't look away.

"How can my best friend be a burden? I love you, Catherine, didn't you know? It was me calling you my lady and my love earlier—for myself, not Romeo. Good God, I parked the Bronco a block away and spied on you like a damn kid when you got home. You're making me crazy, and there's only one thing I know that will cure me, Counselor."

He lowered his head and brushed her lips gently. "Marry me." His tongue traced the corners of her mouth and dipped inside for a quick taste. "Marry me." He trailed his mouth along her jaw and nibbled her earlobe. "Marry me, Catherine. Maybe one day I'll be in a position to give you the things Carl can now, but don't make me wait to give you my love. We're good together, you know we are. We'll laugh a lot and fight a lot and make up like rabbits if I have anything to do with it. Say you'll marry me." His voice was soft, cajoling, seductive.

Her eyes drifted shut as the sincerity of his love sank in. And still she said nothing, for to be wooed like this after a lifetime of emotional deprivation was rainfall to a parched field.

"We'll go to Colorado for our honeymoon. There are some cabins I know of right in the heart of an aspen forest. During the day we'll watch the leaves shiver in the wind. At night we'll make love by a fire, maybe make a little brother or sister for Allie while we're at it. I'd like that, wouldn't you?"

Her heart was too full to contain.

"Ah, sweetheart, honey...don't cry." His tongue caught the tear welling at the corner of one lid before it spilled free. "You can take your time deciding."

She wrapped her arms around his waist and held him close, vowing to make her rugged gentleman happy until her dying breath. Pulling back, she opened her eyes and offered a wobbly smile.

"I never had any intention of marrying Carl after our night together. I just didn't want you to feel obligated to do your gentlemanly duty." She hugged him more tightly. "I want a houseful of kids, Joe Tucker. And Allie for a junior bridesmaid. And a regular game with Earl at The Pig's Gut to keep my aim sharp. Oh...and about that honeymoon?"

His mouth showed signs of breaking into the devilish grin she loved. "Yes, ma'am?"

"I really don't see any point in waiting to start it, do you, Joe?"

And there it came, spreading white and wicked and delicious across his face. "No, ma'am!"

Opening the door and dropping the key in her purse, he handed her the bag and gave her a look that melted her bones. In one powerful swoop he lifted her high against his chest and crossed the threshold.

"Guess who's got his touch back, Juliet?" he crowed before kicking the door shut with his heel.

Take 4 bestselling love stories FREE

Plus get a FREE surprise gift!

Special Limited-time Offer

Mail to Harlequin Reader Service®

3010 Walden Avenue
P.O. Box 1867
Buffalo, N.Y. 14240-1867

YES! Please send me 4 free Harlequin Superromance® novels and my free surprise gift. Then send me 4 brand-new novels every month, which I will receive before they appear in bookstores. Bill me at the low price of $3.34 each plus 25¢ delivery and applicable sales tax, if any.* That's the complete price and a savings of over 10% off the cover prices—quite a bargain! I understand that accepting the books and gift places me under no obligation ever to buy any books. I can always return a shipment and cancel at any time. Even if I never buy another book from Harlequin, the 4 free books and the surprise gift are mine to keep forever.

134 BPA A3UN

Name	(PLEASE PRINT)	
Address		Apt. No.
City	State	Zip

This offer is limited to one order per household and not valid to present Harlequin Superromance® subscribers. *Terms and prices are subject to change without notice. Sales tax applicable in N.Y.

USUP-696

©1990 Harlequin Enterprises Limited

Weddings by DeWilde

Since the turn of the century the elegant and fashionable
DeWilde stores have helped brides around the world
turn the fantasy of their "Special Day" into reality. But now the
store and three generations of family are torn apart by the
separation of Grace and Jeffrey DeWilde. Family members
face new challenges and loves in this fast-paced, glamorous,
internationally set series. For weddings and romance, glamour
and fun-filled entertainment, enter the world of DeWilde...

**Watch for *TERMS OF SURRENDER*,
by Kate Hoffmann
Coming to you in November 1996**

Merchandising manager Megan DeWilde had major
plans for the expansion of DeWildes' Paris operation.
But Phillip Villeneuve, scion of a rival retailing family,
was after the same piece of real estate Megan had her eye
on. Caught in the middle of a feud neither understood, they
were powerless against the sizzling chemistry that overrode
property, family and every shred of common sense.

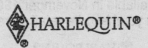

HARLEQUIN®

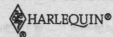

The collection of the year!
NEW YORK TIMES BESTSELLING AUTHORS

Linda Lael Miller
Wild About Harry

Janet Dailey
Sweet Promise

Elizabeth Lowell
Reckless Love

Penny Jordan
Love's Choices

and featuring
Nora Roberts
The Calhoun Women

This special trade-size edition features four of the wildly
popular titles in the Calhoun miniseries together in
one volume—a true collector's item!

Pick up these great authors and a chance to win
a weekend for two in New York City at the
Marriott Marquis Hotel on Broadway! We'll pay
for your flight, your hotel—even a Broadway show!

Available in December at your favorite retail outlet.

NEW YORK
Marriott®
MARQUIS

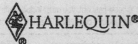 HARLEQUIN®    Silhouette®

NYT1296-R

Free Gift Offer

With a Free Gift proof-of-purchase
from any Harlequin® book, you can receive
a beautiful cubic zirconia pendant.

This stunning marquise-shaped stone is a genuine cubic
zirconia—accented by an 18" gold tone necklace.
(Approximate retail value $19.95)

Send for yours today...
compliments of ◈HARLEQUIN®

To receive your free gift, a cubic zirconia pendant, send us one original proof-of-purchase, photocopies not accepted, from the back of any Harlequin Romance®, Harlequin Presents®, Harlequin Temptation®, Harlequin Superromance®, Harlequin Intrigue®, Harlequin American Romance®, or Harlequin Historicals® title available in August, September or October at your favorite retail outlet, together with the Free Gift Certificate, plus a check or money order for $1.65 u.s./$2.15 can. (do not send cash) to cover postage and handling, payable to Harlequin Free Gift Offer. We will send you the specified gift. Allow 6 to 8 weeks for delivery. Offer good until October 31, 1996 or while quantities last. Offer valid in the U.S. and Canada only.

Free Gift Certificate

Name: _____

Address: _____

City: _____ State/Province: _____ Zip/Postal Code: _____

Mail this certificate, one proof-of-purchase and a check or money order for postage and handling to: HARLEQUIN FREE GIFT OFFER 1996. In the U.S.: 3010 Walden Avenue, P.O. Box 9071, Buffalo NY 14269-9057. In Canada: P.O. Box 604, Fort Erie, Ontario L2Z 5X3.

REBECCA

43 LIGHT STREET

YORK

FACE TO FACE

*Bestselling author Rebecca York returns to "43 Light Street"
for an original story of past secrets, deadly deceptions—and
the most intimate betrayal.*

She woke in a hospital—with amnesia...and with child.
According to her rescuer, whose striking face is the last
image she remembers, she's Justine Hollingsworth. But
nothing about her life seems to fit, except for the baby
inside her and Mike Lancer's arms around her. Consumed
by forbidden passion and racked by nameless fear, she
must discover if she is Justine...or the victim of some mind
game. Her life—and her unborn child's—depends on it....

Don't miss *Face To Face*—Available in October, wherever
Harlequin books are sold.

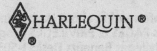

HARLEQUIN ®
®

43FTF

You're About to Become a *Privileged Woman*

Reap the rewards of fabulous free gifts and
benefits with proofs-of-purchase from
Harlequin and Silhouette books

Pages & Privileges™

It's our way of thanking you for
buying our books at your
favorite retail stores.

**PROOF OF
PURCHASE**
HS-PP181
Offer expires October 31, 1996

Pages
& Privileges ™

**Harlequin and Silhouette—
the most privileged readers in the world!**

For more information about Harlequin and
Silhouette's PAGES & PRIVILEGES program call the
Pages & Privileges Benefits Desk: 1-503-794-2499

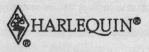